SOMEONE HAD TO LIE

SOMEONE HAD TO LIE

a James Butler mystery

JACK LUELLEN

Vista, CA

ISBN: 978-1-61153-370-5 (paperback)

ISBN: 978-1-61153-383-5 (ebook)

Library of Congress Control Number: 2024914949

Someone Had to Lie is published by: Torchflame Books, an imprint of Top Reads Publishing, LLC, USA

For information about special discounts for bulk purchases, please direct emails to: publisher@torchflamebooks.com

Cover design: Jori Hanna

Book interior layout: Jori Hanna

Printed in the United States of America

To Isabelle Faith

You inspire me to be better and to do more, every day.

PREFACE

This is a work of fiction with references to actual events based on the author's recollection and documentation. The names and details of some individuals have been changed to respect their privacy. All characters, events, and incidents are the product of the author's imagination, and are used in a fictitious manner. Any resemblance to actual persons living or dead is entirely coincidental.

In Mexico, as in other nations of Hispanic or Latino culture, individuals usually have double surnames. A child is given a double surname composed of the "male part" of both the mother's and father's surnames. The male surname is the first of the two surnames.

If parents are of Hispanic or Latino descent, it is probable that each of them has a double surname composed in a similar fashion. Thus, if the mother is named Anna Peréz Garcia, and the father is named Servando Morales González, their son Fernando would be named Fernando Morales Peréz.

To Anglos unfamiliar with this naming system, the second surname looks like the person's last name, but is the mother's family name. The first surname, which looks like the person's middle name, is the father's family name.

ONE

A GUNSHOT SOUND blares from the microphone. "Aguilar! Aguilar!" James's face turns ashen. "Aguilar?!"

The salty mist engulfing the Newport Beach shoreline during the morning and early afternoon hours has ebbed back out to sea, leaving, in its wake, a clear sky and unseasonably warm temperatures.

The Newport Beach Country Club sits across the Pacific Coast Highway from Newport Beach, looking out toward the vast Pacific Ocean, interrupted by stunning views of Balboa Island and Balboa Peninsula. The country club is not a mecca for the masses. Home to a par 71, 6,584-yard golf course composed of meticulously manicured Kikuya grass, the club is private and selective, with membership by invitation only and sponsorship by multiple current members required. The club's website notes its staff are not permitted to provide a prospective member with membership information, as such information is provided only to club members. The club's code advises that "Members and Guests are to conduct themselves as ladies & gentlemen and are not to interfere with other's enjoyment of The Club."

On this early spring evening, the club bustles with activity for the spring kickoff gala and charity fundraiser. Tiki torches and several outdoor fire pits illuminate the grounds against the methodically darkening skies. A gentle breeze refreshingly cools the warm air.

James Butler and Erica Walsh stroll among the fashionable guests, exchanging idle pleasantries. James is one of the younger and newer full members, while Erica has participated in club activities since she was a child. Moving to the edge of the crowd, their walk slows to a stop as they gaze up the hill toward the shops of Fashion Island and Big Canyon behind it.

"I do love a man in a tuxedo," Erica remarks, softly kissing James.

"I do what I must to try to keep up." As James speaks, he checks the cell phone in his chest pocket, declines a call, and returns the phone. "Aguilar," he informs Erica.

"Why would he be calling this late on a Saturday night?" she asks.

"I have no idea."

"What's he been up to?" Erica asks.

"No idea there either. I talked to him a week or two ago, just for a few minutes. He said he was puttering around on a couple of things to keep himself from being too bored at home. I told him it was more likely Rosalia was tired of seeing his face and made him find a hobby."

"Funny," Erica says wryly. "Did he say anything specific about what he was doing?"

"No, and I didn't ask."

"You can check in on him tomorrow. Let's head back and see if we can find my dad. He should have been here already," Erica says.

"The infamous Castle casual tardiness in full swing?" James teases.

"Would you expect anything different?"

"No, I would not. On our wedding day, I assumed he'd meet us at the altar and someone else would walk you down the aisle."

James and Erica lock hands and weave toward the clubhouse before the vibration of another call causes James to pause. He glances at the phone screen and returns it to his pocket without answering.

"Aguilar, again?" Erica inquires.

"Yeah."

"Okay, that's a little weird," Erica observes.

"It's very weird," James concurs.

About eighteen months ago, their adventure in Mexico resulted in the arrest of Mexican drug lord Rafael "Rafa" Caro Quintero for the 1985 murder of DEA Agent Enrique "Kiki" Camarena in Guadalajara. Since then, James and Agent Joe Aguilar have kept in close touch and become fast friends.

"Erica!" calls a voice from the patio.

"Dad," Erica replies, guiding James by the hand to Brian Castle, standing by the firepit. "I'm happy you made it. Finally."

Hugging Erica and shaking hands with James, Brian responds to his daughter's chastening. "I'm sorry. You know how it is."

"Of course, we do," James replies. "We're just happy you're here now. It's a gorgeous night."

James and Erica return their focus to the cell phone, vibrating yet again inside James's pocket.

"Aguilar? Again?" Erica inquires, as James shows her the phone screen.

"You should call him back. Do you want me to try to find a room you can hide out in?"

"Nah, I'll walk over toward the parking lot. I know how twitchy Karl gets about cell phones. Maybe not for you, but definitely for me."

"Okay. I'm concerned."

"I'm sure it's fine," James reassures, before kissing Erica and heading into the clubhouse.

"What's going on?" Brian asks.

"I'm not sure Dad, but I have a very bad feeling."

James darts through the clubhouse to an area near the parking lot, searching for a more private spot to make his call. Dialing the number from the recent calls list, James is surprised to hear Aguilar's voice mail. Pacing back and forth, James waits to try again, only to connect with voice mail once more.

What do I do now?

James wipes his brow with the back of his hand, staring at the moon shimmering above the horizon. Moments later, a call comes in from an unknown number.

"James Butler."

"James?"

"Aguilar, what's going on? I'm at a reception with Erica and her dad. You have us worried."

"I'm sorry to interrupt, James, but we were wrong."

"Whoa, whoa. Slow down and tell me what's going on. Who's we, and wrong about what?" James asks.

"I can't slow down, James. I don't have much time. It was bigger than we thought and now we're in danger."

"You aren't making sense. What was bigger?" James asks

"All of it. I can't explain now, but you need to watch your back and take care of Erica until I can get a handle on this," Aguilar says.

"Where are you? I tried your cell phone, but it went straight to voice mail," James asks.

"I'm in Yuma, Arizona. My phone's dead. I'm at a pay phone," Aguilar answers.

"I didn't know there were any of those left."

"Look, I don't have time to discuss recent changes in telecommunications. I need you to promise to be careful and to stay out of this."

"You know perfectly well I can't—I won't—promise to stay out of this, whatever the hell this is," James says firmly.

James is startled by the roar of a gunshot blasting from his phone's tiny microphone.

"Aguilar! Aguilar!" James's face turns ashen. "Aguilar?!"

The phone receiver rustles, interrupted by a deep voice. "Goodbye. For now."

Oh my God. What has happened?

TWO

March, on average, is the rainiest month in San Antonio. True to form, this late March day is damp, dark, and gloomy as James and Erica drive to the Fort Sam Houston National Cemetery, which sits north of downtown San Antonio, just east of the San Antonio Zoo and Botanical Gardens.

The cemetery spans nearly 155 acres, has more than 150,000 internments, and is listed on the National Register of Historic Places. Among those interned at the cemetery are thirteen Medal of Honor recipients; Colonel Doc Blanchard, the 1945 Heiman Trophy winner; General Richard E. Cavazos, the Army's first Hispanic four-star general; Lt. Colonel Richard E. Cole, a Doolittle Raider; and Lt. Colonel Granville C. Coggs, a prominent African American doctor and a bombardier pilot with the Tuskegee Airmen.

Since his death two weeks ago, James had learned much about Aguilar. Born in 1948 in Bandera, Texas, the self-proclaimed Cowboy Capital of the World, Joseph Michael Aguilar moved to San Antonio to attend Trinity College on both athletic and academic scholarships. His college life was cut short when he joined the US Marines in 1968. His college experience and general aptitude made Aguilar a natural leader. He was made a second lieutenant and sent to Vietnam. Aguilar stayed in Vietnam an inordinately long time, not leaving until 1973, during which time he was involved in too many combat missions to count, in addition to some "unofficial" missions as well. For his service, Aguilar was awarded three Purple Hearts, a bronze and silver star, and the Navy Cross.

Aguilar received an honorable discharge in 1973 and returned to Texas, working first as a constable in Bandera County, then as a deputy sheriff in Bexar County, which includes the city of San Antonio. In 1984, Aguilar joined the DEA in the San Antonio field office and the rest, as they say, is history.

James and Erica enter the cemetery turning left off Harry Wurzbach Road. A long gradual turn leads to the east side of the cemetery, as the funeral site slowly comes into view. Dozens of vehicles line the road, and James parks behind a Texas limousine: a huge, black, four door Ford F-350.

James plucks his umbrella from the back seat and walks to the other side of the car to open the door for Erica. Erica, her own umbrella in hand, takes a deep breath, looks to the sky, holds out a hand, and returns it to her car seat. James closes his umbrella, takes Erica's hand, and leads her on their solemn march to the gravesite.

The gravesite has a flag-draped coffin surrounded by more flowers than a Derby-winning stallion. A queue has formed to offer condolences to Aguilar's widow, Rosalia, who sits in the middle of the first of several rows of folding chairs forming a semi-circle around the grave. James and Erica wait to pay their respects.

"Our deepest condolences, Rosalia," Erica says.

"Thank you both for coming. Joe would have appreciated you being here."

"We are honored to be here," James affirms. "Joe meant a lot to us."

"The feeling was mutual, though I doubt he ever put it into words for you," Rosalia says.

"We didn't need words," James says.

"You'll be at the house later, right?" Rosalia asks.

"Of course, we will," Erica says.

"Good. We will have a nice celebration of Joe's life, with some music, drinks, and a huge pot of the discada I know you love. And I have something to give you."

"We will be there." James and Erica each kiss Rosalia on the cheek and move to the back row. James dries a chair for Erica with his handkerchief and stands silently behind her as more mourners arrive, pay their respects, and take their places.

"Look around," James whispers. "There must be a representative or more from every law enforcement institution in Texas, and every military branch."

"He obviously had quite an impact on a lot of people," Erica says.

The funeral is a unique blend of Mexican Catholic service with full military honors. The cemetery's Memorial Service Detachment provides military funeral honors for veterans, above and beyond what the Department of Defense offers. In Aguilar's case, the service includes a twelve-gun rifle salute, the playing of Taps, and a flag presentation to Rosalia.

Following the ceremony, James and Erica wait as the others slowly make their way to their cars and out of the cemetery. James takes a seat next to Erica, holds her hand on his thigh, and together they sit in silence.

"Where was Tim?" James asks in a hushed tone despite almost no one being near.

Tim Speer, a CIA operative, had played a critical role in their efforts to bring Rafa Quintero to justice. Afterward, they all remained close, with Erica and Tim bonding over similar musical tastes.

"I don't know," Erica replies. "He texted earlier and said he couldn't make it, but he wasn't specific on why."

"Top-secret spy stuff I assume."

"Likely," Erica responds. "You know he doesn't say much about what he's up to."

"Yeah, but I still thought he'd be here."

"Everyone handles their grief in their own way, I guess."

"That's true." James pauses, looking around the cemetery as darker clouds roll in, casting a somber shadow over the cemetery. "I guess we should be going soon. It's a pretty good drive to their house in Hill Country."

"Okay." Erica scans the funeral plot and the American flags gently flapping in the misty wind, as workers begin stacking the chairs onto a small tractor-trailer. "I've looked forward to seeing their house, but, damn, not this way."

James and Erica make the thirty-minute drive to the JW Marriott San Antonio Hill Country to make a quick change into less dour attire and freshen up a bit before the next forty-minute leg to the Aguilars' residence.

Their house sits near the end of a small peninsula jutting into Canyon Lake. On his last visit, Aguilar and Rosalia regaled James with the story of how they bought the parcel of land for next to nothing in 1983, right before Aguilar joined the DEA, and long before any of the area's stunning development. Their friends in San Antonio thought they were crazy. But, over another fabulous Rosalia-prepared meal, they described how they were able to turn the plot of land into a waterfront house they could never dream of affording today. It would make a great inheritance, but for reasons James never asked about, the Aguilars never had children of their own.

James drives in quiet, as Erica looks at the clouds passing outside the car window, until she asks, "You really don't know why Aguilar was in Yuma?"

"I have absolutely no idea."

"I checked the map to confirm, and Yuma's less than an hour from Calexico and Mexicali," Erica notes. "That, of course, made me think of our border escapade. Could there be a connection?"

"Logic would suggest there might be, but, again, I don't know."

"He said nothing helpful?" Erica asks.

"Do you think I've been holding back information, or I forgot to say something?"

"No, of course not," Erica replies contritely. "I'm just grasping at straws, trying to find something sensible."

"I understand, but the only thing meaningful he said was it was bigger than we knew. There was nothing more specific, nothing at all. I asked him what he meant, but he was shot before he could answer."

Erica reaches over to hold James's hand. "I'm sorry, babe. I didn't mean to make you relive it."

"It's okay. I've gone over it in my head a thousand times."

"Maybe Rosalia knows something?"

"I intend to ask her," James agrees. "When the time is right."

"If there ever is a right time."

"True," James mutters, focusing on the road.

After a few minutes, James breaks the silence. "Maybe I did omit something. Playing the conversation over in my head, I was so focused on the 'it was bigger' part, but before that he said, 'We were wrong.'"

"Should we assume the 'we' in both statements refers to the same people?" Erica asks.

"I think so, don't you?" James replies.

"I do," Erica agrees. "So, 'we' were wrong, and it was bigger than 'we' knew. Since he called you, I have to believe you are part of the we, which …"

"Must relate to Mexico," James interrupts.

"Right, but how?" Erica questions.

"I have no idea," James answers.

Colleen Drive leads to an intersection with Janet Drive followed a few blocks later by the Aguilar house on the left. James turns into the long drive connecting the main road to the house, passing the few parked cars.

"For some reason, I thought there'd be more people here," Erica observes.

"I think Rosalia wanted to keep it small, for those who were close to him. I'm touched we were included."

"Of course, we were. He loved you. Rosalia does too," Erica says.

James parks the car next to a brick wall separating the drive from the neighboring parcel. James opens Erica's door as Rosalia waves to them from the large wrap-around porch hugging the rustic, wood-framed home. James and Erica ascend the stairs to greet Rosalia.

"Thank you, for being here. Both of you."

"Thank you for including us," Erica replies, gently kissing Rosalia on the cheek.

Rosalia takes Erica by the hand, leading her to the back porch where the activities are already under way, as James follows. A large pot, sometimes referred to as a Mexican wok, rests on the flames of a fire pit. A couple of coolers are filled with ice, Pacifico beer, and bottled water. Pitchers of margaritas sit on the three tables just beyond the deck. Rosalia returns to the kitchen, leaving James and Erica to mingle with the other guests.

The rest of the afternoon and evening is spent exchanging stories about Aguilar, including James's heavily redacted description of their rendition of Rafa Quintero from Mexico, about which some had heard rumors but heretofore had no confirmation.

Later, James and Erica retreat to a pair of chairs away from the fire, each sipping on a fresh margarita, listening in on the discussions around the fire pit. The moon has assumed its position high over the lake, its light dancing on the water's gently rippling surface. Rosalia leans between Erica and James. "Can you come inside with me for a moment?"

"Of course," James replies, rising to follow Rosalia, while Erica remains seated.

"Both of you," Rosalia says to Erica.

Erica stands, and together they follow Rosalia into the house and then to an office just off the main living room. Rosalia gently shuts the door behind them.

"This was Joe's office, his sanctuary. I almost never came in here. Not because he forbade it, or didn't want me to enter, but out of respect. The day before he left for Yuma, he asked me to come in so he could show me a safe behind the desk. We've been in this house for thirty some years. In all those years, I had no idea he had a safe." Rosalia walks behind the solid mahogany desk, moves the large leather chair, and slides a piece of paneling to the left, exposing a small safe, about one foot square.

"He gave me the combination," she says while spinning the locking mechanism, "and put a file inside. He told me if anything should happen to him, I was to open the safe, find the file he left, and make certain it got to you, James. He was very clear. It was for you and no one else." Rosalia opens the safe door and hands James an unmarked, letter-size manila envelope, bulging at the seams.

"What was Joe working on, and why was he in Yuma?"

"I don't know. I wish I did. He never said. I asked him, but he shrugged it off and said he was just poking around, and it was nothing important. But the day he left, I knew it was more than nothing. The last time he called, he worried me something terrible. I'd never heard him sound so anxious. I almost called you to ask you to talk to him, but I convinced myself he could take care of himself, and he would be home in two days' time."

"Do you happen to have his cell phone?" James asks. "When he called me, he said he was at a pay phone because his cell phone had died."

"No, the police said it wasn't on him. They assumed whoever shot him grabbed the phone and were spooked before they could steal anything else."

Would a thief go for the cell phone before the wallet? I guess. Maybe?

Rosalia's words are followed by a roar of laughter from the porch. "I should go back to my guests but, before I go, please promise me one thing, James."

"Of course. Anything."

"Make someone pay for killing my husband."

THREE

FOLLOWING quick goodbyes to the remaining guests, James navigates the long driveway and finds his way out of the Canyon Lake community, starting the drive back to the hotel. A few minutes into the drive, just past Canyon Lake Fire Station No. 2, James makes a left turn onto FM3159 and breaks the silence.

"Well, that did *not* go as expected," James comments, with a Chandleresque emphasis on the word "not."

"My husband, the master of the understatement. Any ideas?"

"None," James responds. "And I'm not sure if I'm more annoyed or curious."

"Annoyed?" Erica questions.

"Yeah. Pissed off, is more like it. What the hell was he thinking being so reckless? To fall into something so dangerous by himself?"

Erica adjusts her position to face him. "I understand, James, but you know he had to have believed he had it under control. And, if he'd thought it was dangerous, I doubt you would have been the first person he'd call."

"Not me?" James asks.

"You saw all those people at the funeral. Your rank on the list of people to have Aguilar's back in a dangerous situation, I'm sorry to say, would not be high."

"Fine. I can accept that. But now he wants me to clean up his mess."

"I don't know what he wanted or what he intended. But I suspect the answer is in the envelope. But, more to your point, while Aguilar might not have seen you as back up in a dangerous situation, it does seem he saw you as the person he knew he could trust to do the right thing. Of the two, I'm proud you fell into the latter category, and you should be too."

The drive to the hotel passes by quickly, and soon the car is passing the In Contrada Vineyard & Kitchen, the oldest vineyard in Bexar County, before turning onto TPC Parkway and into the JW Marriott property. James glides the car to valet parking and hands off the keys with the minimal small talk required to be polite. Taking Erica's hand, the two race to their room, a small suite accented by a gas fireplace and a view of the TPC San Antonio golf course.

Once inside, James sits on the sofa, resting the folder on the coffee table in front of him. Erica settles in at his side, placing a bottle of water in front of him and opening one for herself.

"Thanks," James remarks. "I may need something stronger soon."

"These are the occasions for which room service was designed," Erica replies. "Are you going to open it?"

"I am. Just wondering what could be so important."

"Only one way to find out," Erica says.

James retrieves a nail clipper from the front pocket of his slacks. Sliding out the attached nail file, he cuts open the sealed envelope before pulling the contents out in one jumbled heap.

"You might want to call room service now."

Erica leaves James to make the room service order from the bedroom, as James starts to sort through the materials. He unfolders each item, giving it a brief examination before placing each into categorized piles. Erica soon returns from the bedroom, wearing a silk robe.

"How am I supposed to concentrate now?" James says as Erica returns to her spot next to him.

"Don't even think about it," Erica advises. "I'm way too tired."

"Just as well," James replies with a smile.

"Who says romance and passion are dead?" Erica observes.

"Funny."

"Making any progress?"

"Not much," James says. "I'm trying to identify topics and material types and segregate them before looking at them in detail. So far, the only consistent theme is an interest in fentanyl trafficking."

"Fentanyl? I wonder what the interest was?"

"As do I, but at the moment, I have no idea."

Erica pulls a newspaper article from a pile and reads aloud as James continues his sorting process.

"'From June 2020 to May 2021, fentanyl and synthetic opioids accounted for roughly two-thirds of the more than 100,000 deaths in the US from drug overdoses, the report found. The fatalities were mostly among Americans ages eighteen to forty-five. Fentanyl, a type of synthetic opioid, has been the primary driver of the US opioid epidemic and is 50 times more potent than heroin, according to the report. It found that while 70 to 80 percent of fentanyl seized by federal authorities between 2014 to 2019 had come from China, Mexico is now the dominant source of fentanyl in the US.'" Erica hands the article to James who places it back on top of his stack.

"I've heard a lot about the fentanyl crisis," Erica states, "but have to admit, I'm not well-versed on the specifics."

"I'm not either, but I think changes are coming soon for both of us."

The discussion is interrupted by a knock on the door. "I'll get the door," James says. "You're not dressed for guests."

As Erica slips back into the bedroom, James greets the room service attendant who wheels in a cart with two bottles of a pedestrian zinfandel and a cheese and crackers plate. After signing the bill, including an appropriately hefty tip, James shuts the door and returns to the couch, as Erica joins him.

"The fentanyl crisis is scary, but I don't understand why Aguilar was looking into it," Erica says, followed by a guttural yawn.

"Babe, why don't you go to bed?" James suggests without responding. "I'll join you soon."

"Yeah, I think I will. I wish I knew why I've been so draggy lately."

"We've both been wiped out. It's been a stressful few weeks."

Erica glides to the bedroom door before looking back at James. "Are you sure you don't want to join me?"

"I need to get through this pile tonight, or I'll never be able to sleep," James says.

"There's the focused, obsessive lawyer I married. Love you."

"Love you too. I'll be in soon."

Later in the night, Erica awakens and reaches across the king size bed feeling in vain for James. The green LCD alarm clock shows 2:14 a.m. Erica quietly rises, covering herself with the silk robe neatly laying across the golden-brown chaise lounge at the foot of the bed. As she moves from the bedroom into the living room, Erica stops to watch James on the sofa as he pours over the documents, his athletic frame illuminated by a small light and the fireplace.

Gently stepping into the living area, Erica inquires softly, "Still at it?"

"I hope I didn't wake you."

"Oh no, not at all. I just missed you in bed." Erica sits, sipping from James's wine glass on the end table, gazing at the papers spread across the coffee table.

"I've been methodically going through these, trying to make sense of this . . . this mess," James explains. "I would have expected an organized file, but this is a mishmash of notes, newspaper clippings, and website printouts."

"Any conclusions?" Erica asks.

"Not any. There is a fair amount of information relating to fentanyl, the trafficking of fentanyl from Mexico, but not a lot more. There are things from all over and in no obvious order. So no—no conclusions."

"Maybe it was a work in progress he intended to organize later?" Erica surmises.

"Possible. Very possible. But no less difficult to decipher."

"Okay, then let's back up," Erica asserts. "He said 'it' was bigger than we thought, right?"

"Right," James answers.

"Okay, then based on *these* materials, do you think the 'it' relates to fentanyl somehow?"

"I've been wondering the same thing," James says.

"And?" Erica prods, taking another sip of wine.

"I'm not sure. He said it was bigger than any of us knew. My immediate assumption was it went back to Rafa somehow, but only as a gut level reaction," James opines before pausing, deep in thought.

"I'm just having a hard time seeing how something relating to Rafa could have gotten Aguilar killed *now*," Erica inserts.

"I know. The timeline is wonky," James agrees.

"The timeline doesn't make sense, and I'm struggling to see a connection to fentanyl," Erica admits.

"Trust me," James says, "I've been going in circles since you went to bed. There is a key to tying these things together, but I just can't figure out what it is."

"Yet," Erica adds.

"Yet," James agrees.

"Did you find anything at all helpful?"

"I won't say helpful, but would you settle for potentially intriguing?"

"James, it's 2:30 a.m. Right now, I'd settle for a possibility of not completely irrelevant."

"There is a name and phone number scribbled on a scrap of paper: Bill Belmonte. 719-555-1222," James says.

"Any ideas?" Erica asks.

"None. But I say we call tomorrow when we're back home and see."

"Sounds like a good plan, for tomorrow." Erica stands, gently squeezes James's hand, and leads him into the bedroom.

FOUR

FOR UNKNOWN REASONS, air travel from Orange County to San Antonio is inconvenient with almost no direct flights. On this trip, James and Erica opted to fly in and out of San Diego to avoid LAX.

Following their late-night discussion, they rise late but secure in the knowledge of San Antonio Airport–one of the smallest, most functional airports at any big city in the US. After checking out, a short twenty-minute drive takes them to the airport. A quick stop at the rental car return, and minutes later they are seated in seats 2A and 2B, juices in front of them, ready for departure.

Erica leans back into the chair. "We haven't talked much about Aguilar's folder this morning, but I'd bet anything you've been thinking about it."

"A little. I'm letting it all percolate in my mind and waiting for an epiphany to appear."

"Still waiting?" asks Erica.

James takes a drink of his juice. "As a matter of fact, I am."

"Please be sure to alert me when it comes."

For an airport serving a large metropolitan area, San Diego's airport is akin to San Antonio's for its general efficiency and ease of use, though some would suggest both have waned somewhat over the years. A bonus, depending on the seat and direction, can be great views of Coronado Island and the Coronado Bridge, the North Island Naval Air Station, and the San Diego Naval Base, which occasionally provides a view of an aircraft carrier or the rarer sighting of a nuclear submarine.

Pilots, on the other hand, universally hate landing in San Diego, due to the omni-present gusty tailwinds and a steep approach path uncomfortably close to several city buildings and, in particular, a nearby parking structure.

Landing today is smooth and with only carry-on luggage to slow them down, Erica and James are soon in James's car, exiting the airport on North Harbor Drive. A right turn onto Laning Road, followed by a quick right onto Rosecrans Street, has them merging onto Interstate 5, heading north for the near straight shot home.

"What does GPS say about traffic?" Erica asks as James puts the car on cruise control but rejects the impulse to employ the car's self-driving features.

"Says an hour fifteen," James replies.

"Still better than dealing with LAX," Erica states.

"Much better, and looking at the route, there are no real traffic issues."

"Don't say that aloud. You'll rile up the traffic gods."

"Heaven forbid. I meant no offense dear gods of the freeways," James says.

As James is talking, Erica rummages in her purse before pulling out a piece of paper. "I grabbed the note with that Belmonte guy's number. Should we call him?"

"What the heck. Let's get it done," James says.

Erica pulls her cell phone from her purse and touches the Tesla's keypad to connect the car to her phone. Dialing the numbers, Erica pauses before hitting the green dial button. "What if this takes us down a road we don't want to know about?"

"We need to know," James says.

"Do we? Maybe the police are right, and maybe we should stay out of it."

"Maybe they are, but Aguilar left the folder for us for a reason. And he included the name and number. Despite my petulant protests last night, you were right—he would have expected us to follow up if anything happened to him," James states.

"I'm sure he did. And since he did . . ." With renewed vigor, Erica activates the dialing of the phone number, returning the paper to her purse as the phone dials and rings. One ring. Two rings. Three. Four. And then a fifth ring. Erica almost reaches to disconnect the call when a voice mail message plays:

"This is Special Agent Bill Belmonte of the Drug Enforcement Administration's Los Angeles Division, Orange County Office. If this is an emergency, please hang up and dial 911. Otherwise, please leave me a message, and I'll return your call as soon as possible."

Erica nods to James to leave a message after the ubiquitous tone. "Agent Belmonte. My name is James Butler, and I'm an attorney at Castle, Smith, and Palmer in Irvine. I have an unusual matter I'm working on I'd like to discuss with you at your convenience. I'm usually easier to reach on my cell phone at 949-555-2222. Thank you and have a nice day."

James barely disconnected the call when he and Erica exclaim harmoniously, "DEA!"

"What does that mean?" Erica asks. "Was Aguilar working with someone in the DEA while he was looking into fentanyl? While he was in Yuma?"

"I guess you were right," James states.

"About what?" Erica asks.

"Maybe he did find someone better than me to have his back."

The sunrise starts its climb as Erica descends the stairs to find James in his running gear, drinking water in the kitchen.

"You're up early," Erica says.

"Couldn't sleep," James replies.

"Thinking about the call?" Erica asks.

"Yep."

"And now you're . . ."

"Going to go for a very long and very cathartic run," James explains.

"So, no office today?"

"I emailed Brian, Billy, and Sonja. They know how to find me if they need to. Plus, I'm taking advantage of the lull since both the Lawrence and Omni-Tech cases settled. You know my philosophy . . . take advantage of the lulls when you have them."

"I may do the same. Do you mind?" Erica asks.

"Of course not," James answers.

"Great. I'm going back to bed. Enjoy your run."

Erica kisses James on the cheek and re-climbs the stairs to the bedroom. "Can we install an elevator?!" she yells to the closing front door.

James sets out on his run, taking side streets to reach the Buck Gully Trailhead off Poppy Avenue, a popular hiking trail, but a deserted trail on this early Monday morning. James intends to do an easy, head clearing, out-and-back to the other trailhead on San Joaquin Hills Road near the Newport Coast Shopping Center, some five and a half miles each way.

Despite his best efforts to clear his head, questions continue to invade his thoughts.

If Aguilar had involved someone from the DEA in his investigation, why did he leave the folder of documents for Erica and me?

And what was he investigating? Why would he care about fentanyl?

He was bored—but not so bored he would start looking into something dangerous for no reason, and not in Yuma.

When James returns to the condo, Erica is dressed and chipper sipping coffee on the balcony.

"Good run?"

"Not bad," James replies while retrieving a bottle of water and a bottle of Coke Zero from the kitchen.

"Solve any mysteries?"

"No, but I did come up with more questions."

"Very helpful," Erica jests.

"Do you know where I left my phone?" James asks.

"I think it is on the end table where you were putting your shoes on this morning."

"Found it."

"Any calls or messages?" Erica asks.

"Not the one we're waiting for," James says.

"Damn it. You'd think a DEA agent would be anxious to talk to a defense attorney on a Monday morning," Erica says.

"Well . . ."

"Sarcasm, my dear. Sarcasm," she says.

James sits next to Erica, downing the water in one swift drink before opening the Coke Zero bottle. "I will never not love this view."

"Me neither," Erica replies. "Though there may come a day when a house is more practical."

"I know. I've been thinking about it too."

"You have?" Erica asks.

"Of course. It sucks that interest rates are where they are, but I've been thinking we need to start looking for something more 'family' and less 'bachelor.'" James smiles at Erica.

"Well said. I love you." Erica's intended romantic kiss is interrupted by the opening notes of "Take It Easy" playing from James's cell phone.

"It's him."

James moves inside, with Erica following, closing the sliding glass door behind them. James breathes out a long breath, then answers.

"James Butler."

"Mr. Butler, this is Bill Belmonte with the DEA. I'm returning your call."

James waves Erica over to the couch next to him. "Thank you for the return call. Do you mind if I put you on speaker so my wife and paralegal—one woman, two roles—can participate?"

"That's fine."

"Thank you, Agent Belmonte. This is Erica Walsh."

"Nice to meet you. How can I help you?" Agent Belmonte asks.

"I'm going to start for both of us," Erica remarks with a nod of approval from James. "We were close friends of Joe Aguilar, a retired DEA agent who, as you may know, was murdered in Yuma, Arizona, a few weeks ago."

"Yes. I heard about Agent Aguilar. I'm sorry for your loss."

"Thank you. We were at his house after the funeral this past weekend, and we found a note with your name and phone number and, well, we were just curious what your relationship was with him," Erica says.

"That's peculiar," Belmonte ruminates.

"Peculiar? Why so?" Erica prods.

"Peculiar because I've never met or talked to Agent Aguilar. Until the news and internal discussions surrounding his death, I'd heard his name only a few times, though, as it turns out, I'd heard stories about things he had done but didn't know it was him. I guess, technically, I still don't."

"You never met him or talked to him?" Erica asks.

"Never."

"You're right. It is a bit strange. Any idea why he had your name?" James interjects.

"I know it's not helpful, but I'm at a total loss," Belmonte says.

Erica pauses for a moment. "Would you have any time to meet this afternoon? I can come to you. I'm just thinking maybe a short discussion might be a path to some ideas and I prefer in person."

"I'll be here all afternoon, but I doubt you'll learn anything more. I'd hate to waste your time."

"If it's all the same to you, I'll risk it. How would 2 p.m. be for you?" Erica suggests.

"Fine with me, Ms. Walsh. Do you know where we are?" Agent Belmonte asks.

"I've been there before. I'll see you at two?"

"Sounds good."

Erica hangs up. "Seemed like a good idea to establish a rapport with him."

"I agree. Certainly, no harm," James says.

"Do you want to come with me?" Erica offers.

"Nah, I think you might be better without me. I'm thinking about calling Javi while you're gone. Maybe he'll have some insights," James says.

"Will the call be before or after your nap?" Erica teases with a smile.

"Probably before the nap, but after a shower," James says.

"I'm going to head out now and stop by the office on my way to Santa Ana and see my dad."

"Okay. This might get interesting. It's feeling like there is more going on here than we know," James says.

"Why would it be any other way?"

FIVE

The US Central Intelligence Agency is a civilian foreign intelligence service involved in the gathering, processing, and analyzing of national security information from around the world. After the Office of Strategic Services (OSS) was dissolved at the end of World War II, President Truman created the Central Intelligence Group under a director of central intelligence by presidential directive on January 22, 1946, and this group was transformed into the Central Intelligence Agency by implementation of the National Security Act of 1947.

The CIA has no law enforcement function and is focused on overseas intelligence gathering, with only limited domestic intelligence collection. This jurisdictional scope differentiates the CIA from its domestic counterpart, the FBI.

When the CIA was created, its purpose was to collect, maintain, and distribute foreign policy intelligence and analysis. Over time, its central mission has evolved. At present, its primary purpose is to collect, analyze, evaluate, and disseminate foreign intelligence, and to carry out covert operations made the subjects of book and movie lore.

The CIA has five key priorities: counterterrorism, nonproliferation of weapons of mass destruction, indications and warnings for senior policymakers, counterintelligence, and cyber intelligence.

The CIA also has an executive office and five major directorates: digital innovation, analysis, operations, support, and science and technology

The director of the CIA is appointed by the president with senate confirmation and reports directly to the director of national intelligence. In practice, the CIA director interfaces with the director of national intelligence, Congress, and the White House. The deputy director is the internal executive, and the chief operating officer is the agency's head of day-to-day activities.

Many of the duties and functions of several of the intelligence agencies, including the CIA, are outsourced and privatized. According to an article in the *Washington Post*, in 2007, Mike McConnell, former director of national intelligence, was about to publicize an investigation report of outsourcing by US intelligence agencies, but the report was classified before it could be released.[1]

Speculation is that in the report, among other issues discussed, the CIA identified different standards for government employees and contractors, an assessment of the appropriateness of outsourced activities, and best practices for accountability mechanisms.

According to an article published in *Salon* in 2008, many senior officials leave their national security and counterterrorism jobs for similar positions in the private sector that pay double or triple what the government agencies offer: "It's a privatization of the highest order, in which our collective memory and experience in intelligence—our crown jewels of spying, so to speak—are owned by corporate America."[2]

While estimates vary, one evaluation asserted that 70 percent of

1. R.J. Hillhouse, "Who Runs the CIA? Outsiders for Hire," Washington Post, July 8, 2007.
2. Tim Shorrock, "Former High-Ranking Bush Officials Enjoy War Profits," *Salon*, May 29, 2008.

the de facto workforce of the CIA's National Clandestine Service is contractors.

Within the CIA, the Special Activities Center (SAC) is the division responsible for covert and paramilitary operations. The SAC itself is comprised of two separate groups: Special Operations Group (SOG for tactical paramilitary operations and Political Action Group (PAG for covert political action.

The Special Operations Group is responsible for clandestine or covert operations that the US government does not want to be connected to. SOG is considered the most secretive special operations force and is said to comprise fewer than one hundred operators.

The Political Action Group is responsible for covert activities related to political influence, psychological operations, economic warfare, and cyberwarfare.

The CIA's budget and expenditures are not publicly released, though there were some disclosures in response to congressional investigations in the aftermath of the 9/11 tragedy. It is estimated that the CIA has the largest share of the National Intelligence Program budget, believed to be around $63 billion in fiscal year 2020.

Interestingly, shortly after the assassination of President Kennedy, former President Truman, the president who essentially created the CIA, openly questioned both the purpose and operation of the CIA. In a piece he wrote for the *Washington Post* dated December 22, 1963, President Truman reflected on the reasons that compelled him to organize the agency in the first place and his vision for reining it in going forward. He argued the CIA should be restored to its original role as the intelligence arm of the presidency and its operational duties should be terminated or moved elsewhere.

> We have grown up as a nation, respected for our free institutions and for our ability to maintain a free and open society. There is something about the way the CIA is

> functioning that is casting a shadow over our historic position and I feel we need to correct it.[3]

As soon as Erica leaves the condo, James scampers up the spiral stairs to the office. Once seated at his desk, he places a call to Dr. Javier Mirada. Javi, as he is known, is a professor at UC San Diego in the history department with a specialty in modern Mexican history and a focus on the development of the Mexican cartel structure and the influence of the cartels on Mexican society.

"James! Good to hear from you, my friend. I was very sorry to hear about Agent Aguilar."

"Thank you. Javi, I need your help," James states.

"You're looking into his murder, aren't you?" Javi asks.

"Why on Earth would you assume that?" James asks.

"You, my friend, are not one to sit by," Javi says.

"I'm just looking at a few things that don't quite add up," James states.

"What about the police?" Javi asks.

"A robbery gone bad, they say," James says.

"No kidding? I wonder how long it took them to come up with that idea," Javi says sarcastically.

"I think he was looking into the flow of fentanyl from Mexico into the United States."

"That's an area you probably know more about than I do," Javi states.

"But that's not the exact reason for my call. Aguilar left some documents for me, and included in them were a few web page printouts where an alleged link between the CIA and cocaine trafficking in the US is discussed."

"Well," Javi muses, "there is fertile ground there. Lots of allegations for many years. But—"

---

3. Harry S. Truman, "Limit CIA Role to Intelligence," *Washington Post*, December 22, 1963.

"But," James interrupts, "what does it have to do with the fentanyl crisis in America?"

"Exactly," Javi says.

"I don't know. But I'm married to a great investigator, so we are dividing and conquering."

"Ah, yes. How is your beautiful bride?" Javi asks.

"Wonderful, as always. She's visiting a DEA agent right now to talk about fentanyl, while I try to figure out if these CIA pages are of any significance. Starting with you."

"Look, James, if you want to understand what role, if any—and I emphasize the word *if*—the CIA has played in drug trafficking over the years, I think you should go way back and look in two areas," Javi suggests.

"Okay, and those are?" James asks.

"First, look at the reports from the Iran-Contra affair."

"Reports?"

"The Tower Commission, the Kerry Committee, the CIA Office of Inspector General. There are many, many reports," Javi explains.

The Iran-Contra Affair is the name given to a secret operation pursuant to which the United States traded missiles and other arms to free some Americans held hostage by terrorists in Lebanon, but also used funds from those arms deals to support the anti-Sandinista government Contra rebels in Nicaragua, in contravention to the Boland Amendment.

The Boland Amendment was a rider to Defense Department appropriations that prohibited military assistance to the Contras. The amendment applied to any agency or entity of the United States involved in intelligence activities. The amendment was signed into law by President Reagan, who opposed the amendment on policy grounds, each year from 1982 to 1986.

The term "Iran-Contra Affair" also refers to the ensuing scandal when the operation was exposed.

In the scandal's aftermath, several investigations were conducted, each with their own reports and conclusions. In November 1986, President Reagan announced the creation of a special review board to look into the matter and appointed former Senator John Tower, former Secretary of State Edmund Muskie, and former National Security Adviser Brent Scowcroft to serve as members. This review board became known as the Tower Commission.

At the request of Attorney General Edwin Meese III, a panel of three judges appointed Lawrence Walsh, a former judge and deputy attorney general under President Eisenhower, as an independent counsel to investigate the legal issues of the Iran-Contra affairs on December 19, 1986. Walsh requested an official appointment by the US Department of Justice on March 5, 1987, in order to avoid challenges over the constitutionality of using an independent counsel.

On March 5, 1987, the joint hearings of the House Select Committee to investigate covert arms transactions with Iran and the Senate Select Committee on secret military assistance to Iran and the Nicaraguan Opposition—later referred to simply as the Iran-Contra hearings—began and lasted for forty-one days and produced its own report.

A more wide-ranging investigation was conducted by a US Senate subcommittee led by Senators John Kerry and Christopher Dodd, referred to as the Kerry Committee. The Kerry Committee report—formally titled "Drugs, Law Enforcement and Foreign Policy"—was released on April 13, 1989, included discussions of drug trafficking in the Bahamas, Colombia, Cuba, Nicaragua, Haiti, Honduras, and Panama.

A significant portion of the Kerry Report discussed narcotics trafficking and the Nicaraguan Contras and concluded substantial evidence that the Contras and those working with the Contras engaged in drug smuggling and that money provided by the US to support the Contras was paid to drug traffickers.

"Okay, and why?" James asks.

"When the whole arming the Contras fiasco hit the fan, there were many allegations of the CIA using drug money to fund the Contras," Javi says.

"Including claims they were working with Rafa Quintero and/or Félix Gallardo. I remember some from my research on Rafa," James says.

"Correct. The primary reports did not support the more grandiose theories and accusations, though there was no reason to think they would, but they did draw some links between support for the Contras and the drug trade. As I said, I don't think there is anything concrete or definitive in them, but it's good background," Javi says.

James takes a moment to consider this. "I suspect the areas of interest they touch upon might also be fertile ground for some additional review, assuming the most egregious evidence of a link might not have made it into a public report."

"Probably a fair assumption," Javi concedes.

"Okay, I'm sold. And the second place to look?" James asks.

"Go back to Gary Webb. Read his book and articles," Javi says.

"Gary Webb? I know you've talked about him before, and I read a bit of his work in the past, but his book doesn't mention Camarena or Rafa Quintero, and since they were our focus, I moved on. Besides, wasn't he discredited?" James asks.

"Don't be so quick to judge. First, ask yourself *who* would want to discredit his reporting. Second, more recent 'analysis' both in the academic community and otherwise is much kinder to Webb and his research than were his contemporaries. And third, even if Webb went astray or made dubious connections, perhaps not *everything* he reported was wrong," Javi says.

"I'm not sure how researching Gary Webb is going to help me figure out who killed Aguilar," James says.

"I don't know either. But do you think the CIA clipping was in Aguilar's materials randomly or by mistake?" Javi asks.

"Not for a second."

"Then, my friend, start from the beginning."

"Okay, makes sense, but a lot of work," James says.

"I can't help you much there, but one of Webb's old colleagues has talked about Webb from time to time. His name is Brian Wilson —not from the Beach Boys—and I think he lives, or did live, in Phoenix," Javi says.

"A good start. Thanks. Anything else?" James inquires.

Javi pauses before speaking. "I'm going to be super candid with you, James, and trust you'll understand. I love my job and I think I'm good at it. I love teaching, especially grad students. I thoroughly enjoy the research, the conferences, the collaborations, the travel. I have a great life. When I look at the cartels, and Mexico, and drugs, there is an entire tapestry of threads I can pull on, and rabbit holes to fall down, to mix metaphors.

"I choose not to pull on many of those threads. Not because they aren't interesting and not because I'm afraid, but because they are of no benefit to my career or my research.

"I work at a public institution and my work is supported, in large part, by public funds. I have great relationships with government officials and agencies on both sides of the border and those relationships make my job easier and more rewarding.

"In my position, there is no value for me to tug on the CIA threads—threads I know full well are there. I'm not convinced there is a single, definitive answer and it's tangential to my main interests. But more to the point, doing it could put what I have and what I do at risk. I'm not saying I wouldn't look deeper at something if it presented itself, but I'm not looking for it.

"But, my good friend, I'll help you in absolutely any way possible," Javi states.

"I totally understand and respect your position, Javi. And I recognize I'm in a unique position to pull on many of those threads —carefully. Erica and I have chosen to continue on this path—for now—but to do so with open eyes and only if we both believe in what we are doing," James says.

"I appreciate the understanding," Javi says.

"Of course. You're my friend and I have a huge amount of respect for you and your work, which I probably should let you get back to," James says.

"Yeah, I should. Good luck, James. Call me if you want to talk about anything."

"You know I will. Be well, Javi."

SIX

The DEA's Orange County office is in a nondescript building near downtown Santa Ana, with no visible signage or any indication of who or what occupies the building. A chain link fence surrounds the building, a gate and a call box the only signs of occupation. Notably, when the call box is utilized, the usual response is an equally nondescript "hello," further adding to the building's anonymity and mystery.

Erica knows the drill and responds to the monotone voice by noting her appointment with Agent Belmonte. A couple of minutes pass before Agent Belmonte arrives and lets her in, leading her down the single sidewalk pathway to a glass door with the appearance of a side entrance.

"Did you find it okay?" Belmonte asks as they walk toward the building.

"I did. Thankfully, I've been here before. I'm sure you know GPS takes one next door?"

"Yes, so we've been told. One of the benefits of having high security, though the Uber drivers hate it," Belmonte says.

"I expect they would," Erica says.

Arriving at the door, Belmonte swipes his key card and holds the door open for Erica.

"Just to the left is the elevator. We will be on the second floor."

Erica turns left and onto the open elevator, with Belmonte following. The doors open on the second floor. Belmonte steps to the side, allowing Erica off the elevator first, before taking the lead.

"I have a conference room down the hall for us. The art on these walls is almost all the work of retired DEA Agent Abel Reynoso, who has a gallery in Florida. Fort Lauderdale, I think."

Belmonte stops and opens the door to a small, sparse conference room. Erica enters and Belmonte shuts the door, before the two sit across from one another at a small table.

"Can I get you anything to drink?" Belmonte asks.

"No, but thank you."

"Tell me, Ms. Walsh, how might I help you, aside from what I told you on the phone?"

"It's Erica, please, and as we discussed briefly on the phone, we found your name and number on some paper among some items left by Agent Aguilar. We were just hoping you might have some information—any information—that could help us as we look into his murder."

"I hate to say you drove all this way for nothing, but, as I already said, I never met Agent Aguilar, and, until his death, knew next to nothing about him," Belmonte states.

"I understand, but let me ask you this, Agent Belmonte, have you always been assigned to the Orange County office?" Erica asks.

"Oh, heck no. We agents tend to move around a lot. I started as a police officer in Chicago before moving to the San Francisco PD to follow my wife who got a job at one of the big accounting companies there. A few years later, I joined the DEA out of Santa Rosa and Stockton, California, then I went to Lima, Peru, for a bit more than five years. After I returned to the US, I was assigned to the Phoenix division, mostly in Nogales and Tucson. I've been here in Santa Ana a bit more than a year."

"You did a lot of traveling for a married man," Erica says.

"My wife maintained our family home, and she was able to

work from Peru; her firm has an office in Lima. These days, we have a house in Los Altos Hills, and I have a condo in Huntington Beach. We go back and forth often. The advantages of having a wife who's a partner in a big accounting firm."

"Do you have a family?" Erica asks.

"We have a daughter who is in medical school at UC San Francisco, and our son lives in New York City where he is working to be a chef after culinary school." Belmonte says. "Do you and Mr. Butler have kids?"

"No, not yet. We've talked about it, and we keep trying to find the right time, though we know there never will be such a thing."

"I'm sure you've heard it a thousand times but there is nothing more challenging or more rewarding than being a parent," Belmonte says.

"I have no doubt." Erica gathers her thoughts. "When you were in the Phoenix division, did you work on any cases involving fentanyl from Mexico?"

"Ms. Walsh, I'd venture to say most agents in the agency have dealt with fentanyl at some point in the last few years. It's reached true epidemic proportions, as I'm sure you know."

"Did you ever work out of the Yuma office?" Erica asks.

"Not directly, but of course I had contact with the agents there and went to the office a dozen or so times while I was in Arizona. What does this have to do with Agent Aguilar?" Belmonte asks.

"I'm not sure, but we think his interest in Yuma might have been related to the fentanyl traffic," Erica says.

"Do you know how?" Belmonte asks.

Erica shakes her head. "I don't know if we are right. At this point, we're just taking baby steps and exploring all angles to look for something helpful or constructive."

"I'd think the authorities covered this ground?"

"And they may have. But, in any event, James and I want to do some snooping around on our own. He was a dear friend. Maybe our relationship with him will help us identify things others would miss."

"I'm sorry I can't help, but you have my number. If something comes up, feel free to give me a call," Belmonte says.

"I suspect I'll be taking you up on that offer," Erica says.

"Before you go, may I ask, is it true?"

"Is what true?" Erica asks hesitantly.

"Did Aguilar go to Mexico and come back with Rafa Quintero?" Belmonte asks.

"There are stories suggesting he did," Erica says.

"Before our meeting, I was talking to someone else in the office. He said he knows only the rumors and gossip, but he was told it was a four-person team. Three men and a woman. Were you and Mr. Butler with Aguilar?"

"I think it would be prudent if I neither confirmed nor denied the veracity of such tales," Erica says.

"I understand. But let me ask this. My friend said he also heard the woman went nose-to-nose with Rafa and got him to confess to killing Agent Camarena, though the confession, as it were, could never be used in court or be told publicly. Was it you?"

"Agent Belmonte, you're putting me in an awkward spot."

"I'm sorry. It's not intended. I do wonder, hypothetically, what the woman thought of Rafa," Belmonte says.

Erica thinks for a moment. "You know, I've heard rumors and stories too. As has James. Those stories suggested that the sight of the blood draining from Rafa's face as he realized he'd gone too far and had no hope was a sight to behold and to cherish."

"I can only imagine. I wonder why the others, besides Aguilar, haven't sold their stories. I'd think they could have networks fighting each other in the streets to get the first exclusive interview," Belmonte says.

"I don't know, maybe. But maybe, at least for some, there are emotions and personal satisfactions that money and notoriety cannot compete with. Maybe having secretly done the right thing, for the right reasons, is enough," Erica suggests.

Belmonte nods and they sit in silence for a moment.

"But there I go again speaking in grand hypotheticals," Erica comments.

"Fair enough, Erica. Fair enough."

"One last question before I go, if I might?" Erica asks.

"Of course. Ask away."

"I know fentanyl is a huge business—an epidemic as you said—but I'm wondering what the DEA thinks the size of it is in dollars?"

"I don't have a number off the top of my head, but I do remember at one point seeing some estimates putting it at more than $3 billion annually," Belmonte answers.

Erica releases a short whistle. "Someone would only need a small piece of a very big pie to make a lot of money," Erica muses.

"Perhaps more importantly," Belmonte replies, "someone with a small piece of a very big pie would be willing to do an awful lot to hold onto it."

SEVEN

JAMES'S OFFICE is more cluttered than normal. Deposition and trial transcripts are stacked high on his working table, and piles of documents dot the office floor. Despite the abundance of work in front of him, James had taken Dr. Mirada's words to heart and looked into Gary Webb and some of his associates, including Brian Wilson. Having spent many fruitless and frustrating minutes trying to locate Webb, James stops, smiles, and dials four numbers for an inter-office call.

"Hi, babe. Miss me?"

"Always! Can you do me a favor?" James asks.

"Name it," Erica says.

"Javi suggested I try to talk to a former reporter named Brian Wilson, who I believe was friends with Gary Webb in the past. He might live somewhere in the Phoenix area, but I'm coming up totally empty on an address or phone number for him. But . . ."

"But I can."

"Exactly," James says.

"Happy to do it. Give me an hour or so," Erica says.

"You're the best."

"Don't ever forget it!"

Within an hour, Erica sends James a virtual dossier on Brian Wilson, who in fact lives in Phoenix and has an AOL email address. James smirks, surprised that such accounts still exist.

Abandoning his usual preference for phone conversations, James composes a quick email:

Mr. Wilson. I am an attorney in Orange County, California. I'm working on a matter that has led me to look at many of the writings of Gary Webb. I'm told you were a colleague and friend of his. I'm wondering if I could visit you to talk about him and his work. Do you still reside in Phoenix?

After hitting send, James returns to work, and, trying to utilize some time management tools, does not look at his inbox for a few hours. When he does open Outlook, he is relieved to find a reply from Wilson:

Gary and I worked at competing papers for many years. We were rivals and friends. I hate what happened to him. As for meeting, I am retired and spend most of my days reading and doing an occasional article. I'm in the Phoenix suburbs. Come by if you want. 1705 West Tyson Street, Chandler. 480-555-3333

James presses a speed-dial button on his office phone.

"Mr. Butler. How may I help you?"

"Do you know any drug dealers in Phoenix?"

Bobby stifles a laugh. "If you need a hookup, we can probably arrange it here."

"Good to know. But no. I need to go to Phoenix to meet with someone, and while I'm there, I was hoping to find someone who might be able to talk about the flow of drugs from Mexico into the US. Someone more at the street level," James says.

"You causing trouble again?" Bobby asks.

"Maybe, which is why I was going to ask you to come with me," James says.

"You're learning. I know someone. Let me try to set up something. When are you thinking?" Bobby inquires.

"Thursday?"

"Works for me, and I'll try to set up the meeting then too," Bobby says.

"Awesome. I'll book it and send you the info," James says.

"Always a pleasure, Mr. Butler."

"See you soon."

Gary Webb authored a three-part series "Dark Alliance" published in the *Mercury News* from August 18 to 20, 1996. The overall thesis behind the series, and the essence of Webb's claims, was that a San Francisco Bay area drug ring sold cocaine to the Crips and Bloods in Los Angeles for almost ten years, and funneled millions of dollars from the profits to a Latin American guerrilla army run by the CIA.

In his first article, Webb claimed that this drug ring essentially created the pipeline between Colombian cartels and Black communities in Los Angeles, and this open channel fueled the crack epidemic in urban America.

Webb's articles focused on three men: Ricky Ross, Oscar Danilo Blandón, and Norwin Meneses. Ross was a major drug dealer in Los Angeles. Blandón and Meneses were Nicaraguans who smuggled drugs into the US and supplied dealers like Ross. Webb attributed much—perhaps too much—of the rise of crack cocaine in the United States to these three men, with particular emphasis on the disparate impacts crack had on Black communities.

Looking back, the initial press reaction to Webb's series and its accusations is stunning. Rather than being supportive of Webb's efforts, most of the response could best be described as decidedly hostile. The first detailed piece on Webb's articles appeared in the *Washington Post*, where reporters Roberto Suro and Walter Pincus claimed Webb's allegations were not supported by the available information and further maintained the rise of crack was "a broad-based phenomenon" driven in numerous places by diverse players.[1]

By mid-October, the *New York Times* had published two articles characterizing Webb's evidence as thin and questioning the importance of the drug dealers discussed in the series, both in the crack cocaine trade and in supporting the Contras.

The *Los Angeles Times,* utilizing a team of seventeen—yes seventeen—reporters, ran a series of articles on the Webb allegations from October 20–22, 1996, and concluded Webb "significantly overstated" the contributions of Blandón and Meneses to the Contras and Contra-supporting organizations and further maintained the men had not been protected by the CIA.[2]

Despite the general rejection of Webb's assertions by the press, the "Dark Alliance" series prompted at least three federal investigations. As a group, the reports denied most of Webb's primary assertions, but, at the same time, were critical of some CIA and law enforcement actions.

The *Mercury News* conducted an internal review of Webb's series, which resulted in a column published on May 11, 1997, where the paper's executive editor, Jerry Ceppos, defended parts of Webb's work, writing the series had "solidly documented" that the drug ring described in the series had connections with the Contras and did sell large quantities of cocaine in inner-city Los Angeles.

The Ceppos column, however, went further, concluding Webb's series did not live up to the periodical's standards in four areas: (1) it presented only one interpretation of conflicting evidence and in one case "did not include information that contradicted a central assertion of the series"; (2) the series' estimate of the money involved was presented as fact instead of as an estimate; (3) the series oversimplified how crack epidemic in American cities grew;

1. Robert Suro and Walter Pincus, "The CIA and Crack: Evidence Is Lacking of Alleged Plot," *Washington Post,* October 4, 1996.
2. Jesse Katz, Doyle McManus, John Mitchell, and Sam Fulwood, "The Cocaine Trail," *Los Angeles Times,* October 20–22, 1996.

and (4) the series "created impressions that were open to misinterpretation" through "imprecise language and graphics."[3]

Soon after the Ceppos column, Webb resigned from the *Mercury News* and expanded the "Dark Alliance" series into a book in which he responded to some of the criticisms he had endured and described his experiences writing the story and dealing with the controversy. His experience left him disillusioned with the industry he had dedicated his career to:

If we had met five years ago, you wouldn't have found a more staunch defender of the newspaper industry than me. . . . The truth was that, in all those years, I hadn't written anything important enough to suppress.[4]

Webb was found dead in his home on December 10, 2004, with two gunshot wounds to the head. The Sacramento county coroner's office ruled Webb's death a suicide but did not quell the allegations of a conspiracy and cover-up.

Webb's ex-wife, Susan Bell, told reporters she believed his death was a suicide. According to Bell, Webb had been unhappy for some time over his inability to get a job at another major newspaper, and Webb had sold his house the week before his death because he was unable to afford the mortgage.

---

3. Jerome Ceppos, "To Readers of our 'Dark Alliance' Series," editorial, *Mercury News*, May 11, 1997.
4. Gary Webb, *Dark Alliance: The CIA, the Contras, and the Crack Cocaine Explosion* (New York: Seven Stories Press, 1998).

EIGHT

JAMES APPROACHES Brian Wilson's suburban Phoenix home, which sits at the end of a cul de sac abutting the lake at Fountain Park. James parks on the street before ringing the doorbell of the stylish patio home.

Wilson answers the door, looking as if he has been summoned from Central Casting. Wilson is short, with only faint traces of a former head of hair, his soft blue eyes hidden behind wire rimmed glasses, wearing a blue Oxford shirt, khakis, and brown loafers. Wilson looks to be approaching seventy, but he puts out an aurora suggesting more vitality than his age might suggest.

Wilson greets James and shows him around the house, highlighting some of his more notable achievements reflected among the many plaques, news clippings, and mementos adorning the light grey walls.

Two glasses of ice-cold water later, and the men sit on the patio looking toward the park, enjoying the moderate spring weather.

The small talk about the weather soon leads to James asking about Gary Webb.

"They killed him. Directly or indirectly, they killed him," Wilson asserts.

"Let me ask an admittedly overly simplified question," James responds, treading lightly. “Why? I mean, why would someone be so concerned about what he wrote to be willing to go so far as to kill him?”

“Don’t worry, James, you won’t offend me. I’ve heard all of these questions and then some for years,” Wilson says.

“Good,” James says with a smile. “I’m not in any way disagreeing with you, but, rather, trying to learn more and understand better.”

“The answer to your question is, in my opinion, simple: because he was right. Nearly thirty years later, we know he was right. The CIA was involved in and profited from the flow of drugs, mostly cocaine, from Mexico into the United States.”

“Again, respectfully, so what? Don’t we assume the CIA is into all sorts of nefarious things, and no one paid a price for what he wrote?” James presses.

“It’s a fair question, James, and I think there are two answers to it.” Wilson’s eyes are passionate, but his words are deliberate. “First, think about the time frame. When Gary’s work came out, people were maybe less jaded, and evidence pointing to the CIA bearing a significant responsibility for the proliferation of crack cocaine in the United States was, to many, shocking. Second, who says the efforts of the CIA started or ended with the events Gary wrote about?”

“I’m not sure I follow,” James says.

“Meaning, if Gary was right, and people believed Gary was right, there would be more scrutiny on operations past and present and more rats would have been exposed by the light,” Wilson says.

“I imagine then, following that logic, you think that’s why so many came down so hard on him and his reporting? When I was researching Gary and the aftermath of his articles, I was taken aback by the vociferousness of the criticism from those within the journalism world,” James says.

“In all fairness, it is a complex issue, and remember, I was part of his world professionally. Some of my good friends, then and now, turned their backs on Gary, as did journalists I respected. I think there were a number of factors. Professional jealousy played a part. I think there was a lingering naiveté, even within the professional press, and it led to a reluctance to believe the government could be involved in these things, notwithstanding the events of Vietnam and Watergate. I'm sure, and I think there has been some evidence to prove, there were elements of the press doing the bidding for the CIA to discredit his reports, whether knowingly or naively.

"But, again, to be fair, I must admit Gary didn't always help himself. It's apparent, at least to me, there were places where he took things farther than he needed to. Times where he extrapolated too much. Some of his assertions of 'fact' probably were larger than the evidence supported. Grander than they needed to be. But those errors on his part don't change the fact that his base allegations—the core of his reporting—were true," Wilson says.

"Why, then, has there been so little work in support of his allegations or follow-up reporting to vindicate the bulk of his reporting?" James asks.

"James, I suspect you know the answer at least as well as I do."

"Perhaps, but for discussions sake, what do you think?"

"As with so many questions, there are many potential, and not mutually exclusive, answers. For example, who in the media had the interest in following in his footsteps? Woodward and Bernstein end up at a Hollywood premier to see their images on the silver screen—by Redford and Hoffman no less—while Gary was run off and to his death." Wilson says.

"And," James inserts, "I suppose, someone in a position to do such reporting would be aware if there *were* elements in the media, government, or elsewhere who tried to destroy Webb's credibility, those elements would still be out there—whether the same names and faces or not—the interests were still there exactly."

"Some more objective reporting did come along, just decades too late," Wilson says.

"Long after it made any difference to Webb," James adds.

"In 2014," Wilson continues, "a reporter by the name of Ryan

Devereaux wrote about documents released by the CIA, including a previously unreleased six-page article titled 'Managing a Nightmare: CIA Public Affairs and the Drug Conspiracy Story.' Devereaux said the documents showed that the CIA viewed Gary's reports as 'a genuine public relations crisis.'"

"Somehow, I'm shocked the CIA was worried about public relations. But, I suppose I shouldn't be surprised," James says.

"What's worse, James, is what they did in response to the PR crisis. There is a line from Devereaux's article I remember. The quote might not be perfect but it's something like using 'a ground base of already productive relations with journalists,' the CIA 'watched with relief as the largest newspapers in the country rescued the agency from disaster, and, in the process, destroyed the reputation of an aggressive, award-winning reporter.'"[1]

"I'm having trouble wrapping my head around this. Would the CIA be so worried about Webb's reporting?" James asks.

"Let me answer your question with a question of my own. What do you know about Operation Gladio?" Wilson asks.

"I think I'm going to be embarrassed when I say nothing," James admits.

"Don't worry, not many do. Gladio was part of a post-World War II program set up by the CIA and NATO to thwart future Soviet/communist invasions or influence in Italy and Western Europe. But there are allegations, most notably from a Swiss historian, Daniele Ganser, that Gladio became a decades-long, state-sponsored, right-wing terrorist network, involved in false flag operations and activities to subvert democracy. At a minimum, it was a secretive and unsupervised operation by the CIA spanning decades. The existence of Gladio was confirmed and admitted by the Italian government in 1990, and several other countries, including the United States years later.

---

1. Ryan Devereaux, "How the CIA Watched Over the Destruction of Gary Webb," *Intercept*, September 25, 2014, https://theintercept.com/2014/09/25/managing-nightmare-cia-media-destruction-gary-webb/.

"As I understand it, Ganser and others believe the Gladio-style groups, in the absence of Soviet invasion, took steps to discredit left-wing groups and politicians through the use of 'the strategy of tension,' which included acts of false-flag terrorism. Tension allows for control and manipulation of public opinion. The idea, I think, was to instill fear into the populace while placing the blame for terrorist attacks on communist and left-wing opponents." Wilson takes a sip of water.

"This is all documented?" James asks.

"It is, James. There are the Ganser publications. There were hearings here and in Italy. There were news reports. There is a good book compiling much of the information on the matter by Paul Williams. Of course, not everyone agrees with all of Ganser's conclusions, but the 'stay behind' operations are irrefutable. Heck, there are some articles asserting a connection between the CIA, the Operation, and the Kennedy assassination, but I have steered clear of that very deep rabbit hole," Wilson says.

"Then why have I not heard about it?" James asks.

"To ask the question, James, is to answer it," Wilson states.

"So you're saying this is just one example of CIA activity the agency would have been concerned about becoming publicly exposed?" James asks.

"Exactly."

James pauses and thinks for a moment. "Okay, since you zigged left, I'm going to zag right and ask what you know about Genaro Garcia Luna."

"Only what I read in the paper. He was, what, the head of Mexico's anti-drug efforts but in practice was cooperating, on some level, with the Sinaloa Cartel?" Wilson asks.

"A good summary of the ten-thousand-foot view," James says.

"But you're going to tell me there are more interesting things at a different view." Wilson smiles.

"I am. As I've been able to unravel it, Garcia Luna was not just working with the Sinaloa Cartel—including having some type of personal relationship with El Chapo—but he was also well connected and likely working with both the FBI and the DEA. A tangential thread of investigation suggests, at a minimum, that El Chapo, for many years, had a relationship with the CIA," James says.

"How far back can you trace the CIA's involvement with him?" Wilson asks.

"Maybe back to the beginning of his real power; the early 1990s. But a hard maybe. Information on the activities of the traffickers during the 80s and into the 90s is far more difficult to come by than one would expect," James says.

"It does make sense to me." Wilson pauses, gazing at the fountain in the park. "Let's piece this together for a second. Gary asserted he found direct connections between the CIA and drug trafficking in the US, mostly coke and crack and mostly to inner cities."

"Okay . . ." James intones.

"And you say there may have been connections between the CIA and El Chapo a few years later?" Wilson asks.

"Right," James replies, puzzled, as he leans on his knees looking at Wilson.

"Don't you have to wonder how far back or how widespread it was?" Wilson adds.

"The CIA's connection with the traffickers?" James asks.

"Right," Wilson affirms.

"I think about it all the time."

"Then, of course," Wilson continues, "are the allegations connected to the Camarena case?"

"Hold on. I've done a lot, and I mean *a lot*, of work and study and investigation around the Camarena case. If you are referring to claims that the CIA was somehow involved in Agent Camarena's murder, I've found nothing, nothing substantive or verifiable to support such a connection," James says.

"You sound pretty convinced. All I know are the allegations I've heard," Wilson offers.

"You're right." James takes a deep breath. "There are allegations. Allegations I've looked at, about people I've talked to, and I can't accept them. More importantly, I've not been able to find any corroboration for the statements of a few criminals desperate to stay in the US and a prosecution almost frenzied in their efforts to convict someone for Camarena's murder."

"I'm convinced. Are you saying the CIA wasn't involved with the drug traffickers around then?" Wilson asks.

"No, no, I'm not prepared to go so far," James says. "They may well have been connected to Félix Gallardo in some way—"

"Through Matta?"

James lets out a short laugh. "So, you know more than you let on. There likely were connections between Matta, Félix, the Colombians, and the CIA. I might be willing to consider the possibility that some of the other traffickers, including Rafael Caro Quintero, might have had CIA contacts or connections, at some level. But none of it means—"

"The CIA killed Camarena," Wilson interrupts. "No, it does not."

"Look," James continues, "I'm sure we've both seen enough evidence to assert, with some element of persuasiveness, the CIA was somehow involved with drug trafficking in the US and in Mexico, and probably South America, for a large part of the 80s and 90s, at a minimum. In my mind, Webb's reporting, accepting some of its flaws, remains perhaps the most comprehensive exposure of those connections."

"I can live with that summary," Wilson says, standing to take both water glasses to the kitchen, returning with filled glasses. "The question I have is why, knowing what you know about the CIA, about Webb and, I suspect, about the traffickers, past and present, why are you asking more questions? What's in it for you? Why is a high-profile Orange County lawyer sitting on my patio asking questions about my friend Gary, who's been dead for, what, twenty-ish years now? Wouldn't it be easier and maybe safer to let the past stay in the past?"

"I understand the logic of what you're saying, and I have no good retort. But I'm afraid I've gone too far down the road to look back now," James says.

"And which road is that, James?" Wilson asks.

"As I mentioned earlier, my current interest is in understanding the current flow of drugs, fentanyl in particular, from Mexico into the United States, and to understand the players involved in the trade, on both sides of the border," James says.

"I'm no direct help there. I only know what I've seen or heard on the news or in the papers," Wilson asserts.

"Fentanyl is not why I wanted to talk to you. My suspicion is, and you've helped solidify that suspicion, that there are threads running from the fentanyl trade, back to Garcia Luna, to El Chapo, to the Contras, and the events Webb disclosed—or at least some of them. It's like one flowing river of malfeasance through time." James stands and paces as he talks. "But now I think there must be more. Paradoxically because there is precious little material supporting information from around the time of the Camarena murder."

"I'm not sure I follow. If there is the river you refer to but nothing that ties to the Camarena case, the absence of ties says something in and of itself?" Wilson asks.

"Yes, as I said before, I've looked. A lot. And nothing I've found even hints at a connection. There's not one piece of paper I'm aware of supporting the claim. His name never comes up in Webb's book," James says.

"But," Wilson retorts, "going back to our prior discussions, if many of the CIA's operations are 'off the books' then isn't it possible some were kept under wraps better than others?"

"Sure, and I know someone who might have an answer to the question," James states.

"But there is more, James."

"More is good. Let's hear it," James says.

"There was a hearing before the House Intelligence Committee in March 1998 where CIA Inspector General Fred P. Hitz said he found examples where the CIA did not always cut ties with certain individuals supporting the Contra program who were allegedly involved in drug trafficking. Hitz was asked whether any of the allegations he referred to involved trafficking in the United States. Hitz answered with a simple yes," Wilson says.

"Wow," James says in awe of what he's hearing.

"But I haven't yet gotten to the most remarkable part. Hitz went on to assert that from 1982 to 1995 there was no official requirement to report on allegations of drug trafficking with respect to 'non-employees' of the agency, defined to include agents, assets, and contractors. And, most significantly, Hitz testified that there had been a secret agreement to that effect between the CIA and US Attorney General William French Smith," Wilson says.

"No kidding?" James exclaims. "No wonder the argument so often focused on the lack of evidence of any drug trafficking operations involving between the CIA and the Contras. They were playing a game of semantics."

"And the press perpetuated the semantic deception."

According to the CIA's inspector general, the agreement had its roots in Executive Order No. 12333, which President Reagan signed into law in 1981. It is said the order was signed the same week Reagan authorized the CIA's operations in Nicaragua.

The executive order set forth the rules on the conduct of US intelligence agencies around the world. The new rules differed from the Carter Administration's rules in how crimes committed by American operatives were to be reported. Following the executive order, the rules stated that the attorney general and the head of an intelligence agency had to agree on procedures related to crimes reporting. This requirement for agreement, in effect, gave the CIA veto power over crimes the Justice Department might want to prosecute.

In 1982, CIA director William Casey and Attorney General

French Smith executed a Memorandum of Understanding delineating those crimes to be reported to the Justice Department. Two key elements of this policy distinguished the policy from the policies of prior administration.

First, crimes committed by people "acting for" an intelligence agency were not required to be reported to the Justice Department. But any crimes committed by official "card-carrying" CIA officers were required to be reported.

Second, drug offenses were removed from the list of crimes the CIA was required to report, apparently revealing one of the policy's primary motivations. Several reports indicated the drug crimes removal was thoroughly discussed and coordinated between the CIA and DOJ. This led some to speculate that the CIA was well-aware, in advance of the completion of the agreement, that some working with the CIA would likely be selling drugs.

"Why is it I have heard almost nothing about this?" James asks. "The Administration behind the infamous 'Just Say No' campaign structured a deal to overlook agency-related drug crimes. It's . . . it's . . . I hate the word but it's incredible."

"The truth is, with the exception of a few reports, the media either ignored the story or buried it," Wilson states.

"Intentionally?" James asks.

"Someone else can make that judgment, but, to me, the evidence speaks loudly."

"Can I go back to Webb and ask another question?" James asks.

"Fire away," Wilson says.

"Who do you think killed him?" James asks.

Wilson pauses before responding. "In short, all of them. They all played a role in what happened to him, what he did. The media, the government, people he thought were his friends."

"So, you think it was a suicide?"

"I don't know. I don't. I could see how it could have been. He'd lost everything," Wilson says.

"What about the murder speculation?" James queries.

"Maybe." Wilson looks down as he talks. "But, as his friend, it didn't matter much, he was gone, and no amount of finger pointing was going to bring him back."

"No, I guess not," James says.

"Before you go, James, I have a last thought," Wilson offers.

"What's that?"

"Assume the CIA was involved with drug traffickers as Gary reported, and as the DOJ agreement might indicate, and then assume the CIA profited in some way from those connections and maybe collaborated with El Chapo. In those circumstances, what do you suppose the money would have been used for?" Wilson asks.

"By the CIA?" James asks.

"Right," Wilson concurs. "I mean, I assume they weren't making deposits in the national treasury or Bank of America."

"Black ops? Off the book, non-congressionally funded operations?" James surmises.

"I agree," Wilson says lifting himself to sit upright. "And if they had been receiving such dark funding over the course of many years, isn't it likely to have amounted to a lot of money?"

"Enough money to fund a number of pet projects, and enough money to miss if it suddenly went away," James says.

"Exactly. Which leads to one inevitable and critical question, James."

"Which is?" James asks.

"Why would anyone think the money flow ever stopped?"

NINE

JAMES RETURNS to his modest rental car in front of Wilson's house. He turns the car on to activate the air conditioning before placing a call to Bobby.

"How was your meeting?" Bobby asks.

"Illuminating. Well worth the trip. Do we have a schedule for this evening?" James asks.

"We do. We are meeting at 6 p.m."

"How far from the hotel?" James asks.

"Not far at all. Ten minutes max," Bobby answers,

"Meet in the lobby at 5:45?"

"Sounds good. And one more thing, James," Bobby says.

"Yeah?" James asks.

"Try not to look like a lawyer."

James pulls out of the Wilson driveway, considering his path back to the hotel. Once on I-10 toward downtown Phoenix, he thinks more about his discussion with Wilson.

I've read so many conspiracy theories involving the CIA, I might have become too cynical. Maybe Tim can steer me in the right direction.

James uses voice command to place the call. Tim answers on the second ring.

"James, how are you?" Tim asks.

"I'm good. Hey, I'm in Phoenix looking into Aguilar's case, and I had a witness give me some interesting information about the CIA in Mexico. I had a few questions, and who better to ask than you?"

"Damn, James, I'd be happy to help but I'm in the middle of a 'thing' right now. Can we talk later?" Tim asks.

"Sure. Do you want me to call you later?" James asks.

"Why don't I call you instead . . . when I free up?" Tim says.

"Sure. Thanks, Tim."

"You bet. Bye," Tim says and hangs up.

That was . . . unusual. I wonder what he's working on.

The Westin Phoenix is located in downtown Phoenix, within easy walking distance of the federal courthouse, Civic Space Park, The Arizona Republic, and the Sandra Day O'Connor College of Law and is a quick Uber to Chase Field and other downtown landmarks.

After returning from Wilson's, James goes to his room to type up some basic notes of his conversation with Wilson and to prepare a few key talking points for the meeting this evening. Following a hot shower to relax, James admires his view of the South Mountain Park and Preserve before heading to the valet.

James hands the valet his parking ticket and finds a spot to wait sheltered from the spring wind carrying a chill defying the low sixty-degree temperature.

James watches Bobby exit through the hotel's revolving door, wearing jeans, a solid black T-shirt, and white Converse sneakers.

"Mr. Butler, how are you?" Bobby asks, reaching out to shake hands.

"I'm great, Bobby. I had a chance to unwind a little, so all is good. A little chilly, but good."

"Hah, how often do you get to wear your cashmere sweater in Phoenix?" Bobby asks.

"Aren't you cold in just a T-shirt?" James asks.

"You forget, I played in Buffalo."

"Yes, but you grew up in Southern California," James replies.

"Trust me, Buffalo winters will toughen you up real fast," Bobby explains.

As Bobby speaks, the valet pulls up with their modest rental car, and James and Bobby hop in.

"Where are were headed?" James asks.

"Lo-Lo's Chicken & Waffles on Central Avenue."

"You're joking right?" James asks.

"No, why?"

"Could this be any more stereotypical? Heck, I feel racist just thinking about it," James says uneasily.

Bobby shrugs. "It's where C-3 wanted to meet so it's where we're meeting. Plus, he says the food is really good."

"Okay, okay. Tell me about C-3 again. Like, how did he get the name?" James asks.

"Cedric, I should call him Cedric, he doesn't go by C-3 these days. Cedric Charles Carter. C-3," Bobby states.

"Oh, got it. Frankly, it's not a very intimidating name."

"Maybe not, but you might want to keep that opinion to yourself," Bobby says.

"Duly noted," James agrees.

"In any event, Cedric is an old-school gang banger from South Phoenix. For a time in the early 2000s, he was the head of the West End Gangsters, and from what I've heard, he was a major player and a major bad ass. So, again, best not to tell him his nickname was wimpy," Bobby reiterates.

"Point taken. How do you know him?" James asks.

"His brother, Derek, was a safety for the Bills when I played with them. We became good friends, so I've hung out with Cedric on occasion. He's legit now, teaches at Maricopa Community College, but he remains well connected to the streets."

"What else should I know?" James asks.

"He is very smart and very quick. He's a straight shooter and comes across as pretty mellow, but I'm told he was a scary SOB back in the day. He knows the players and the history in this area as well as anyone. If he trusts us, he could be a tremendous resource," Bobby says.

"If he trusts us. Got it."

Phoenix, as with many cities, has its own gang history. The early gang structure in Phoenix was neighborhood oriented. Phoenix Police Sergeant Paul Ferrero, a former member of the department's street gang enforcement unit and someone referred to as the department's unofficial historian, has been quoted as saying: "It wasn't like you were in a gang; you were from a neighborhood. There were certain neighborhoods you knew if you had no business going there, you wouldn't go."[1] Ferrero also said those earlier groups, especially in the Hispanic communities, had a tight connection, which grew from already being bound together by familial, cultural, and racial ties.

In 1978, the Phoenix police documented one of the oldest, still operating street gangs, the Wedgewood Chicanos. Urban legend says the Wedgewood Chicanos started when a young man from California, who had been in a gang there, was sent to live with relatives in Phoenix. By 1981, police documented 150 street gangs in Phoenix alone.

By the mid-90s, there was a documented rise in the Black California gang influence in Phoenix, many of whom were associated with factions of the Crips. There were other groups as well, most of which hoped to exploit the growing drug markets in Arizona.

By the early 2000s, police say there were more than 300 gangs

---

1. Patti Epler, "Gang Influence Runs Deep in Phoenix's Roots," *Phoenix New Times*, September 16, 1999, https://www.phoenixnewtimes.com/news/gang-influence-runs-deep-in-phoenixs-roots-6432147.

on record in Phoenix, although authorities say only about three dozen pose any real criminal threat.

It is a short five-minute drive down First Street, then over to South Central Avenue via East Buckeye Road to Lo-Lo's. James makes a right turn into the parking lot just before reaching West Yuma Street.

Lo-Lo's occupies a red brick building with its name shining from large neon letters. A smaller neon sign, highlighted by a red rooster, has a yellow arrow pointing to the parking lot. The inside maintains the brick walls, which feature pictures from black history and unique boards highlighting the restaurant's history and features, including one noting that Kool Aid is always on tap.

Bobby walks to the front door with James following. Entering Lo-Lo's, James and Bobby look around before Bobby hears a familiar voice.

"Bobby Burgess. As I live and breathe." The voice comes from Cedric Carter, who rises from a booth in the back corner of the restaurant as Bobby and James walk toward him. Despite the restaurant being moderately busy, the tables near the booth are completely empty.

Cedric, nearing forty, stands at only five-feet nine-inches, but he carries himself in such a manner to appear taller. He dresses in a novel amalgamation of corporate and street—black slacks and a plain, black, close-fitting T-shirt, offset by a gold "C-3" chain and a gold watch. His shoes are far more expensive than they look. A black leather jacket rests, neatly placed, on the booth next to where he was seated.

"You get better looking every time I see you," says Cedric.

"Good to see you too, Cedric," Bobby says.

"You look like you could suit up right now."

Bobby and Cedric shake hands and exchange a bro hug.

"Cedric, this is James. The man I told you about."

"Nice to meet you, James," Cedric says shaking hands before gesturing to the booth. "Please have a seat."

"How's Derek?" Bobby asks, as the men slide into the booth.

"He's okay. You know, he didn't handle the transition from his playing days as well as you did, but he's doing okay," Cedric says.

"Still in Buffalo?" Bobby asks.

"He is, for some reason. He says he's comfortable there," Cedric says.

"It's too damn cold there for me to ever be comfortable!" Bobby exclaims.

"I hear you there. I think he doesn't want to come home until he is in a better place," Cedric reasons.

"Good evening, Mr. Carter," says Sonja, the waitress. "Do you know what you want?"

"Sonja, it's my friends' first time. Give us a minute, but I'll take an iced tea."

"Okay. And you sir?" she asks Bobby.

"An iced tea for me too."

Sonja glances at James. "Make it three," he says before Sonja walks away.

"Mr. Carter?" Bobby notes.

"I come here often, so I get some respect and the corner of the restaurant."

James and Bobby look at the menu. Lo-Lo's is popular for its Southern soul food listed on the menu as "Lo-Lo's Hood Classics" and "The Eats." It also serves from an all-day breakfast menu.

"The food is great. Everything on the menu," Cedric explains.

Sonja returns with the three iced teas. "Are you ready to order?"

"I think we are," Cedric replies. "I'll have the Baby Ray."

"As usual," Sonja notes.

Bobby speaks next. "I'm looking at Uncle Brotha's Shrimp and Grits. Do you recommend it?"

"Highly. It's very good," Sonja says.

"Okay, I'll take that, with some extra hot sauce."

"And you, sir?" Sonja asks James.

"I'm having a hard time saying no to Betty's Boob."

"Oh," Cedric says, "and some catfish beignets and fried green tomatoes for the table."

"Got it. I'll be back soon."

Cedric waits until Sonja is out of hearing range before he speaks. "So, how can I help you two?"

"We are looking into a matter," Bobby begins, "and could use some background information I thought might be right up your alley. But I'll let James provide more detail."

"James, the floor is yours," Cedric says.

"We are interested in understanding the flow of drugs from Mexico to the US and the distribution of those drugs, particularly as it relates to Mexican cartels and US gangs. And anything specific to those issues in Yuma would be even better," James explains.

"That's a broad ass question, James," Cedric says.

"I know, and I promise I'd be more specific if I could. More than anything, we are hoping for some insights beyond what we'd find looking at Google and Wikipedia. And, of course, we appreciate any information you can share."

"It's not a problem; just yanking your chain. I'll tell you what I know. But we have to start with a basic proposition or two. Most importantly, you should assume any gang in the southwestern US dealing drugs in any volume is affiliated in some way with a Mexican cartel," Cedric states.

"Would the list of drugs associated with the Mexican cartels include fentanyl?" James asks.

"Of course. These days, most gangs with any real drug trade have someone connected to someone in a cartel in Mexico, often through family, but not always. Sometimes a direct connection has been lost but the relationship and trust remain and so too does the business."

Cedric pauses, seeing Sonja approaching with the meals, which she places in front of the men. "Will there be anything else?"

"Not right now, Sonja. Thank you," Cedrick replies. "Eat up guys, while it's hot."

"Oh my god, this shrimp and grits is great," Bobby says after a single bite while adding more hot sauce to the dish.

"How's yours, James?" Cedric asks.

"I'm not saying Betty's Boob is my favorite boob ever, but it's damn close."

"You guys eat, and I'll talk between bites," Cedric offers. "Speaking in broad generalities, it's most common for the cartels to handle getting the drugs over the border. They have the logistics, the experience, the routes, the connections, and the money to complete that task. Once over the border, the drugs are taken to what you might think of as a central distribution hub before being shipped either to other hubs or out to the dealers on the streets. It's a lot like the hub and spokes distribution models they talk about in economics or marketing. In the US, the main hubs include places like Denver, Chicago, and Atlanta, with a number of smaller regional hubs.

"Law enforcement often says each of the functions—transportation, distribution, sales, collections, and money laundering—are separated and one doesn't know what the other is doing. I can't speak for everywhere, but in my experience with the larger gangs—which by the way is a term I'm not real fond of but will use in this conversation for convenience—they provide more than one function and have their own internal organizational structure and methodology.

"As you probably know, the cartels have preferred hand-off type arrangements, and as a result, don't often move into territories in a hostile manner trying to co-opt an area. There have been some stories of violence, of course. Some are true, some just plain wrong, but where it *does* happen, it's more isolated and not standard operating procedure," Cedric says.

"What about the stories I see on the news saying that people arrested in the US are connected to the cartels?" James asks.

"Semantics generally," Cedric answers. "I'd say a significant portion of those that traffic in narcotics in the US can be said to be affiliated with a cartel. But often times that affiliation is quite attenuated. Now I'm not saying there aren't some direct cartel folks in the States, but it's not a substantial number and the cartels by-and-large have not taken over and displaced local infrastructures and procedures."

"How do the cartels move the drugs into the US?" James asks.

"It's usually much simpler than you would think," Cedric states. "There are the 'sexier' methods like drug tunnels and air drops, but the majority of it crosses the border by land in commercial and passenger vehicles. Some cartels also have significant maritime operations. But, again, most of the drugs enter through ports of call along the southwestern US border with Mexico; the DEA calls it the SWB. And it's a bit of a numbers game. The traffickers send a lot of product through border crossings with lots of commercial traffic, and most of it gets through because border agents can't search everything. Plus, many of the traffickers—the ones actually getting the stuff across the border—are smart and adaptive; there's too much money at stake and the risks are too great not to be."

"What do you know about Yuma?" Bobby asks. "Sorry to jump in, James."

"Jump in any time you like," James responds.

"Yuma is interesting and has become a bigger hub over the years. Think about this: If you look at the border, Tijuana and Mexicali are reasonably close to one another and just by their nature have more visitors and more patrols. After Yuma, other than the tiny crossing at Lukeville, there isn't anything until Nogales, which is about three hundred miles, if you could drive along the border, which you can't.

"Historically, Yuma was connected to the Sinaloa Cartel, but it's become a bit more unsettled in recent years. I've heard about the Caborca Cartel, in whatever form it is in these days, CJNG, and some smaller groups, trying to gain influence in Yuma, not to mention the internal issues between El Mayo's soldiers and La Chapiza, the Ninis, and others," Cedric says.

"Do you mind me asking how you know so much about the cartels?" James inquires.

"In my former line of work, knowledge was power, and power was everything. I made it my business to know as much as I could about everything that could affect my business or the people who associated with me. And I mean everything. In my current role, I help kids find the right path and hold a number of training seminars for law enforcement at all levels of government. So, I have to stay aware of what's going on."

"Makes sense. I hope the question did not offend you," James says.

"Not at all. I'm spouting a lot of facts at you. You should know whether it's all BS or not."

"Thanks," James says. "What about the gang influence in Yuma?"

"Yuma, like a number of smaller communities, has some homegrown gangs, but more frequently is dominated or controlled by larger gangs from somewhere else, from a bigger city, with greater access and more resources."

"In this case Phoenix?" James volunteers.

"A logical guess, James, but no, and the reason is geography. Yuma is actually closer to San Diego than Phoenix, and only fifty-some miles from Calexico," Cedric says.

"So, a San Diego gang?" Bobby tries.

"Also logical, but also incorrect. In this case, from everything I hear, it's an LA-based group with the largest influence in Yuma."

"Interesting," James reflects.

Sonja, who had been careful not to approach the table while the men were talking, seizes the opportunity provided by a brief lull in the conversation. "It looks like you gentlemen enjoyed the meal. Would you like any dessert or anything else, Mr. Carter?"

"No thanks, Sonja. Just the check," Cedric says.

Sonja reaches out with the check, which James tries to grasp, before it is snatched away by Cedric. "Simple rules, James. My town. My check."

Cedric stands up, reaches into his front pocket for a wad of cash, swipes three large bills from the top and places them on the table next to the check. James and Bobby stand as well and all three stride toward the exit.

"A hefty tip," Bobby notes.

"It is. Why do you think they call me Mr. Carter, put me in the corner, and have someone wait on me? It's at least part of the reason."

"Works for me," James says.

The men exchange pleasantries in the parking lot before heading to their cars. As James opens his door, Cedric shouts at him. "James! A word of caution if I might?"

"Of course."

"Be careful. I don't have a personal relationship with anyone in Yuma anymore, but the street says there are some wild cards down there."

TEN

WHILE JAMES and Bobby are returning from Phoenix, Erica heads to the DEA's Santa Ana office, responding to an email from Agent Belmonte letting her know he had an internal DEA report she might find interesting.

"There is a public version of this report," he says, handing a document to Erica, "but this version is more detailed and extensive." Agent Belmonte allows Erica a few minutes to review the report.

"Officially, the DEA refers to Mexican cartels as transnational criminal organizations or TCOs. Currently, the DEA considers the following nine Mexican TCOs as having the greatest drug trafficking impact on the United States: Sinaloa Cartel (CDS), Jalisco New Generation Cartel (CJNG), Beltran-Leyva Organization, Cartel del Noreste and Los Zetas, Guerreros Unidos, Gulf Cartel, Juarez Cartel and La Linea, La Familia Michoacána, and Los Rojos.

"We think TCOs maintain drug distribution cells in cities across the United States and those cells either report to TCO leaders in Mexico or through intermediaries. These TCO's dominate the drug trade in the United States market, with most cartels creating a polydrug market for maximum flexibility and resiliency of their operations," Belmonte says.

"Helpful information," Erica notes. "But if we are trying to get a handle on this, is there any way to narrow it down?"

"Let's start with the usual suspects," Belmonte says. "The Sinaloa Cartel is one of the oldest and most established in Mexico. CDS controls drug trafficking activity in various regions in Mexico, particularly along the Pacific Coast in northwestern Mexico and near Mexico's southern and northern borders. Additionally, the Sinaloa Cartel maintains the most expansive international footprint compared to other Mexican TCOs, providing the group an added advantage over its rivals. The Sinaloa Cartel exports and distributes wholesale amounts of fentanyl, heroin, methamphetamine, cocaine, and marijuana in the United States by maintaining distribution hubs in various cities.

"Some have concluded the CDS is the primary fentanyl threat to the United States due to their ability to run clandestine fentanyl synthesis labs in the areas they control in Mexico."

"So, we should be looking for traffickers in Yuma connected to the Sinaloa Cartel?" Erica asks.

"Maybe. But—not trying to be too obtuse here—there are other possibilities, such as the CJNG, which has a significant presence in at least twenty-three Mexican states with most of its growth and territory being in central Mexico and strategic locations on the border between the Unites States and Mexico.

"The CJNG smuggles illicit drugs into the United States by accessing various trafficking corridors in northern Mexico along the southwest border, including Tijuana, Juarez, and Nuevo Laredo.

"There are conflicting analyses, but some suggest the CJNG controls Puerto Vallarta and uses it as a base of operations, together with its influence over the busiest port in Mexico, the Port of Manzanillo. CJNG, like CDS and most other cartels, is a poly-drug trafficking group, manufacturing and distributing large amounts of fentanyl, heroin, methamphetamine, and cocaine. And, of course, there could be another cartel or faction, or an unaffiliated wild card."

"Not helpful, Agent Belmonte, not helpful at all."

"Also, perhaps the most concrete action regarding fentanyl in the US was the indictment of Los Chapitos."

Los Chapitos is the name given to four sons of the infamous former cartel leader Joaquín Guzmán Loera, better known as El Chapo. The sons, who are only four of many of El Chapo's children, are Joaquín Guzmán López, Ovidio Guzmán López, Iván Archivaldo Guzmán Salazar, and Jesús Alfredo Guzmán Salazar. Joaquín and Ovidio have a different mother than Iván and Jesús Alfredo, who is often referred to as Alfredillo. Los Chapitos have followed in their father's footsteps and are key figures in the leadership and operations of the Sinaloa Cartel .

Of these brothers, Joaquín kept the lowest profile until his arrest in July 2024, while Alfredillo and Iván are said to have the most direct roles in the CDS. Los Chapitos are believed to control a significant CDS faction with Ismael Mario Zambada García, a.k.a. El Mayo, controlling the other. There is no consensus on the scope of their respective control or the degree of cooperation between the factions, particularly in the CDS's battles with other cartels. The uncertainty increased when El Mayo was arrested with Joaquin after a plane they were riding in landed at a small airfield in Santa Teresa, New Mexico, which borders Teas near El Paso

Ovidio was captured by the Mexican military in an early morning raid in a neighborhood of Culiacán on January 5, 2023. The US soon sought his extradition, and in September 2023, Ovidio was flown to Chicago.

In April 2023, the US Department of Justice unsealed indictments against Los Chapitos and their associates in the Southern District of New York, the Northern District of Illinois, and the District of Columbia.

According to a DOJ press release, the Southern District of New

York charges included fentanyl trafficking, weapons, and money laundering charges against twenty-eight defendants, including

three of the Chapitos; top lieutenants and leadership of the Sinaloa Cartel; alleged manufacturers and distributors of the Sinaloa Cartel's fentanyl; the managers of the violent armed security apparatus protecting the Sinaloa Cartel's drug trafficking operations; the sophisticated money launderers who repatriate the Sinaloa Cartel's drug proceeds back to Mexico; and multiple chemical precursor suppliers in China who fuel the Sinaloa Cartel's fentanyl distribution operation.[1]

In the Northern District of Illinois, the charges included narcotics, money laundering, and firearms against all four of Los Chapitos.

Narcotics, firearms, and witness retaliation charges also were unsealed in the District of Columbia against Néstor Isidro Pérez Salas, a.k.a. El Nini, the head of security for Iván or perhaps all of Los Chapitos. Pérez Salas also is the apparent leader of Los Ninis, an organization made up of people between twenty and thirty-five years old with a violent profile, who support Los Chapitos in the inter-cartel rivalry with the El Mayo faction.

At a press conference, the DOJ representatives spoke in grand terms regarding Los Chapitos and the efforts to bring them to justice.

> The DEA and our law enforcement partners took down the previous leader of the Sinaloa Cartel, Joaquin Guzman Loera, or "El Chapo," who is now serving a life sentence in a U.S. prison for his crimes.
>
> But El Chapo's sons—Ovidio, Ivan, and Alfredo, known as "Los Chapitos"—became the new leaders of the Sinaloa

1. Office of Public Affairs, "Justice Department Announces Charges Against Sinaloa Cartel's Global Operation," press release number: 23-412, April 14, 2023, https://www.justice.gov/opa/pr/justice-department-announces-charges-against-sinaloa-cartel-s-global-operation.

> Cartel. They inherited a global drug trafficking empire and they made it more ruthless, more violent, more deadly, and they used it to spread a new poison—fentanyl.
>
> Let me be clear: The Chapitos pioneered the manufacture and trafficking of the deadliest drug our country has ever faced, and they are responsible for the massive influx of fentanyl into the United States. . . .
>
> Today's indictments strike a blow against the Chapitos and the global network they operate, a network that fuels violence and death on both sides of the border. . . .
>
> Today's indictments are only the beginning. This case should send a clear message to the Chapitos, the Sinaloa Cartel, and criminal drug networks around the world that the men and women of the DEA will relentlessly pursue you to save American lives and to protect the national security of the United States of America.[2]

DEA Administrator Anne Milgram told a press conference the DEA infiltrated the Sinaloa Cartel and the Chapitos network over the past year and a half. She also asserted the agency "obtained unprecedented access to the organization's highest levels, and followed them across the world."[3]

2. Department of Justice, "DOJ and DEA Announce Charges against Chapitos in the Latest Actions to Disrupt Flow of Illegal Fentanyl and Other Dangerous Drugs," press conference prepared remarks, April 14, 2023,
https://www.dea.gov/sites/default/files/2023-04/DOJ%20and%20DEA%20Announce%20Charges%20against%20Chapitos%20in%20the%20Latest%20Actions%20to%20Disrupt%20Flow%20of%20Illegal%20Fentanyl%20and%20Other%20Dangerous%20Drugs.pdf.

3. Office of Public Affairs, "Justice Department Announces Charges Against Sinaloa Cartel's Global Operation," press release number: 23-412, April 14, 2023, https://www.justice.gov/opa/pr/justice-department-announces-charges-against-sinaloa-cartel-s-global-operation.

"Yes, I do remember when that happened. Did it have much of an effect on the fentanyl trade?" Erica asks.

"I don't think any one event, or even a series of events, is ever going to have much of an effect on the drug trade as a whole. There are lots of drugs and lots of people willing to manufacture and transport them," Belmonte states.

"Not to mention," Erica adds, "the number of people willing to buy them."

"A very good point. I think there is not enough attention paid to the bilateral nature of the drug trade. It's supply and demand and each element fuels the other. I should also note the products are continually evolving, serving both criminal elusiveness and commercial appeal."

"A complex problem," Erica summarizes.

"Far more complex and diverse than most people know, or care to understand," Belmonte says.

"While this has been informative, and with no offense intended, you could have shown me these things in an email, so, I'm wondering why you had me come down here to meet?" Erica implores.

"You're right. There is more."

"Spill it, Agent Belmonte," Erica says.

"Upon reflection, I felt bad after our last discussion."

"Why?" Erica asks.

"I didn't know you or Mr. Butler, or Aguilar for that matter, and though I'd asked around a little, I was a bit skeptical of your intentions when we first met," Belmonte admits.

"And now?" Erica asks.

"Let's just say, since our meeting, several people I trust have expressed a lot of confidence and trust in your husband, and in you by extension, and encouraged me to help if I can."

"That's nice to hear. James is an exceptionally good lawyer."

"And a straight shooter I'm told. Law enforcement doesn't often speak well of criminal defense lawyers. I suspect you are quite good at your job as well," Belmonte says.

"Is that all you wanted to tell me?" Erica asks.

"No. I have one other thought. Are you sure looking into fentanyl trafficking is what got Agent Aguilar killed?"

"Agent Belmonte, at this point I'm not sure about much of anything. But are you telling me you think it was really a robbery attempt?" Erica asks.

"No. Based on what you have told me about the call James had with Aguilar, a robbery doesn't make sense to me either, but I'll hold open the possibility that the police are correct," Belmonte says.

"Then what are you thinking?"

"I made some phone calls and did some checking. No one in our organization heard anything about a significant shipment or movement of fentanyl in the days leading up to his murder."

"Which says what to you?" Erica asks.

"Look, it is possible Aguilar asked the wrong thing to the wrong person at the wrong time and got himself killed," Belmonte says.

"But . . . ?"

"Agent Aguilar was an experienced investigator," Belmonte asserts, "so I doubt he was reckless or careless. And I think drug dealers don't kill strangers unless they have no option or have something significant to protect, irrespective of what they show in the movies."

"So, you think something else was going on?" Erica reasons.

"Or *someone* else. What if the assumption he was killed because he was looking into fentanyl is wrong?"

"Then," Erica reflects, "there is the very real possibility we've been looking at the whole case the wrong way."

"Maybe so," Belmonte says.

"But, being the devil's advocate, we know—we think—he went to Yuma to look into the fentanyl trade," Erica states.

"Okay, but what if *being* in Yuma was what got him in trouble, not what he was looking into?" Belmonte suggests.

"Like maybe his mortal enemy happened to be lurking in

Yuma, waiting in silence for his one opportunity?" Erica says with a reassuring giggle.

"Not exactly, but you get the idea."

"Kidding aside, the thought is an excellent one. You must have done this kind of investigating before."

"Once or twice, ma'am. Once or twice," Belmonte replies.

"The key then," Erica summarizes, "is to understand better what else was happening in Yuma when Aguilar was there and/or who else was there."

"And why," Belmonte adds.

"And why. Good point," Erica concurs.

"I should also note the obvious."

"Which is?"

"If Agent Aguilar was killed while poking around, it likely means someone, or a group of someones, either had something very important to hide or a serious vendetta against Aguilar. Either way, you know what that means?" Belmonte asks.

"What?" Erica asks.

"Those same people may well have an issue with you and James as well."

"Just what I wanted to hear, Agent Belmonte. Thanks. Thanks a lot."

ELEVEN

James and Erica sit under a green umbrella on the patio of Sapori Ristorante, an elegant Italian bistro located just off Bayside Drive in Newport Beach: left, then a block from Beacon Bay.

Erica's father has been coming to Sapori almost since it opened in 1989. James and Erica had their first "date" here some four years ago when Erica told James she and Brian would meet him for dinner and then Brian had something come up. It still took James another two years and a life altering quest in Mexico to realize he was in love with Erica, though Erica tells her friends she knew it that night.

On this evening, a heat lamp has been placed near the table, warming the chilly sea air. Tonight, James and Erica prefer the privacy afforded on the patio, though the hostess politely asked if they would be more comfortable at a table inside at least three times. Declining the wine list and opting instead for sparkling water with lime, they request a few minutes before ordering.

"Who wants to go first?" James asks excitedly.

"You should," Erica replies with a knowing smile.

"Okay. If you insist. No major breakthroughs but some interesting information," James says, before giving Erica an abbreviated, but animated, breakdown of his conversations with Wilson and Cedric.

"Bottom line, then, is Wilson suspects the CIA in everything, and the fentanyl and other drugs running through Yuma are likely connected to Mexican cartels, including, but not limited to, the Sinaloa Cartel?" Erica summarizes.

"Well, yes, but I liked my way of explaining it better," James says.

The waitress, Ambra, who has been hovering inconspicuously, senses an opportunity and strikes. "Would you like to order now?"

"Oh, I'm sorry. We got wrapped up in our conversation. Are we holding you up?" James asks.

"No, sir, I'm fine. I just didn't want to interrupt. If you're not ready, I can come back," Ambra offers.

"Nonsense, you are right. We should order. By the way, Ambra is a beautiful and unique name," James says.

"It means an amber-colored jewel in Italian, I believe," Erica imparts as she continues to look at the menu.

"Thank you, and yes it does," Ambra replies.

"As many times as I've been here over the years, and I still look over the menu every time. I think I'll settle on the minestrone and the ravioli d'aragosta," Erica says.

"That's my favorite pasta, but don't tell Chef Maniaci. He has a soft spot for the penne otero, the chef's signature dish. And for you, sir?"

"I'll go with the insalata Sapori and the salmon alla griglia."

"Very good," Ambra notes. "Would you like anything else to drink with dinner?"

"Not for me," James replies, "but Erica may want something else."

"No, I'm good too."

"Okay, I'll be back with the soup and salad," Ambra announces before walking away.

"Who are you, and what did you do with my husband in Arizona?" Erica asks.

"Whatever do you mean?" James asks.

"No wine, and salmon instead of the filet? This is not the James Butler I know."

"You're funny. After a couple of days with Bobby, I started to feel like I should be taking better care of myself."

"You do just fine, babe. It's Bobby's business," Erica says.

"Maybe, but moving on, tell me about your meeting with Belmonte today, please and thank you."

"He thinks it's possible Aguilar was in Yuma looking into fentanyl trafficking, but it might not be what got him killed," Erica says.

"Really? What does he think it might have been?" James asks.

"To quote the great Irwin M. Fletcher, 'Well, there we're in kind of a grey area.'"

"He thinks it's not fentanyl but isn't sure what it might be?"

"Ding, ding. We have a winner," Erica exclaims.

"What do you think?" James asks.

"He makes some sense. Essentially, he says drug dealers don't usually kill random people, and nothing he was able to find indicated there was anything unusual or unique going on in Yuma at the time. And he gives Aguilar credit for being a smart investigator."

"The police did label it a robbery attempt," James adds.

"Would they have closed the books so quickly if it was a drug dealer who shot a retired DEA agent?" Erica questions.

"Somehow, I think not likely," James says.

"Nor do I."

"I still think it had to be more than a robbery, otherwise Aguilar's words don't make sense. 'It's bigger than we knew,'" James notes.

"Another good point," Erica agrees.

"If not fentanyl dealers, then who and why?"

"Those, my love, are the questions yet to be answered," Erica replies.

Ambra arrives in time to stifle any follow-up from James and places the minestrone and salad in front of them before returning to the main restaurant.

"Apropos of nothing," James says, "and before we get back to Aguilar, would you like to hear a crazy theory on the Camarena kidnapping?"

"What, you just came up with a new theory and decided now was a good time to discuss it?" Erica replies.

"I see your point, but on the trip back from Phoenix I had a thought and it's congealed to the point I think I can articulate it, though it's not yet completely thought out. And I thought you just might be interested."

"Of course, I am, silly. Hit me with it."

Nearly four decades after the tragic kidnapping, interrogation, and murder of DEA Special Agent Kiki Camarena, there remain many unanswered questions about the case, including a definitive answer to who ordered Agent Camarena's abduction.

Conventional wisdom has been that Agent Camarena was abducted because of the DEA's success in identifying marijuana fields controlled by drug trafficker Rafa Quintero. Others have pointed to Ernesto Fonseca Carrillo, known as "Don Neto," a long-time drug trafficker with familial ties to Rafa. Carillo and Rafa conducted drug trafficking operations with Miguel Ángel Félix Gallardo, often known as El Padrino ("The Godfather") or El Jefe de Jefes ("The Boss of Bosses"). The exact relationship between the three, especially near the time of Camarena's abduction, remains subject to debate and conjecture.

Various other theories have been proposed, some with more plausibility than others. Javier Barba-Hernández was a lawyer turned trafficker who had ascended to a role as a key associate of Carillo. Some have proposed that Barba was more involved in the planning and execution of the kidnapping and interrogation of Agent Camarena than previously assumed.

Another key player in the abduction of Agent Camarena was Samuel Ramírez Razo, known as "El Samy," a former officer with the Direccion Federal de Seguridad (DFS), a Mexican intelligence agency and secret police, created in 1947 with the assistance of the US CIA and its predecessor organization. Most investigators believe El Samy took the lead role in abducting Agent Camarena off the street outside the American Consulate.

After Camarena was abducted, he was taken to a house in a nearby residential section of town located at 881 Lope de Vega (commonly referred to simply as "Lope de Vega"). Records indicate that, at the time of the kidnapping, Lope de Vega was owned by Rafa Quintero. In all likelihood, Agent Camarena was interrogated and brutally tortured at Lope de Vega.

"What if the kidnapping was a brilliant plan by Félix Gallardo?" James asks.

"I'm listening," Erica says.

"Consider this. Félix is tired of both the DEA and Rafa. The DEA is being, at a minimum, a nuisance, and Rafa is reckless and has expressed an interest in getting into the cocaine side of the business. I suspect he could manipulate Rafa into executing the actual kidnapping."

"You're not going to get an argument from me," Erica concurs.

"Félix hypes Rafa up to kidnap Camarena and have him taken to Lope de Vega knowing there will be evidence left at Lope de Vega, which is Rafa's house," James says.

"Any chance Félix was involved in the acquisition of Lope de Vega?" Erica questions.

"I hadn't thought about it, but now I will. In any event, after Camarena is taken to Lope de Vega, Félix either has his men interrogate Camarena there or he has him moved and interrogated," James says.

"With the latter idea perhaps providing some explanation for why no one heard about Lope de Vega for a couple of months," Erica suggests.

"Right. Then either Félix plans for or expects Camarena to be killed, or things go south, and Rafa and his men take the interrogation and torture too far. Under either scenario, Félix sets up Rafa to be captured at the airport. Rafa is the fall guy, and Félix has solved two problems at once," James posits.

"Which is why," Erica adds, "later, when the DFS 'cleans' Lope de Vega, all of the evidence left points to Rafa and to the torture and murder occurring at Lope de Vega."

"Correct," James asserts. "Of course, Félix expected his political connections to protect him."

"Which they did, for four years," Erica notes.

"Right."

"Okay, then," Erica continues, "what if I add on and posit that Javier Barba Hernandez was more involved than most people consider?"

"Color me intrigued."

"Think about it," Erica continues. "When Kuykendall wrote about the interrogation tapes, he noted there were a lot of questions about Barba, and he said one of the interrogators was angered when Camarena did not have the right answers. Kuykendall suggested the angry interrogator was Barba himself."

"Okay, I do remember that," James says.

"It's also noteworthy that Harrison and Plascencia Aguilar both testified that Barba had started off working *for* Carillo and then became an equal," Erica says.

"Right. Didn't Harrison suggest Barba displaced El Samy in that role?" James asks.

"He did. Add in that Barba was an educated lawyer with police knowledge. If there was any real planning by the traffickers involved, wouldn't it make sense to involve the one person, maybe aside from Félix, most likely to have the ability to do the planning and stay out of the fray?"

"But wasn't Barba in the fray if he was in the interrogation?" James queries.

"Not if no one knows for sure it was him. Kuykendall said he suspected it, but I've never seen evidence of a voice identification. And think about it. Barba has never been talked about as one of the main planners," Erica says.

"Maybe because he was killed not too long after the kidnapping?" James suggests.

"Under, shall we say, questionable circumstances," Erica replies.

On Erica's observation, Ambra returns with the rest of their dinner as a busboy clears the soup and salad dishes, following close on his heels, laying the dishes on the table. "How does everything look?"

"Lovely, Ambra, just lovely," Erica says

"Great. Let me know if you need anything else. Bon appetite."

The salmon alla griglia is grilled salmon in a lemon and caper sauces, with steamed asparagus aside. James takes a bite, making sure plenty of sauce makes it onto the salmon.

"How's the salmon?" Erica asks.

"It's excellent," James answers.

"But you wish you had gotten the filet, don't you?"

"Yes, I do. Am I so predictable?" James asks.

"Not predictable, dear. It's just how well I know you. But back to Barba, if he had been behind the kidnapping and had government connections who were either aware of it or knew about it, there would be any number of people who would want him dead and have the power to have the MFJP do it. I suspect there were a lot of people who wanted him dead."

"Which make me think," James asserts, "we might be able to swap Barba for Félix in my theory and end up in the same place. Barba wants to be a trafficker. He's close to Carillo but not a relative like Rafa, and he doesn't have the same history with Carillo as Rafa. If Félix thought Rafa was too reckless, Barba likely did as well. Maybe Barba tried to move up the ranks by getting rid of him."

"Two possible issues," Erica states. "First, Harrison said Félix was unhappy with both Rafa and Carillo. Setting up Rafa only gets rid of one problem. Second, if it was Barba, does Félix need to set up Rafa at the airport?"

"Good questions," James comments. "And here's how I'd respond. First, Carillo is older, and I suspect some of his wild behavior was because he was with Rafa. Rafa had to have been the one Félix—"

"Or Barba," Erica inserts.

"Félix *or* Barba was most concerned with. As to the airport, I think the same answer applies no matter who was behind the kidnapping. If the blame is placed on Rafa, and he is in custody, whatever heat there is on Félix dissipates, at least temporarily," James says.

"I can accept both of those thoughts. Maybe Carillo was still valuable to Félix and whatever organization they had," Erica suggests.

"I like that thought too. I don't think we should disregard Carillo either. He's always struck me as being wiser and craftier than how he's portrayed. I accept the stories saying he was mad about Camarena being close to death, but he still could have been behind the kidnapping plot itself. If my initial premise was that Félix could manipulate Rafa, then I'm sure Carillo could as well."

"But," Erica notes, "if Carillo was behind the abduction, I still have a few questions: Why take him to Rafa's house? Why does Carillo come and go? Why is Rafa, apparently, one of the interrogators?"

"More good questions," James says. "Maybe if Barba was an interrogator, he was getting the information Carillo wanted?"

"Which takes us back to what? Basically, to the current version—it was Rafa and/or Carillo?" Erica speculates.

"True, but I have an affinity for the idea of Félix or Barba being behind it. But we still are left with two theories, if not more."

"Is there any way to prove either of them?"

"Nope," James reluctantly asserts. "None I can think of."

"Imagine that. More plausible theories defying proof." Erica shakes her head ruefully.

She takes a few bites of her ravioli filled with lobster and bufala mozzarella before asking, "Where do we go from here?"

"Yuma is the epicenter, and there must be some answers there," James states.

"Agreed. But, while I hate to overstate the obvious, Aguilar got killed asking questions there."

"True, but we know it could be dangerous going in, of which Aguilar might not have been aware," James says.

"And we'll have Bobby with us," Erica adds.

"No, no, and no. Back the truck all the way up. There is no we. You aren't going anywhere near Yuma," James says.

"But it's okay for you to go?" Erica asks.

"If I had my druthers, I wouldn't go either."

Erica lets a little giggle slip out.

"What's so funny?" James asks.

"Every so often, you slip in a Midwestern colloquialism that strikes me as so . . . so not you. It's quite cute."

"I'm glad I amuse you."

"I kid you because I love you. And because I love you, I am not a fan of you going to Yuma," Erica says.

"I know, but I'll have Bobby right there with me," James says.

"And so would I!" Erica protests.

"Look, I don't want to be overly protective—"

"Or misogynistic," Erica offers.

"Or that," James agrees. "But doesn't it make more sense for one of us to stay here, keep everything under control at the office, and be available for the police if anything does go bad?"

"Not funny, Butler. Not even a little funny. I'm worried about you," Erica says.

"I know. But we don't move this forward without going to Yuma. I almost wish we had just driven there when we were in

Phoenix, but the timing wasn't right." James takes a drink before resuming. "I know there's a risk, but I think Bobby and I can navigate it by going in eyes wide open."

"I so badly want to argue with you, but I won't," Erica says.

Ambra returns to the table, though the plates are only half eaten. "How is your dinner? Can I get you anything else?"

"The dinner is excellent, as usual," Erica replies.

"Can I have a glass of a nice zinfandel?" James requests.

"I thought we weren't drinking tonight?" Erica asks.

"Suddenly," James responds, "I think I could use a glass."

"Would you like one too, ma'am?" Ambra asks Erica.

"No, thanks. I'll just take another bottle of Perrier."

"Coming up," Ambra replies before slipping out of sight.

"When do you think you'll go?" Erica asks James.

"Let me check in with Bobby. I'm sure he'll be thrilled to take another trip to Arizona. I have two prelims next week, so it will have to be the following week at the earliest."

"Just remember, James. If Belmonte is right, and fentanyl is a red herring in this, then you could be walking into something different, or more dangerous, than you know. With or without Bobby."

"Thanks for the reassurances. I'll give Bobby the full rundown, and we'll be careful. Very careful."

TWELVE

YUMA, Arizona, is the seat of the eponymous county, with a population of about one hundred thousand. Yuma has a place in the Guinness World Records as the sunniest city on Earth, with sunny and warm weather an estimated 91 percent of the year. Yuma County is a huge agricultural center and accounts for the growth of 90 percent of all leafy vegetables in the US. Yuma is also home to a Marine Corps Air Station.

The city of Yuma is also twenty-five miles from the border with Mexico. On the US side of the border is the city of San Luis, Arizona, a rapidly growing city of more than thirty-five thousand residents. The lowest point in Arizona is located on the Colorado River in San Luis, where it flows out of Arizona and into the Mexican state of Sonora.

San Luis is immediately across the border from Mexican Federal Highway 2 and the town of San Luis Río Colorado, with the San Luis I Land Port of Entry connecting the two towns and two countries.

San Luis Río Colorado is situated in the extreme northwestern corner of Sonora and is the fourth-largest city in the state with a population nearing two hundred thousand. Manufacturing is a key component of the San Luis Río Colorado including maquila factories for companies such as Daewoo Electronics, Bose, and other international companies. Maquila factories are largely duty- and tariff-free factories that take raw materials and assemble, manufacture, or process them and export the finished product.

James and Bobby drive separately to Yuma, which sits about three hours east of San Diego on I-8. James has booked two rooms at the Quechan Casino Resort just off the interstate a few miles west of Yuma.

James is mindlessly feeding a video poker machine at a casino bar when Bobby finds him.

"Mr. Butler, nice to see you."

"Bobby, thanks for coming my friend."

"It's my pleasure."

"How was the drive?" James asks.

"Uneventful, but this is just far enough to be far," Bobby says.

"I know. Sorry we couldn't combine trips. I'll blame it on the Los Angeles County Superior Court," James says.

"All good, my friend. Do you want to talk now or in the morning?" Bobby asks.

"You already know most everything, so we can just chat in the morning," James says.

"Sounds good. I'm wiped out, so I'm going to head to the room. What time do you want to leave in the morning?"

"Can we say 9 a.m.? I'll drive," James offers.

"Works for me. You going to hang here?"

"For a bit, I think." James says, staring vacantly at the video screen in front of him.

"You okay?" Bobby asks.

"Yeah, I am. Just hating why we're here," James answers.

"I get it. Call me if you need anything before the morning."

Before Bobby can walk away, James presses "Deal" hitting a royal flush, with the accompanying bells and sirens showing James has not only won the hand but also a $127,820 jackpot. Smiling at Bobby, James reiterates, "Yes, I'm fine."

"That is so very wrong," Bobby says shaking his head as he walks away.

James waits by the front desk just before 9 a.m. when Bobby arrives in jeans and a tight T-shirt showing off the hard-earned, sculpted physique that carried him to the NFL.

"Cedric was right. You are a freakin' rock," James says.

"Sometimes flaunting my assets helps prevent confrontations," Bobby explains.

"Then by all means, flaunt away."

James and Bobby walk to James's Tesla for the short drive on I-8 to Yuma.

"So, I think I understand the basics from our conversations," Bobby says as James navigates out of the parking lot and onto the highway, "but tell me again the objectives for today."

"As I mentioned last week, Aguilar had a great nephew who was a stud athlete in Texas, with D-1 scholarship opportunities. At a post-graduation party, he tried some drugs laced with fentanyl and overdosed."

"Damn, what a shame." Bobby sighs and shakes his head.

"The local, low-level street dealer was arrested and charged, but no one higher up was ever arrested. I think Aguilar was on a mission to identify whoever supplied the dealer," James says.

"Okay, simple enough," Bobby says.

"Perhaps. We know the vast majority of fentanyl in the US comes from Mexico, by land, over the border. So, it's reasonable to assume some substantial quantities come through Yuma and the surrounding areas. Aguilar could have asked questions to the wrong people, at the wrong time," James says.

"But you're not convinced?" Bobby inquires.

"But I'm just making assumptions, and one could theorize that his death was only tangentially related to fentanyl trafficking, if at all," James says.

"I'm not sure I follow," Bobby says.

"It's okay. I can't say I understand much of anything at this point. Maybe Aguilar's investigation implicated the Sinaloa Cartel and raised concerns that Aguilar knew too much about the cartel because of his involvement in the Camarena kidnapping. His investigation could have become something much larger in their eyes, leading to his death," James posits.

"Seriously? That's incredible," Bobby says.

"Maybe. Right now, I'm just trying to put some puzzles pieces together and hope a picture starts to emerge," James says.

"Which leads us here," Bobby reasons.

"Right. Aguilar used his credit card when he was in Yuma, so we can trace his movements around Yuma. I was thinking we could just follow his path and look and ask around. Find anyone who saw him, who he was with. That sort of thing."

"You mean like a private investigator would do?" Bobby asks.

"Exactly. Do you know a good one?"

Bobby laughs a loud and hearty laugh. "It's a good thing I like you, James."

Aguilar had stayed two nights at the Howard Johnson on Fourth Avenue, across Thirty-Second Street from a Lowe's, Pep Boys, and a Dodge dealer. He also hit several of the fast-food joints on Fourth Avenue. James also noted Aguilar had eaten dinner two nights in a row at Taco Salsa, further north on Fourth Avenue.

James parks at the Howard Johnson, now a Wyndham branded property. "Might as well start here, don't you think?" James asks.

"Agreed," Bobby says.

James and Bobby enter the empty lobby, and James rings the bell on the counter. A man, wearing a Larry name tag, emerges from the office. "How can I help you boys?"

James holds out his phone showing Larry a picture of Aguilar. "Do you recognize this man?" James asks.

"Sure," Larry replies. "He was the man who was murdered a month or two ago. I saw his picture on the news."

"Did you meet him when he stayed here?" James inquires.

"What do you mean?" Larry asks.

"He stayed in this hotel the two nights before his murder," James states.

"Really? I had no idea," Larry says.

"You never met him?" James asks.

"Never."

"Is there anyone else working who might have met or talked with him?" Bobby asks.

"Of course. There are a few people who work the front desk, but I'm the only one here now," Larry says.

"It would be a great help if you could ask your coworkers if they remember anything about him," James says.

"Sure, I can do that," Larry says.

"I'll give you my business card. If anything stands out about him or his time here, I'd appreciate a call," James says.

"Irvine, California. You're a long way from home."

"Anything you find out would be helpful," James reiterates.

"Sure," Larry says, setting the business card on the counter. "I can do that."

"Thank you, Larry. We appreciate it," James says as he and Bobby walk out to the sidewalk.

"Well, that was disappointing," James says.

"Get used to it. In my experience the ratio of questions to productive answers is painfully low," Bobby says.

"That's not how it works on TV," James complains.

"No, it's not. I suspect *L.A. Law* was not an accurate depiction of the day-to-day life of a lawyer in Los Angeles either," Bobby says.

"Not by a long shot. A good show, but my daily life is far more routine and boring than anything suitable for a television audience," James says.

"Same is true for investigators. Far more leg work than exciting gotcha moments," Bobby states.

"We've been duped," James says with a laugh.

James and Bobby spend the morning working their way along the three-mile stretch between the hotel and Taco Salsa, learning almost nothing. They decide to grab lunch at Taco Salsa.

The restaurant is located at the north end of a small strip mall, appropriately named the Fourth Avenue Shops, next to the Yuma Bagel Company, while an embroidery shop, a nail salon, a barbershop, and a cash advance store occupy the south half.

"I'm ready for lunch," James says as the two enter the restaurant. The men briefly look at the menu before approaching the counter to order.

"What can I get you gentlemen?" says Elena, a middle-aged woman working behind the counter.

"I'll take the number nineteen combination plate—two sopes, both beef—and an iced tea," James orders. "What about you Bobby?"

"I'll take the number twenty-one combination plate and a water please."

"Is that one check or two?" Elena asks.

"One check, please," James says handing over his credit card.

"Here are your drinks, and we'll bring your plates out to you shortly," Elena says, handing James his credit card and the check, which James promptly signs.

James and Bobby find a seat at a two-person table with pale orange bench seats. "So, any thoughts?" James asks.

"I'm not sure. It certainly has been easy to trace Aguilar's steps," Bobby responds.

"It has. As I hinted at this morning, that says to me either he wasn't worried, or he was leaving breadcrumbs for someone to follow," James says. "In other words, he was worried enough that he wanted someone to be able to track his movements, or he wasn't concerned in the least."

"Not exactly an analytic breakthrough," Bobby notes dryly.

"Not yet at least," James says.

Suddenly, Elena appears with the meals. "Wow, that was fast," James notes as Elena sets the plates in front of them.

"Can I get you anything else?" Elena asks.

"No, I think we are good, but may I ask you a question?" James asks.

"Sure," Elena answers.

"Do you recognize this man?" James asks, showing Elena a picture of Aguilar on his phone. "He ate here two days in a row about six weeks ago."

"The man who was murdered?" Elena asks.

"Yes, that one. He was a friend of mine. Do you remember him coming in?" James asks.

"I do, mostly because he was an out-of-towner and, as you said, he came in two days in a row," Elena says.

"Do you remember anything about him? Was he alone? Nervous? Anything that stood out about him?" James asks.

"I'm sure this is not going to be helpful, but there was nothing special about him. He was very nice and polite. He sat in that corner, facing the door, and was very leisurely with his meals. There was nothing remarkable about him, and I probably wouldn't have remembered even that much if he had not been murdered," Elena states.

"Thank you, Elena, that is super helpful," James says.

"No problem. Let me know if you boys need anything else," Elena says before returning to the counter.

After finishing their meal, and as they are about to leave, Elena approaches.

"Guys, I thought of one more thing about your friend," she says.

"What's that?" James asks.

"As he was leaving the second day, he received a phone call as he was about to leave, and he went back to his table to talk. He was probably on the call for ten minutes or so. He seemed distracted when he left," Elena says.

"What do you mean by distracted?" Bobby asks.

"I said goodbye and asked if we would see him again. He barely responded on his way out the door. Not in a rude way, but, as I said, as if he was distracted, his mind was somewhere else," Elena says.

"That helps a lot," James says. "Thank you," he says, handing Elena a one-hundred-dollar bill.

"You don't need to do that," Elena says.

"I appreciate you talking to us." James presses the bill into her palm.

"Well, thank you," Elena says before James and Bobby leave through the front door.

"That was nice of you," Bobby says.

"I'm a nice guy," James says.

"So you say. To the car?" Bobby asks.

"I think so," James replies. The men walk back to the hotel parking lot where James left his car.

"Where to next?" Bobby asks as they get in the car.

"Next is the one I've been dreading. Near where Aguilar was shot. A gas station and convenience store close to the airport," James says.

"It's disconnected from the other places we've been to. Out of the way, you might say," Bobby notes.

"I agree. He drove out from Texas, so he didn't need to go to the airport, and there are other gas stations closer to town. He made a small purchase here the evening of his murder, but there is nothing else in this area at all," James says.

"So, what, he makes the purchase and then goes to the pay phone and gets shot? How far from the store is the pay phone?" Bobby wonders aloud.

"Take a look for yourself." James pulls into an empty area just off the road and before the gas station. "The pay phone is there across the street and the store is right here."

"If in a hurry, maybe a two-minute walk?" Bobby speculates.

"Sounds about right. I need to grab something to drink before we look around," James says.

"Works for me. How many more places after this?" Bobby asks.

"Three. Or two more after this one, however you want to look at it."

James and Bobby stride into the store and look around. "I'm going to find the restroom," Bobby announces as he walks to the back of the store.

James retrieves a bottle of Coke Zero from the cooler and approaches the young man behind the cash register. After paying for the soda, James pulls up a photo of Aguilar on his phone and shows it to the clerk. "Any chance you remember seeing this man?"

"Nope." The man is stoic as he stares at James.

"Are you sure? He was the man murdered just across the street a few weeks ago," James says.

"I don't remember anyone being murdered. I might have heard someone got shot for sticking his nose into other people's business. Asking too many questions is not safe," the cashier says.

James stands tall, seeking to convey the impression that he is not intimidated by the veiled threat. "I'm not trying to pry into anyone's business. I'm just looking to find out what happened to my friend. Is there anything you can tell me about him and his time in Yuma? Anything at all?"

A voice emanates behind James. "I thought I heard Ricky here tell you that asking too many questions is not safe. And then you ask more questions?" James turns to see a tall, slender man, wearing a black Harley Davidson T-shirt, with tattooed arms, and a large neck tattoo.

James starts to speak but is interrupted as the man moves closer. "If you want to walk out of here, you better walk now. Quietly."

"I told him, Leo," Ricky proclaims. "I told him I didn't know nothing, and he should leave."

"I heard someone's been asking questions around town," Leo states.

James looks at Leo and then back at Ricky behind the counter, his mind searching for a solution to his predicament just as one appears from the back of the store.

"What's up, James?" Bobby asks, assessing the situation as he approaches.

Leo wheels around, responding before seeing Bobby's figure behind him. "It's none of your damn business."

"There you are just wrong. See, I'm making it my business." Bobby walks slowly until he is only inches from Leo, who's now frozen in his tracks.

"Look," Ricky says, "we don't want no trouble, but no one wants some stranger asking questions in our town."

"Fair enough," Bobby replies calmly, then asks James, "Did you get the information you needed?"

"I suppose I did," James replies.

"See," Bobby says to Leo, "we are leaving. No harm done." Bobby takes a few steps toward the door before turning back, keeping his focus on Leo. "But threaten him again, and I'll cancel your ticket, permanently." James and Bobby don't wait for a response and walk out the front door toward James's car.

As James nears the Tesla, he starts to look over his shoulder to check for anyone following.

"Don't look back," Bobby demands. "Badasses don't look back."

"Do badasses get shot?"

James starts the car and begins to pull out of the parking lot, noticing Ricky and Leo watching from the front doorway.

"A suggestion, James, if I might?" Bobby offers.

"Suggest away!"

"Forget the last two places . . . let's get my car and leave town."

A few minutes pass when James's cell phone, plugged into the car's entertainment system, rings. Not recognizing the number, James answers cautiously.

"Hello?"

"Leaving town is a good idea. Better for your health." The caller is a man with a deep, Hispanic-sounding voice.

"We weren't causing any trouble," James insists.

"Mr. Butler, if you play with scorpions, you get stung."

"Wait. How do you know my name?" James asks.

"Mr. Butler, I've known you, and Ms. Walsh, since Mazatlán."

THIRTEEN

James calls Erica immediately after dropping Bobby off at his car to let her know he is fine and heading home. Adrenaline and his active mind keep him alert as he lets the Tesla's onboard system manage the drive through the California desert on I-8. Throughout the drive, James thinks through the multitude of questions raised by the day's events, and the phone call replays in James's head over and over and over. But, in the end, he arrives in Newport Beach with the same questions and no good answers.

Despite liberal compliance with the posted speed limits, which knocks twenty minutes off the drive, it's still almost 3 a.m. by the time James walks into the condo. Exhausted, James crawls into bed, promising Erica all the details in the morning before falling into a hard, deep sleep.

The next morning, Erica wakes early but vows to let James sleep in, at least a little. She keeps herself busy working out in the building's gym, cleaning the kitchen and bathroom—though they were spotless to begin with—and answering a few work emails. A morning chat with her college roommate, Rebecca Talbot, occupies her until a bit after 9 a.m., at which point her curiosity will not let her wait another moment.

Bringing a bottle of Coke Zero with her to the bedroom, she

opens the bottle and places it on the nightstand next to James. "Good morning, sunshine."

A groggy James rolls over to find Erica sitting on the edge of the bed. "What time is it?" James reaches for the bottle and takes a long drink.

"A little after 9 a.m.," Erica answers.

"Your restraint is impressive," James says.

"Hey, it wasn't easy."

"I expect not." James props a pillow behind him and sits up, leaning against the headboard.

"So?" Erica asks.

"What?" James asks.

"Start talking this minute, Mr. Butler."

"Yes, ma'am," James replies. Following another drink, James gives Erica the basic rundown on the day in Yuma, stopping just short of the phone call as they left town.

"So maybe it was fentanyl trafficking behind Aguilar's murder?" Erica asks.

"Well, I haven't yet gotten to one important thing," James says.

"You're burying the lede, James. Spill it."

James recounts the mysterious phone call, in exact detail.

"He said what!" Erica shouts. "How in the hell does he know you? And me? And what does Mazatlán have to do with any of this?"

"I don't know, babe. Trust me, I thought about each of your questions, and so many more, the entire way home," James says.

"Mazatlán has to mean a connection to Rafa, right?" Erica inquires.

"It must. But I don't know how. Can we take this discussion downstairs to the patio, so I can use the bathroom?" James asks.

"Sure, I'll meet you down there. Do you want anything?"

"Just another Coke Zero, please."

"Why can't you drink coffee in the morning like a normal person?" Erica asks while heading down the stairs.

Erica takes another two bottles of Coke Zero and a glass of orange juice to the patio, places them on the mosaic tile table, moves the chairs to avoid sunlight in their eyes, and waits for James.

James soon appears on the stairs, wearing black joggers and a matching Arctic Cool T-shirt. Erica begins talking as he approaches, without waiting for him to actually sit at the table.

"So just to recap, Belmonte says it doesn't sound like a fentanyl trafficking crime to him. When asking questions in Yuma, you and Bobby are confronted in a way that suggests that maybe Aguilar was the victim of a 'wrong place, wrong time' drug crime. Then, who-the-hell-knows who makes it about Rafa. What the hell?"

"Is it 'who-the-hell-knows who' or 'whom'?" James asks in a vain effort at lightening the mood.

"You're cute, Butler, but don't push it. All I know is I haven't gotten a good answer to a single question in a few days, and it's starting to irritate me," Erica says.

"I'm sensing that," James notes.

"I'm not kidding. This is serious," Erica responds.

"I know. Trust me. The message was received loud and clear. Thank God for Bobby." James takes Erica's hand in his. "But we will approach this like we do everything else. Methodically, slowly, and together."

"Yes, we will. Damn, I love you."

"Good, 'cause you are stuck with me."

"So where next?" Erica asks.

"Let's go back to the very basics. What do we know for sure?" James asks.

"Okay. We know Aguilar was searching for fentanyl traffickers, and we know he said 'it' was bigger than we knew," Erica says.

"Let's break it down," James imparts. "He was looking for fentanyl connections between Mexico and the US. Can we say it's a given?"

"I feel secure saying we know that," Erica answers.

"Okay, then we know something was worrying—dare I say, scaring—him and that he was afraid when he said it was bigger than we knew."

"I recognize three questions arising from your one short sentence," Erica says.

"Three?" James asks. "Let's hear them."

"One—what or who was he afraid of? Two—what was 'it'? And three—who is 'we'?"

"I hadn't broken it down, but you're right. We also know someone connected to Rafa and Mazatlán knew that Bobby and I were asking questions in Yuma," James says.

"Are you certain? Could they have heard about Mazatlán some other way?"

"I don't think so. I heard his voice. He was smug and certain. I have the feeling he was involved with Rafa somehow. He called right as we were leaving Yuma," James says.

"Did the call sound like it was international?" Erica asks.

"Not really, no. Which means . . ."

Erica speaks before James can finish his thought. "Our Mazatlán friend was in Yuma."

"Damn." James whistles.

"You are lucky to be alive," Erica states.

"You might want to thank Bobby next time you see him. One other thing. I can't shake this nagging feeling the guy's voice is familiar," James says.

"Like you know him?" Erica asks.

"I don't know. More like I've heard it before," James says.

"So, what do we do now?"

"Keep digging," James says.

"Great. Can you be any more specific?" Erica asks.

"We keep following Aguilar's footsteps. That has to lead us somewhere," James says.

"And not get us dead."

"And not get us dead," James agrees.

There is a moment of silence as James and Erica ruminate on the tasks in front of them, until James sits upright in his chair.

"This might not help much, but I think I have a pertinent thought," James states.

"I'm sure I'd be impressed if I knew what it was," Erica says.

"Can we agree we just outlined or touched on several theories as to what exactly got Aguilar killed?" James asks.

"Yes, I think that is accurate," Erica answers.

"If so, I think I know which one is true," James says.

"Great. Please share. Which one?"

"Which *ones*?" James questions back.

"Huh?" Erica replies.

"No one theory alone is correct," James says.

"This semantics game is annoying me. Which of our theories do you think are correct?" Erica asks.

"All of them."

FOURTEEN

FENTANYL IS a potent synthetic opioid drug approved by the Food and Drug Administration for use as an analgesic and anesthetic said to be one hundred times more potent than morphine and fifty times more than heroin. In addition to its use as an advanced analgesic, fentanyl also can be used as a sedative. Fentanyl is a Schedule II narcotic under the United States Controlled Substances Act of 1970.

Similar to other opioid analgesics, fentanyl produces effects such as relaxation, euphoria, pain relief, sedation, confusion, drowsiness, dizziness, nausea, vomiting, urinary retention, pupillary constriction, and respiratory depression.

Illegal fentanyl goes by many different street names including Apace, China Girl, China Town, China White, Dance Fever, Goodfellas, Great Bear, He-Man, Poison, and Tango & Cash.

Illicit fentanyl can be sold alone or in combination with heroin and other substances. Fentanyl has been widely reported to be present in a wide swath of fake pills masquerading as pharmaceutical drugs like oxycodone. Fentanyl also is often imbedded in cocaine, methamphetamine, and other non-opioid substances.

Illegal use of fentanyl is often in the form of powder used for inhalation or injection, blotter paper, and patches. Prescribed fentanyl patches can be abused by removing its gel contents and then injecting or ingesting these contents. Patches have also been frozen, cut into pieces, and placed under the tongue or in the cheek cavity.

Fentanyl is one of the primary drugs fueling the epidemic of synthetic opioid drug overdose deaths in the United States. While prescription opioid deaths remained stable from 2011 to 2021, synthetic opioid deaths increased from twenty-six hundred to more than seventy-six thousand overdose deaths per year. Fentanyl constitutes the majority of all drug overdose deaths in the United States since it overtook heroin in 2018.

Historically, illegal (that is, not medical) fentanyl has entered the United States in two primary ways: from China through common carriers such as FedEx and the US Postal Service and through Mexico via Mexican cartels. The former method has been curtailed significantly through greater awareness, oversight, and enforcement. Thus, today, most of the fentanyl in the US likely comes from Mexico and is the product of Mexican cartels.

The production pipeline for Mexican fentanyl can vary but generally starts with the precursor chemicals necessary to manufacture fentanyl. It is believed that most of those chemicals come to Mexico from China and Southeast Asia, though there are numerous reports of cartels expanding their own precursor capabilities. Often, the chemicals from China are brought by sea and "dropped" from ship to ship to ship (e.g., freight liner to fishing trolley to sightseeing boat) before reaching land.

The chemicals are then often taken to a stash house until they are delivered to a chemist who will produce a final product. Usually that final product is designed in a way to look like prescribed pharmaceuticals.

Before the product is ready to be moved, it is packaged in an effort to avoid detection at the planned border crossing. The product might be wrapped in plastic and then coated so as to escape detection by drug smelling dogs. This masking process usually involves everyday items such as coffee, mustard, or fabric softener. Other steps are taken in an effort to avoid other border patrol detection efforts.

Finally, the product is ready to cross the border, transported by a drug "mule." The transportation can be in a private car or a commercial vehicle but most frequently occurs at a designated port of entry. Often times, those transporting the drugs into the US are American citizens, presumably under the belief they will pass through the border, US Customs, and Border Protection searches more easily. Border agents find significant quantities of drugs (27,000 pounds of fentanyl and 545,000 pounds of drugs in total in 2023) but it is presumed that much more escapes detection then is seized. Once safely inside the US, the product is handed over to a distributor. As with transportation, the distributors are usually American residents, and often citizens.

Frequently, each step in the process is isolated so that only those involved in each step know their roles. In a program on fentanyl production in Mexico, a fentanyl chemist said succinctly: "The cemeteries are full of people who knew too much."[1]

Despite the dangers associated with this process, drug trafficking in general, and fentanyl production specifically, creates a ring of economic opportunity for many who have few other options for work or economic development.

Of course, there are a myriad of variations on this production pipeline, and in the distribution process inside the US. On top of that, domestic production of fentanyl is growing, though reliable metrics are elusive.

The following morning, James pauses from his legal work and retrieves Aguilar's file from his top desk drawer. Though the docu-

1. *Trafficked: Underworlds with Mariana Van Zeller*, episode 2, "Fentanyl," written by Rodrigo X. González, directed by Frederic Menou and Mariana Van Zeller, featuring Mariana Van Zeller, aired December 2, 2020, on National Geographic.

ments had been copied and scanned into the firm's document management system, James prefers to feel and touch the actual documents. Erica and he organized the documents from Aguilar's file in the best order they could, and looked into some items they found interesting, but the documents as a whole remained perplexing. This afternoon, James selects the file labelled "Miscellaneous"—documents not falling into any discernable category.

James flips through the documents, searching for one in particular—a clipping of an article from the *Bandera Bulletin* about the Bandera High Bulldogs winning a Texas regional football playoff game. James scans the article, jots down four names mentioned prominently in the story, closes the file, and places it back atop the other files in his drawer.

Returning to the computer, James accesses Google to research the names.

- Blake Anderson. Playing football at TCU.
- Jesus Gabriel. Joined the army.
- Steve Martinez. Playing basketball at University of the Incarnate World in San Antonio.
- Robert "Robbie" Rivera. Died of a fentanyl overdose six months ago.

"Bingo," James says aloud. *We should have made this connection sooner.*

Looking up the number on his computer, James calls the Bandera County sheriff's office and is surprised when he is soon speaking with Sheriff Harvey Henderson.

"What can you tell me about Robbie Rivera?" James asks.

Sheriff Henderson sighs. "Every overdose death is a tragedy, but his struck a nerve in the community. Robbie was a good kid. Smart, good-looking, a good athlete. He had a lot going for him."

"Do you know how he ended up making such a mistake?" James asks.

"Dumb kids doing dumb kid things. Try something just once. You get it."

"Yes, I do. What about the case? I understand there was an arrest."

"We got the guy who sold the kids the drugs," Sheriff Henderson states.

"No one else in the chain?" James asks.

"We looked. We absolutely did, but the reality is, there weren't many breadcrumbs to follow. We didn't have the resources and this one-off death didn't inspire any of the feds to take up the case. As I'm sure you know, this ain't television. Much of the time we nab who we can when we can and move on. Resources are limited," Henderson admits.

"I understand, Sheriff. Has there been much of a fentanyl problem in your area?"

"Mr. Butler, there is a fentanyl problem everywhere."

"I'm learning as much," James says.

"You didn't ask, but here's the real issue, Mr. Butler. It's not just fentanyl. Just as soon as we started to understand the fentanyl crisis, this potent animal sedative, xylazine, often called 'tranq' or the 'zombie drug,' starts infiltrating illicit substances like fentanyl, heroin, and cocaine. By 2022, it was a major contributor to overdose deaths in the US.

"Then there is another set of synthetic opioids called nitazenes, said to be up to forty times more potent than fentanyl. Don't ask me how it's even possible. Called Frankenstein opioids, they were added to a number of states'-controlled substances lists and are regarded as having no acceptable medical use. Then, health organizations started advising us to be on the lookout for something called carfentanil, which they claim is one hundred times more potent than fentanyl.

"Hell, those are just the ones we know. Soon there will be the newest bad thing, and the next one, and the one following it. It's almost impossible for a poor sheriff like me to keep up, and there are hundreds of others just like me. We do the best we can and work hard, but the playing field isn't level."

"Are most of the drugs in your area coming from Mexico?" James inquires.

"Probably, but there are plenty of sources in the US too. Then, of course, there is the issue of the unrelenting demand for these drugs. As long as the demand is there, the supply will be created, here or abroad. I could go on and on, but I'll spare you."

James reflects on the new information, paired with what he learned in Phoenix, before he calls William "Billy" Garza, now a second-year associate, into his office.

"What can I do for you, James?" Billy says walking into James's office.

"Just one second," James says while typing at his desk.

Billy looks outside toward the ocean. "Damn, it even looks hot, at least for this time of the year."

"I know. Let me ask you, how much do you know about fentanyl?" James asks.

"It can kill you with a little bit. Otherwise, not much," Billy answers.

"I'd like you to spend a little time going through the typical and non-traditional sources for discussions about fentanyl and the trafficking of fentanyl looking for anything noteworthy," James says.

"Meaning?" Billy asks.

"To be honest, I'm not sure, but I'm hoping there is something a bit outside the norm or somehow distinct from what one might call the traditional narrative," James says.

"Got it. Sounds interesting. So, you are thinking DEA and . . .?"

"DEA, Congressional Record, CDC, something called the Center for Advanced Defense Studies. But more than just the typical sites. Almost anything with at least a hint of authenticity and authority to it. My friend, Dr. Mirada, suggested I look into these sources a few weeks ago, but I kinda blew it off."

"No worries. I've got your back," Billy says. "When do you need something? Day before yesterday?"

"Whenever you can. You know me—no memos. Just give me what you find and think would be helpful on a rolling basis," James says.

"On it. I'll stop back if I have questions."

"Thanks, Billy. And bill your time to pro bono."

As Billy starts to leave the office, James calls to him. "Billy?"

"Yeah?"

"This is important. I need not just your intellect but also your instincts," James says.

"Got it. I'll see what's out there. Before I go, can I ask a question?" Billy asks.

"Sure. What's on your mind?" James asks.

"In the past, you said you didn't believe the CIA was involved in Agent Camarena's abduction and murder, but we now know so much more about the CIA and its connections to drug trafficking. I mean, I know Rafa Quintero was the actual guy, but every time you have me look at something, I find evidence of the CIA or someone working with them manipulating something or someone up to and including governments, so I'm just wondering if your thoughts have changed at all," Billy says coolly.

"You ask a good question, and I think about it often. At the end of the day, though, the answer is no, my opinion has not changed. But—and this is important—it's not because I rule out the possibility of the CIA being involved but because it doesn't make sense to me based on the facts we know at the moment.

"In the first place," James continues, "we know there is nothing contemporaneous to suggest Agent Camarena had found something secretive with respect to the CIA. In fact, Agent Berrellez once asserted Camarena was 'about to' uncover something. Do you kidnap and interrogate a federal agent because they are *about* to uncover something? I think not, but, more to the point, if there was something Camarena had found or was about to find, then it stands to reason the CIA's concern would be the 'secret' getting out. What better way to have the 'secret' discovered than to kidnap a DEA agent and have hundreds of DEA and FBI agents come to town looking into everything the agent had done or been involved in.

"That continues to be my thought, though I'm not inflexible. I will note, I do not think Félix Rodríguez was involved in the interrogation in any way, and I find the statements of Godoy and Lopez Romero on the subject wholly unbelievable," James concludes.

Félix Rodríguez is a legendary, or infamous, depending on the point of view, former CIA officer who was a Cuban exile involved in the Bay of Pigs. Rodríguez later was involved in the capture of Che Guevara in Bolivia and was highly decorated for his efforts in the Vietnam War, flying over three hundred missions and being shot down five times.

Later, Rodríguez was a key figure in the Iran-Contra Affair, and he gave extensive—and at times, highly combative—testimony to the Kerry Commission.

Two witnesses, propped up by former DEA Agent Héctor Berrellez and shown in the controversial docu-series *The Last Narc,* claim Rodríguez was present for and participated in part of the interrogation of Agent Camarena. Their testimony, while believed by some, has been critiqued on a number of fronts, including the lack of corroborating evidence.

"But not impossible?" Billy clarifies.

"But not impossible. If impossibility is the bar, though, we'd never make any progress looking at a lot of mysteries—who was Jack the Ripper or D.B. Cooper or the Zodiac. I love the line from

Jules Verne: 'Science, my lad, is made up of mistakes, but they are mistakes which it is useful to make, because they lead little by little to the truth.'[2] That's how I try to approach the law and how I've tried to approach this case. We make reasonable judgments to move the analysis forward, and we build on those judgments until we reach a conclusion, but no judgment or conclusion is ever so profound as to be beyond correction," James explains.

"Were you the one who told me about the D.B. Cooper researcher?" Billy asks.

"Probably. There was one researcher, and I'll be damned if I can remember his name, but he spent a decade or more looking into one suspect and was convinced he had the right one. Then his prime suspect was ruled out, and he went back to square one and later identified a different suspect. He's a legend in my mind, even if I can't remember his name," James says.

"Which puts us where?" Billy asks.

"With our assumptions and informed judgments," James answers.

"Our informed judgment being that the CIA wasn't involved in Agent Camarena's kidnapping, interrogation, or murder, but subject to change in the event additional or contradictory information is received?" suggests Billy.

"I think so. And that applies to everything else about the case," James says.

"Everything?"

"Everything," James confirms. "Nothing—and no one—is too noble or important to be questioned, if the facts demand it."

2. Jules Verne, *A Journey to the Centre of the Earth* (New York: C. Scribner's Sons, 1905), 180.

FIFTEEN

THE ORANGE COUNTY Superior Court is located in downtown Santa Ana off West Civic Center drive, near a number of government offices including Santa Ana City Hall and the public library. Most of the civil litigation courts are housed on the third through seventh floors.

This afternoon, in a courtroom on the fourth floor, Erica had assisted Paul Goss, a partner in the firm's litigation department, in the presentation of materials in a hearing on Goss's motion for summary judgment in a contentious business litigation matter. The hearing, which included Erica manning the computer for the presentation of documents and materials to the court in support of Goss's argument, had lasted a mind-numbing two plus hours. At the end of the presentation, the court took the matter under advisement, promising a decision in a week to ten days.

Erica and Goss had driven separately to the courthouse, each arriving in the early afternoon for the 1:00 pm hearing. By the time they had arrived, available parking spots were few and far between, and they ended up parking in different lots.

After a brief discussion on the courthouse steps following the presentation, Goss walks north on North Flower Street, crossing W.

Civic Center Drive toward his car in the lot behind the corner building housing, among other agencies, the Orange County Public Defender's office.

Erica was parked further away in the lot off W. Sixth Street, one block south and a couple blocks west of the courthouse. The spring air and a gentle breeze refresh Erica even though the temperature is unseasonably warm. Pulling the AV equipment case and her briefcase, Erica slowly makes her way down Sixth Street, thinking through the hearing and making a mental checklist of the items left to be completed today.

Erica enters the parking lot from Sixth Street, but her car is in the far corner abutting North Shelton Street. The lot was packed with cars a few hours ago but now is largely empty.

As she reaches her car, Erica pops the trunk and sets down the equipment cart. Prior to loading the cart, Erica checks her phone and is delighted to discover a text from James.

> I have some news. Maybe. I might have figured out why Aguilar was in Yuma or at least why he was looking into fentanyl.

Erica composes a quick reply.

> Might and maybe aside, it sounds promising. Leaving Santa Ana now and going to the office. Lots to talk about. Dinner out or at home? Love you.

James's response is immediate.

> I'll probably miss you at the office. I'm leaving for Long Beach now. Let's just figure something out for dinner at home. Love you.

Erica responds.

> Dinner in is great. I'm wiped out. Drive safe. Love you.

As Erica loads the equipment into her car, a black Land Rover drives slowly toward her. As the car creeps closer, the tinted glass makes it impossible to glimpse inside. Erica surveys the parking lot as the car slowly passes. *It's a thin line between prudently cautious and paranoid,* she thinks. Seeing nothing, she climbs in, presses the engine start button, and double checks to be assured the doors are locked. *A thin line indeed.*

Within minutes, Erica merges onto the 5 Freeway for the short jog to the Costa Mesa Freeway. Seeking time to digest her conversation before returning to her office, Erica stays in the slow, right lane. As she nears the MacArthur Boulevard exit, Erica switches lanes to pass slowing traffic merging onto the freeway. As she returns to the right lane, a black Land Rover makes the same lane change. *Relax, Erica. It's a busy road. But the thin line gets thinner.*

Preparing to transfer onto the Corona Del Mar Freeway, Erica observes the Land Rover again mimicking her movements. *What do they say? Just because you're paranoid doesn't mean they're not following you.*

Erica exits onto Bristol Street, but rather than turning into the drive for the office building, she continues past and makes a series of right turns to bring her back in front of the office, with the Land Rover continuing to follow. Erica hits a red light at the corner of Dove Street and Birch Street. Erica is in the right turn lane, but traffic prevents her from making a right turn on the red light. The Land Rover pulls up close behind her.

"Call Dad," Erica instructs her Tesla.

"Brian Castle's office," answers the receptionist after a single ring.

"Amy, it's Erica. Is Brian available?"

"He's in his office with Ben. Do you want me to interrupt?" Amy asks.

"Yes, please. Tell him it's urgent," Erica says.

"Okay."

"Hi, Erica. Are you okay?" Brian asks.

"Dad, I'm being followed. I'm getting close to the office. Can you send some cops to the office? I'm afraid to pull up to the building," Erica explains.

"Where are you?" Brian asks.

"I'm circling the building now. It's a black Land Rover," Erica says.

"Keep driving. I'll get help," Brian says before hanging up.

Erica changes her pattern, but the Land Rover maintains both its distance and persistence.

A text from Brian appears on the screen in front of her: *Police coming. Pull up to the front of the building. Reggie and I will be there to meet you.*

Erica makes one last right turn to pull up in front of the office building, spotting Brian and Reggie, head of building security, waiting. To her amazement, the Land Rover almost follows, until correcting its direction and speeding down the street as sirens begin to wail from two police cars approaching the building.

Erica pulls in front and hugs Brian who had raced to open the door for her. "Are you okay?" he asks.

"A little shaken, but okay," Erica says.

"Are you sure it was following you?" Reggie questions.

"Positive," Erica confirms.

"Did you get a license plate or anything else?" Brian asks.

"No. Sorry."

"How many people were there?" Reggie asks.

"The windows were tinted, and I was trying not to crash. I couldn't see a thing. But some things are starting to make more sense now."

Erica had ordered delivery from Il Piacere and has dinner set on the dining room table when James comes home.

"Yum, smells good. Il Piacere?" he asks.

"It is. I hadn't talked to Andre in a while, so it was nice to chat with him for a few minutes," Erica says.

After a brief discussion of the legal matters of the day, Erica's curiosity surfaces. "I think you said you might know why Aguilar was in Yuma. What'd you come up with?"

"In Aguilar's documents, there was an article from the *Bandera Bulletin*," James says.

"Yeah, I remember it. It seemed out of place, so I put it in the miscellaneous file."

"Right. I re-read it and started looking at the football players named in the story, and four names stood out. With a bit of Google sleuthing, I figured out one of them is playing football at TCU, one joined the army, and another is playing basketball at University of the Incarnate World in San Antonio," James says.

"And the fourth?" Erica prompts.

"The fourth was a scholar athlete named Robert "Robbie" Rivera, who died of a fentanyl overdose the night of his high school graduation."

"I'm going to go out on a limb here and surmise Aguilar had a connection to Robbie?" Erica asks.

"Grandnephew," James confirms.

"No mights or maybes about it, babe. This has to be the connection. I wonder why Rosalia didn't say anything," Erica says.

"I wondered that too, but my guess is she just never made the connection. She may have no idea fentanyl is trafficked through Yuma or how it gets from there to Texas," James suggests.

"Makes sense. But we still don't know what the connection is to someone from Mazatlán," Erica says.

"Not yet," James replies, "but we will."

The next morning, before heading to the office or calling Bobby about the Yuma trip, James heads out for a mind-cleansing run. Heading west, James stops at a light at PCH before he can cross over to Balboa Peninsula to the path along Ocean Front West. James checks his watch and evaluates his time while waiting for the light. Looking to his right, a black Land Rover stops at the red light in the center lane. *A black Land Rover. Coincidence? Take it easy, James. There must be dozens of black Land Rovers in Newport Beach.*

The light turns and the blinking walk sign gives James the opening to resume his run. James cruises down Newport Boulevard to Balboa Boulevard arriving at McFadden Square to connect to the beach front path. He follows the path stopping at West Jetty View Park, which abuts the entrance of the Newport Bay Channel.

Turning back, James soon reaches McFadden Square, but he takes a left to run to the end of Newport Pier, resting to take in the clear ocean view and the surfers in wetsuits riding the morning waves. Returning back to McFadden Square, James finds a black Land Rover in an adjacent parking spot.

No way! That can't possibly be the same car, can it?

James looks more closely at the vehicle this time, noticing tinted windows as Erica had described. He checks but finds the car has no license plates.

James accelerates his pace, heading back up the hill. Nearing PCH, James veers to the right and has an opportunity to look behind him. Not seeing the Land Rover, James relaxes for a moment. Heading east, up the hill on Old Newport Boulevard, James resumes his pace past Santa Ana Avenue, but approaching Catalina Drive, he stops in his tracks, seeing a black Land Rover stopped at the approaching intersection.

There's no way I can turn back. There's nowhere to go. If I make it past the intersection, I can play Frogger and sprint to the other side of Newport Boulevard.

James accelerates his pace to a near sprint, passing the car at the intersection, but finds his path across Newport Boulevard blocked by a bus and backed up traffic. Suddenly, the Land Rover appears on his left. The front passenger window descends halfway, before a voice calls out.

"Mr. Butler! You should be more careful than running by yourself. It's not safe."

"Who the hell are you?" James asks.

"Don't worry. We will meet again. Soon." With those words, the window rolls back up and the Land Rover races off on Newport Boulevard, soon evading James's sight.

James stands, breathing heavily, intently following the disappearing Land Rover. *Now they're pissing me off.*

SIXTEEN

"JAMES BUTLER."

"James, it's Bobby."

"Hey, man. What's up?" James replies.

"Are you busy this evening?" Bobby asks.

"Depends on what you have in mind," James says.

"I have us scheduled for a meeting in Los Angeles with someone who may have more information on Yuma and fentanyl. I can explain more later."

"'May have' is good enough for me. I'm in. Where, and what time?" James asks.

"Way up in northeast LA at 7:00 p.m. I can drive and we can talk on the way," Bobby offers.

"Works for me. Would coming to my office be too far out of your way?" James asks.

"Not at all. Accounting for traffic, we probably should leave a bit before five," Bobby says.

"What if I meet you in front at 4:45, more or less?" James asks.

"Perfect. I'll see you then."

James waits outside his office building enjoying the fresh air. Soon Bobby arrives in the black Tesla Model S Plaid James had gifted to Bobby as part of James's share of the reward from the Rafa Quintero matter.

"Good to see you, Bobby."

"You as well, James."

"Nice car," James says.

"Yep," Bobby replies. "I like it a lot."

"So, where are we headed?"

"Montecito Heights. The Ramona Hall Community Center to be more specific," Bobby explains.

"Sounds lovely. Mind if I ask why?" James asks.

"Last night, Cedric called me and put me on a three-way call with a dude named Víctor Florés, who Cedric said led a prominent gang in the Boyle Heights area of East Los Angeles in the 1990s."

"Okay, I'm tracking," James says.

"Víctor's niece's husband is now a key figure in a current and more prominent gang in the same general area. Some say the gang has close ties to the Sinaloa Cartel. Víctor thinks he can convince this guy—Guillermo is his name—to meet with us tonight."

James thinks for a moment. "Let me see if I have this right. We are driving to East LA to meet with a former gang leader we don't know, to maybe be introduced to a current gang member we don't know, to ask him what he knows about drug dealings with the Sinaloa Cartel?"

"Sounds less appealing when you say it like that. Do you want to bail and go back?"

"Oh hell no. Let's see where this goes. I'm starting to love the adrenaline rush of life-threatening situations," James says, only half-joking.

Sometime in the late 1960s, Mexican American inmates of the California state prison system separated into two rival groups, primarily based on the locations of their hometowns. Those from the northern part of the state were referred to as Norteños. Conversely, those from Southern California were referred to as Sureños.

As it has evolved, the north–south dividing line between Norteños and Sureños has been accepted as the cities of Bakersfield and Delano, though the "border" is far from definitive, and various factions can be found throughout the state. Sureños are particularly prominent in Southern California, but they also have notable presences in Nevada, Arizona, Texas, New Mexico, and Utah. Sureños are said to foster relationships with various drug trafficking organizations based in Mexico.

Norteños use the number 14, which represents the fourteenth letter of the English alphabet, the letter N, in order to pay allegiance to Nuestra Familia. Norteños often use images of the Mexican American labor movement, such as the sombrero, machete, and the logo of the United Farm Workers which is a stylized black Aztec eagle.

Sureños use the number 13, which represents the thirteenth letter of the alphabet, the letter M, in allegiance to the Mexican Mafia. Most Sureños are of Mexican descent, but some Sureño gangs allow members from various other ethnic backgrounds to join their ranks.

The Ramona Hall Community Center is located off Figueroa Street, north and slightly east of Dodger Stadium. The Center is a two-story, white stucco building surrounded by a black wrought iron fence, fronted by a small, green lawn and an American flag flying from a tall, lighted flagpole. Serving the general East Los Angeles neighborhood, the center offers a wide selection of sports, fitness, and cultural programs, including afterschool and preschool activities.

The drive, as expected, is slow, with periods of stop-and-go traffic. James and Bobby discuss a myriad of topics on the drive, none having to do with drugs or murder, cartels or gangs. The drive finds Bobby's black Tesla S weaving northeast on the Costa Mesa Freeway to the 5 North, through Santa Ana and Anaheim, past Disneyland and Angels Stadium, through Norwalk, Commerce, and the giant sign for the Commerce Casino and Hotel. Passing Boyle Heights, with downtown Los Angeles glimmering in the evening sun, the road soon turns to the 110 North. Bobby navigates the exit onto East Forty-Third Street. A quick left takes them over the freeway to the intersection at Figueroa Street, stopping at the light with a Jack in the Box to their left and a Donut Factory in front of them. A right turn on red, a few blocks, and another right turn into a parking lot put James and Bobby in the parking area for the community center and several other buildings.

"Ten till seven. Pretty good timing," Bobby says.

"The drive would have been miserable alone. I've become such a wimp with traffic," concedes James.

"Haven't we all," Bobby says.

"What's the plan from here?" James asks.

"Víctor said he'd meet us inside. Said he'd be able to spot us," Bobby explains.

"Not a comforting statement," James says.

Stepping out of the car, the two follow a path to the main entrance for the center. "Ready?" Bobby asks.

"Let's do it," James replies.

Bobby opens a door and follows James inside. Scanning the foyer, James and Bobby soon spot a man walking toward them.

"Bobby Burgess, I assume."

"Víctor," replies Bobby as the two men shake hands. "This is James Butler, whom I mentioned last night."

"A pleasure," Víctor says, shaking James's hand.

"Thank you," James replies.

"I got us a small room over here where we can talk." Víctor begins walking down a hallway to the third door on the right. Inside is a small table and four folding chairs. The wood-paneled walls are dotted with posters of Spanish words with English translations.

"Have a seat. This room is used as a small classroom during the day, but no one will need it this evening." Víctor waits for everyone to settle in before continuing. "Cedric called me a few days ago and explained what you and he had discussed a while back. He also said you were good people and could be trusted. He asked if I could help."

"How do you know Cedric?" James asks.

"I've known Cedric since he went by C-3. We come from similar backgrounds, with similar initial careers. I didn't know him well back then, but I knew who he was. Communication and things were different then, before social media and all. We both moved on, and now we both try to help young men learn from our mistakes and see a better path forward. There aren't many of us in that line of work with our backgrounds, so we've gotten to know each other a bit better," Víctor says.

"We appreciate any information or help you can give us," James states.

"I got out twelve years ago, and over time, my direct knowledge has faded. Now I know only a little. My niece, my sister's daughter, Gabrielle, is the apple of my eye. Smart and beautiful. She goes to UCLA. Against my wishes, she married into the life. She married Guillermo de Leon, an ex-con mechanic who never works on cars, if you get my drift. Because I love Gabby, I tolerate Guillermo. Because of my past, he gives me a certain level of respect. We don't talk about his activities, but I hear enough. I'm confident he knows quite a bit about what you are concerned about. I asked him to come by to talk but didn't say much more."

"Will he be receptive to talking to us?" James asks.

"I don't know, but Cedric said it was important, and then Bobby last night said you were looking into your friend's murder, so I thought it would be worth asking."

Víctor looks at James and smiles. "You're nervous."

"A little. And a bit embarrassed it's that obvious," James says.

"Don't worry. Nothing will happen while I'm here." Víctor pauses. "Probably," he says, followed by a loud and hearty laugh.

Víctor's phone buzzes with a notification. "It's Guillermo. He's outside but wants to talk to me before he comes in. I'll go talk to him. Wait here."

"Okay," James replies. "We aren't going anywhere." James pauses until Víctor has left the room and the door is shut before asking Bobby, "What do you think?"

"Reasonable," Bobby says.

"And safe?"

"I think so. Nothing will go down here for sure," Bobby says confidently.

"Suggestions on how to approach the discussion?" James asks.

"Not many. You are better at this than me, but I think the key is to make sure he understands why you are looking for information."

"Agreed," James says, trying to calm his nerves before they return.

Bobby and James sit in silence, checking their phones for email and sports scores, before the door opens and Víctor walks in with Guillermo. Guillermo is short and stocky, obviously in good shape. He wears jeans and a black T-shirt, sized to accentuate his build.

"Guillermo and I talked, and he is willing to listen to what you have to say," Víctor announces. "Guillermo, this is James and next to him is Bobby."

James and Bobby stand to shake hands with Guillermo, who ignores the gesture. "You didn't mention the big guy here," Guillermo protests to Víctor.

"I told you it was a lawyer from Orange County and his friend," Víctor replies.

"I don't care. He makes me uncomfortable," Guillermo says.

"Too bad," Bobby responds, "we are a package deal."

"Fine. Then I'll leave," Guillermo asserts.

"Wait, wait, wait. Let's all be reasonable for a minute," James requests. "Give us one second."

James leans over to whisper to Bobby. "I think I'll be fine as long as Víctor is here."

"I'm sure, but I don't like him thinking he can dictate things," Bobby says.

"Agreed, but I think we have to go along," James says.

"Okay, but I'll be right outside the door," Bobby says.

"I hope so," James says.

"Fine," Bobby announces to the room. "I'll leave. But I'm not going far. I'll be right outside."

"Thanks, Bobby. Everything will be fine," Víctor states in a soothing voice.

"Wait a second!" Guillermo exclaims as Bobby turns toward the door. "I thought you looked familiar. You're Bobby Burgess, aren't you?"

"I am. How'd you know?" Bobby responds, turning back to the room.

"I'm the black sheep of my family. My brother and sister, on the other hand, both went to UCLA, and my wife does now. I've been a Bruins fan for a long time. What are you doing now?" Guillermo asks.

"After I retired, a started an investigations firm in Orange County, and James here is a good client and a better friend," Bobby explains.

"Man, I loved watching you play. Did you guys ever see him?" Guillermo asks the others.

"I did," James notes, while Víctor shakes his head no.

"I remember one game against Oregon," Guillermo says.

"Oh yeah, what a game," Bobby agrees.

"You should have seen it," Guillermo says to James and Víctor. "Fourth quarter and Bobby dominates and capped it off with a fifty yard—"

"Fifty-three yard," Bobby interjects.

"A fifty-three-yard run where he ran over—I mean ran straight over—a safety trying to shoot the gap. That one got some play on

ESPN. Man, I thought you were going to have a great career in Buffalo. But Buffalo?" Guillermo says.

"I know. They should have a draft rule that cold cities can't draft kids who've never lived in the cold. But, you know what, I started for most of six years, made and saved some good money, and got out on my terms. No messed-up knees, nothing. I'm happy," Bobby says.

"That's great. Bobby Burgess. Son of a …" Guillermo shakes his head in disbelief.

"So, can I stay?" Bobby asks.

"Hell yes. Sorry. You know how it is. Big black guy who looks like he could take on a small army—made me nervous," Guillermo says.

"I get it. No offense taken," Bobby says.

Bobby sits back in his chair before Víctor takes the floor.

"I explained to Guillermo what you are doing, and, not speaking for him, he is willing to help."

"Your friend was killed?" Guillermo asks James.

"He was. Shot in the back. While we were talking on the phone," James says.

"Rough. Why do you need me?" Guillermo asks.

"I'm trying to find out what happened to him. The police conclusions are suspect, and they have not been much help," James admits.

"There's a big fucking surprise. Where was he killed? Maybe I've heard something," Guillermo says.

"He was in Yuma. Arizona," James says.

"I ain't got nothin' to do with anything in Yuma. I'm in East LA. Jesus Christ. This look like Arizona to you? Did you see a fucking cactus in the parking lot?" Guillermo jokes.

"No, no I didn't. Look, my friend was looking into fentanyl trafficking through Yuma. Do you happen to know anything about it?"

"What the fuck? You asking if I'm a trafficker? *¡Chale!*"

"Settle down. The man just asked a question," Víctor says.

"Like hell. The man trying to trick me into saying something stupid. Are you sure he ain't a cop? Is he wired?" Guillermo stands up and pulls a pistol from his waistband.

"Whoa, whoa, whoa. Let's all calm down!" Bobby yells.

"Damn, man," James pleads. "I'm not a cop. I'm just someone trying to find out why my friend was murdered."

"I didn't kill him. I don't know who did. Why you asking about drugs and shit? You trying to get me to confess something?" Guillermo asks.

"No," Bobby interjects. "Truth is, we don't care about you. At all. James here doesn't want or need you to say anything about anything you've ever done or not done. Got it? Nothing. Not a Goddamn thing. He's interested only in what you know, or what you've heard, or what you might believe to be true."

"I don't know. Still makes me nervous," Guillermo says.

"That's fine," Bobby reassures. "These are sensitive areas, but we think there probably is a Mexican cartel connection. We thought you might have some general impressions that could help. That's it. No tricks. No traps."

"What about this?" James offers. "What if I describe somethings we've been told or think we've learned, and you can tell me if you think I'm saying something wrong or off base."

"Sounds sensible to me," Víctor says.

"Fine," Guillermo says as he returns his gun to his waistband under his shirt and sits back down, arms crossed in front of him.

Bobby sits down next to James, who pauses to allow emotions to calm.

"Fine," Bobby says finally.

"Okay. What if we start at the most basic level. There is agreement that a lot or even most of the drugs sold in the US come from Mexico," James starts.

"Everyone knows that," Guillermo says impatiently.

"Right. And drugs often cross from Mexico into the US at or through regular border crossing checkpoints, including places like Yuma," James continues.

"Go ahead," Guillermo says.

"The consensus also is that most of the drugs coming from Mexico into the US are controlled by Mexican cartels," James says.

"Sounds plausible," Guillermo says.

"Some have gone so far as to suggest Mexican cartels have alliances or working relationships with US organizations that some might call street gangs," James says.

"Probably safe to say the cartels don't distribute their drugs inside the US," Víctor asserts.

"Everyone has turf," Guillermo notes.

"And one of the prominent Mexican cartels in drug trafficking is the Sinaloa Cartel, or CDS," James continues.

"Probably," Guillermo says.

"It has been said the Sinaloa Cartel has an influence on the drug trafficking through Yuma." James watches Guillermo for any sign of recognition.

"Go on," Guillermo says.

James knows he has to tread lightly here. "I'm also told Yuma gangs have direct connections to some in Los Angeles."

"I don't want to talk about that," Guillermo says.

"You don't need to say anything except wrong, if I am. But I don't think I am," James says.

"Pretty cocky for a gringo, aren't you?" Guillermo says.

"Not cocky. But I've done my homework. Let me lay out this scenario: CDS transports drugs through Yuma. Some of those drugs are to be transported to networks in different cities, including LA, and the street gangs in Yuma work for or maybe with their counterparts in LA. Now I'll pause."

James waits, but Guillermo remains silent, leaning back in his chair, arms folded.

"If someone, like my friend, was killed while asking questions in Yuma," James continues, "it could be because of the CDS connection, or because of the fentanyl traffickers, or a gang banger getting a little too nervous."

"Maybe, but I don't know," Guillermo says.

"I didn't expect you would," James says.

"Then why am I here? Why are you wasting my time?" Guillermo's rise from the chair matches the change in his volume. Bobby stands to match Guillermo.

"Because you might know someone who does know, or cares who's looking." James pauses to let emotions abate before continuing. "Look, Guillermo. I don't want you to take this as a threat. I cannot tell you how much I do not want you to take this as a threat. But there are two ways this can go down. One is we shake hands and part ways tonight, and the DEA goes into Yuma and investigates everyone and everything connected to the drug trade. Or you can help us nail the people who murdered my friend, and the DEA will arrest them and only those connected to them, with an appropriate show of force, and then go away. Neat and clean. No collateral damage."

Guillermo scoffs. "You don't have that kind of juice with the DEA."

"I didn't say I did, but I have a very, very good friend who does," James says.

Guillermo pauses and thinks, his anger subsiding. "I need to make a phone call."

"Okay," James says.

"I'm going outside. I'll be back."

Guillermo leaves, and Bobby shuts the door behind him.

"Damn impressive, Mr. Butler," Bobby says.

"We don't have anything yet," James states.

"You will," Víctor says.

"No doubt," Bobby agrees.

Time slows to a crawl as they wait for Guillermo to return. All three look at their phones. James calls Erica at the office but gets her voice mail. *Good for her. She left early.* Before James can call her cell phone, Guillermo returns.

Standing, rather than returning to his chair, Guillermo strikes a more subdued posture. "Here's the deal. I can't tell you who killed your friend because I don't know, but I can give you the local dealers."

"That's the best you can do?" Víctor asks.

"I went high up. That's all I can do," Guillermo says.

Víctor nods to James, who looks at Bobby.

"Your call," Bobby states, "but I believe it."

"Okay, Guillermo. If you can provide me with information on the right people in Yuma, I'll make sure the investigation stops there," James says.

"Deal. Give me a couple of days," Guillermo says.

"That's fine," James says, handing his business card to Guillermo. "And thanks."

The men shake hands, and Víctor rises to shake hands with Bobby and James.

"Be well, Víctor," James says. "And thank you."

Guillermo shakes hands with James then Bobby. "By the way," he says, "this never happened."

"What do you mean?" Bobby assures him. "We came for bingo night."

"But I met Bobby freaking Burgess. Pretty cool," Guillermo says.

The men all walk to the parking lot. As Guillermo reaches his car, his phone rings. Guillermo answers it, and walks toward Bobby's car as he speaks, disconnecting just as he reaches James and Bobby.

"I respect you guys. You're doing a good thing, but what I'm going to tell you has to stay between us."

"Completely," James assures him.

"Do you know a Mexican cartel dude by the name of Javier Cruz?" Guillermo asks.

"No. At least not by name," James says.

"Well, I'm told he worked for Caro Quintero and knows you and your wife. You might want to check on her. And you'll owe me," Guillermo says.

"No," James replies, "I *do* owe you."

SEVENTEEN

The secret rendition of Rafael Caro Quintero from Mexico two years ago started when James and Erica sought a way to meet with Rafa himself. Eventually, they were able to connect with anonymous people in Rafa's circle and then with a San Diego lawyer who facilitated a meeting.

James and Erica traveled to the Mexican resort city of Mazatlán. The day after their arrival, they received a call directing them to Joe's Oyster Bar, located on the beach in Mazatlán's main tourist area, commonly referred to as the Golden Zone. At 8 p.m., Joe's converts from a beach bar to a nightclub with dancing inside and in the open beach air.

At Joe's, James and Erica were approached by a man identifying himself as "Javier," who they learned was a key lieutenant to Rafa. Javier transported James and Erica to a house in a residential neighborhood of Mazatlán, where he led them to a bedroom and a meeting with Rafa.

James and Erica's discussions with Rafa were interrupted when three men in tactical gear and masks subdued Rafa's men, forced Rafa, James, and Erica into a black van, and sped off. Soon, it was revealed that two of the "abductors" were Aguilar and Tim Speer.

The two had planned and then executed Rafa's transfer to the United States and into the custody of US officials.

Night has settled in as Erica works in her office, her face framed by the glow from her computer screen and a small lamp on the credenza behind her.

"Still here?" Brian Castle inquires of his daughter.

"I'll be dead in my chair if you scare me like that again. Christ!" Erica says.

"Sorry," Brian replies, taking a seat in the client chair across from Erica. "I've always said if we ever need to perform emergency surgery at work, your office is the closest we have to a sterile operating theater."

"Hey, there is nothing wrong with being neat and tidy," she says.

"Nothing at all, but I will note it is a short walk from fastidious to OCD," Brian says.

"You're hysterical. Was there a point to you gracing me with your presence?" Erica asks.

"Nope. No point at all. Just checking in. But, you know, my last name is on the front door, and you're married to a partner. You don't need to work so hard," Brian offers.

"It has nothing to do with me needing to work hard but rather ensuring our cases are all covered. Besides, with James and Bobby in Los Angeles talking to who knows whom, it keeps me from worrying too much," Erica says.

"I didn't know James was in LA. What are they doing up there?" Brian asks.

"Kind of a last-minute thing," Erica states. "Bobby's contact in Phoenix put him in touch with a former gang leader who knows a current gang member who might know about the movement of fentanyl from Mexico, and they are all getting together for a nice chat."

"What could go wrong?" Brian quips.

"Precisely!" Erica says.

"Okay, well, I have a dinner in Laguna, so I need to get going, but please do your old man a favor and go home soon?" Brian requests.

"Since you asked so nicely." Erica looks up and gives him a reassuring smile.

Brian's lips tighten. "I'm still worried about whoever followed you."

"I'll be fine. It's a secure building, with secure parking. Besides, Reggie is downstairs and won't let anything happen."

"It's Carl tonight, not Reggie," Brian informs her.

"Same difference. I'll be fine. Being tailed freaked me out at the time, but I feel comfortable here. Besides, I think it was more intimidation than anything else," Erica says.

Brian stands, turning toward the door. "Call me if you need anything."

"Of course," Erica replies.

Brian walks toward the lobby, slowly leaving Erica's line of sight. Upon the distinctive tone of the descending elevator, Erica's attention returns to her work.

With the office to herself, Erica slips off her heels and enhances the ambiance. "Alexa, play The Pixies album *Doolittle*. Alexa, volume up." Soon "Debaser" is blasting through the Echo Studio on the bookshelf across from Erica's desk, and Erica is typing feverishly, pausing only after the album finishes playing to instruct Alexa to play the album *Pablo Honey* by Radiohead.

Mid-album, the music stops, the computer turns off, and the lights go dark. Looking outside, Erica spots lit offices in an adjacent building. Curious, she calls down to the security desk, but there's no answer.

Standing to look around, Erica calls down the hall, "Is anyone here?"

Erica walks down the dim hallway, now illuminated only by the moon and ambient light from the street. The reception desk and lobby are at the end of the hall. Newly remodeled, the lobby is now much smaller, replaced in large part by two wellness pods. The three-shaft elevator bank is just past the lobby. On the other side is a locked glass door, opened only by a key card.

Erica passes the elevators and opens the door with a quick swipe. Rather than letting the door close behind her, she props it open with a door stop often used during business hours. *If I'm in a hurry, I might not want to have to open the door.*

Erica walks slowly down the other hall. The recent remodeling added more white marble to the floors and lobby walls and replaced most office walls with glass partitions. The floor is configured in a large square with attorney offices and a large conference room on the windowed outer perimeter and paralegal offices and a smaller conference room on the inside of the hall on one side and legal assistant carrels and a kitchen on the other side.

Erica is startled by the chime from the elevators. *Great. The elevators are working. The power must not be out in the whole building. That's odd; why just this floor?*

Turning to walk back to the elevators, Erica calls out again. "Carl. Is that you?"

Erica's query is met with cold silence rather than the reassuring voice of the security guard. Erica walks to the lobby but neither sees nor hears anyone.

Okay, I'm almost certain someone got off the elevator, but where are they? If I go this way, I might get to my office and my cell phone (why didn't I take it with me!?!), but I also might run into whoever is here.

Erica reverses course and ducks into the first office in the hallway, picks up the phone, and is stunned when there is no dial tone.

This is like a bad horror movie. The computer room is over by my office. But who has a key? Carl does.

Erica returns to the lobby, frantically pressing the down button, which fails to illuminate. Light but pronounced footsteps getting closer to her raise Erica's concern.

"Carl?!" Erica calls.

"No, señorita. *No es* Carl."

Erica remains silent, retreating back just beyond the elevators, enveloped in darkness.

"Señorita, do you remember me?"

Quietly, Erica takes a few steps further down the hallway.

"Señorita, please say hi. You'll remember me."

Erica's mind is racing. *Remember you? Who the hell are you?*

"Señorita!" the voice menacingly sings out. "Señorita. Señor Quintero sends his regards."

Son of a bitch. It's Javier from Mazatlán. Oh my god—he's the one who called James in Yuma. I need to get to my office, but I'm going to have to go the long way and it's much quicker for him. I need to know where he's at.

"What did you do to Carl?" Erica asks.

"Ah, there you are. *Muy bonita,*" Javier says.

"I asked what you did to Carl," Erica repeats.

"Carl is fine. Richer and just fine. *Con dinero baile el perro.*"

With money, the dog dances. I used to think it was a quaint Mexican expression, Erica thinks.

"What do you want, Javier?" Erica asks.

"Ah, you *do* remember me," Javier says.

"I remember you and your bad breath," Erica says.

"Chica, you should be nicer to me, since it's just you and me here tonight," Javier says.

"What do you want?" Erica asks.

"You, chica. Señor Quintero wants you," Javier says.

Erica takes a few steps down the hallway to see if Javier will follow her. "Rafa is in prison. What does he care?"

"We've been watching you. You and your husband," Javier says.

He's following me but not in any hurry, she thinks.

"You were so easy to find. And now that I've found you, I get to kill you myself. But, before I kill you, Señor Quintero sends his regards. He says you are very beautiful, but an evil *puta.* He wishes he could kill you himself," Javier says.

"What's your plan? Come up here and kill me . . . hoping no

one comes, no one sees you, no one misses me? If I'm late for dinner, James will start asking questions," Erica says.

"Good. Then I can kill him too," Javier says.

"You're pretty confident for someone whose boss is going to die in Supermax next to El Chapo," Erica says.

"Vete a la mierda," Javier says.

"Is that any way to talk to a lady?" she says. *If I can keep him talking and focusing on being mad at me, maybe I can get close enough to make a break for my office.*

"Señor Quintero says you are no lady," Javier growls.

"Did he tell you he cried like a little girl missing her teddy bear when he realized he'd been tricked by a woman?" Erica asks.

"You are lying," Javier says.

"The great Rafael Caro Quintero confessing all of his sins to me," Erica says. *A few more steps and I'll be on the backside of the floor. Gotta keep him talking and distracted.*

"What's your plan, Javier? You're gonna shoot me and hope you can somehow leave undetected?" she asks.

"No, chica. I'm not going to shoot you. Señor Quintero wants me to tell him what it feels like when I stab a knife into your heart," Javier explains.

"Too messy, Javier. You haven't thought this through. You're going to get caught the moment you walk out of here," Erica says.

"Not with Carl and my man downstairs," Javier says.

Another few steps . . .

"Why'd you kill Aguilar?" Erica asks.

"Who?" Javier asks impatiently.

"In Yuma," she says.

"The old man asking questions?" Javier asks.

"My friend, you asshole," Erica says.

"Why such language, chica?" Javier asks.

"You're going to kill me anyways. How'd you know who he was?" Erica asks.

"I didn't. I was told to look into who was asking all of the questions in Yuma. When I saw him, I thought his figure looked familiar. Señor Quintero said he was one of the people from Mazatlán," Javier explains.

"Rafa is in federal jail waiting for his trial. How could he tell you anything?" Erica asks.

He clicks his tongue. "Lady, you must know better than that."

One more step and I can run to my office.

Erica sprints down the hall, slips into her office, grabs her cell phone from the desk, and hides under the desk. *Please let the yoga training keep me from breathing too damn hard.*

"Chica!" he sings. "Where did you go?"

Under the desk Erica shields the cell phone's light and sends a text to her father: *911. Rafa's men here. One in office. One downstairs. Carl with them. Send police.*

As Erica hits send, she can see Javier's shadow walking past her office. *I bet he thinks I'm heading for the elevator.*

"Chica, I was going to stab you in the heart, so you'd die quickly. Now I'm going to watch you bleed to death," he says.

Javier's voice indicates he is walking—slowly—toward the lobby.

Erica crawls out from her desk and lays her cell phone face down on the desk. *I almost forgot about my little friend.* Erica reaches behind her door for the aluminum softball bat leaning against the wall. *Every woman should have a bat, or maybe a 7 iron, in her office at all times.*

Erica steps into the doorway before pausing. *What if I just wait for the police? But what if Dad doesn't see the text? I'm not going to sit here waiting for Javier to find me.*

Erica steps cautiously into the hallway, her eyes now well-adjusted to the dark conditions.

"Chica! You are making me angry."

He's at the elevators.

Erica tiptoes until she reaches reception where she ever so quietly hides behind the desk.

"I'm not going to kill just you. Not just your husband. I'm

going to kill your entire family. Their blood will be on your hands," Javier explains.

Erica grabs a stapler from the desk and throws it down the hall toward her office. It lands with a loud thud on the hallway carpet.

"There you are," he purrs.

Erica stands against the wall, hidden from anyone approaching from the hallway, and waits until Javier has passed and is down the hall.

Finally, years of coed softball will have paid off. Just a moment longer.

Erica tosses a set of paperclips onto the lobby floor.

"No more games. Señor Quintero wanted me to tell you goodbye before I kill you," Javier says.

Erica waits, silently counting each of Javier's steps. Soon, she detects Javier's faint outline as he slowly passes her, looking into the lobby to see the paperclips on the floor. Erica takes two silent steps forward and swings the bat hard and fast, landing with a thud on the back of Javier's head. Javier crumples to the ground, and Erica issues another, somewhat softer blow to Javier's head and then one harder still to his ribs.

"Señor Quintero can kiss my ass!" Erica proclaims, kicking the prone figure in front of her for good measure.

EIGHTEEN

FOLLOWING THE TRAGIC KIDNAPPING, interrogation, torture, and murder of DEA Special Agent Enrique "Kiki" Camarena in February 1985 in Guadalajara, Mexico, the media began referring to something called the "Guadalajara Narcotics Cartel," a term not used earlier.

Though not really a cartel in any true sense of the word, the Guadalajara Narcotics Cartel was an over-arching term to refer to the narcotics traffickers in and around Guadalajara, the largest city and capital of the Mexican state of Jalisco. Leadership of this group was attributed (by the media) to three men—Rafael Caro Quintero, Ernesto Fonseca Carillo, and Miguel Angel Félix Gallardo.

The DEA, at the time of the Camarena case, knew, and investigations since then have revealed, that there were others involved with this group of traffickers, including Juan Jose Esparragoza Moreno, Manuel Salcido, and Javier Barba Hernandez.

Esparragoza, known as "El Azul," had been a member of the Dirección Federal de Seguridad (DFS) and is credited by some with being one of the founders of this so-called cartel. A few years later, El Azul was one of the original leaders of the Sinaloa Cartel, a cartel formalized along with other cartels in the aftermath of Félix Gallardo's arrest in 1989. Later, El Azul joined forces with the

Juárez Cartel, then led by Amado Carrillo Fuentes, whose alias was "El Señor de los Cielos" (the Lord of the Skies). El Azul stopped associating with the Juárez Cartel as a leadership void developed following Carillo's death during a plastic surgery operation. He remains at large with multimillion dollar reward bounties offered in the US and in Mexico. Some reports, however, claim Esparragoza died in or around 2014 of a heart attack, though there is an absence of verification.

Juan Manuel Salcido Uzeta, who went by the alias "Cochi Loco" or "El Cochiloco" (the Crazy Pig), left Sinaloa for Guadalajara around the same time as Rafa, Carillo, and Félix Gallardo. Once established in Guadalajara, Salcido continued his trafficking operations working both with and separate from his home state compatriots. Salcido died in October 1991, purportedly at the hands of Colombian traffickers after he stole a portion of a cocaine shipment destined for Baja California. The Mexican government maintains his death was at the hands of the military.

The third under-credited trafficker was a former college activist turned lawyer tuned trafficker Javier Barba Hernandez. Once the leader of a militant student group called the Federación de Estudiantes de Guadalajara, Barba became associated with the traffickers in Guadalajara before becoming a critical confidante to Carillo. Lawrence Victor Harrison, a communications expert for the traffickers and a possible CIA asset, testified that Barba had risen to a point where he was on a par with Carillo. Others have speculated Barba was on an upward trajectory with a clear motivation to be a major player in the drug trafficking world.

James Kuykendall, Camarena's supervisor and friend, noted in his book that during the interrogation of Agent Camarena, one interrogator asked a number of questions about Barba and became very agitated when Camarena did not produce the desired answers. What's more, according to Kuykendall, this interrogator knew a lot about Barba. So much so that Kuykendall and others have speculated Barba himself was the disturbed interrogator.

While the DEA sought to question Barba in connection with

Agent Camarena's murder, Barba was killed on November 13, 1986, in a shoot-out with MFJP officers in Mazatlán. Many, including many within the DEA, believe the shooting was part of a cover-up, evidenced by the MFJP's refusal to give the DEA access to Barba's body or even his fingerprints.

Of the primary traffickers, Félix Gallardo, known as "El Padrino" (the Godfather), has attracted the recent attention through the Netflix series *Narcos: Mexico*. Following some time in college, Félix served as an officer with the Mexican Federal Judicial Police and worked as a family bodyguard for the governor of the state of Sinaloa Leopoldo Sánchez Celis. Some assert Sánchez Celis's political connections were fundamental to the prodigious growth of his drug operations. At the same time, though, Félix Gallardo had the strength of personality, the mindset, and the political wiles necessary to help build a trafficking empire.

Several elements of Félix Gallardo's trafficking activities were notable. First, with the assistance of Honduran Juan Ramon Matta Ballesteros, Félix Gallardo used the established transportation routes in Mexico to connect the Colombian cocaine supply with the market for the drug in the United States. Significantly, Félix Gallardo was able to reach financial arrangements with the Columbian supplier that were uniquely rewarding to him and his associates. Many reports over the years have concluded Matta Ballesteros was the owner of SETCO, an airline that the Contras used to covertly transport military supplies and personnel in the early 1980s.

Second, the role Félix Gallardo played—or did not play—in the Camarena abduction and murder is a matter subject to intense speculation. Some purported witnesses placed Félix Gallardo at some of the so-called planning meetings, while others maintained his presence was limited at best, and still others disputed the very existence of such meetings. A few witnesses also said Félix Gallardo was in the house when Camarena was interrogated and tortured. Others, including Sergio Espino Verdín, a likely Camarena interrogator and former commander of the Mexican

Federal Bureau of Political and Social Investigations, told Mexican investigators that Félix Gallardo was not present during Camarena's interrogations.

In his testimony in the 1990 Camarena criminal trial, Harrison asserted Félix Gallardo had a falling out with Rafa and Carillo in late 1983 and all of 1984 because Gallardo thought they were too wild and too high profile. According to Harrison, Félix Gallardo said he would continue to do business with the men but did not want to be around them.

James, Erica, and Brian sit on the patio at The Dock in Newport Beach for an early dinner. Brian and James enjoy Smoked Old Fashioneds.

"I remember the last time we all were here. I knew there was something going on with you two," Brian pronounces.

"If you did, you were the only one," James replies.

"Well, I could not be happier," Brian says, smiling.

"Nor could we," Erica answers.

"Speak for yourself," James says, eliciting a punch to the shoulder from Erica.

"Not to jump from your romance to cartels, but how are you feeling? I've never been so worried in my life as I was when I saw your text, which, by the way, was perfect," Brian says.

"I'm okay, Dad. Really. It was scary and all, but I wasn't traumatized by it."

"She may not have been traumatized, but I was. That was the longest drive ever from East LA," James adds.

"I will say, though, you cannot imagine my relief when I heard the sirens and then saw the police getting off the elevators," Erica says.

"Well, we are working with Reggie and building management to improve our security . . . a major upgrade," Brian states.

"And I'm doing the same at home. Bobby has worked with the

condo association and should be installing some hi-tech security in the next week or so," James adds.

"I am curious about something in this regard, if you don't mind," Brian says.

"Of course not," Erica replies. "Ask away."

"It's a question for both of you, and maybe it's better to discuss it now and have a more pleasant conversation during dinner," Brian says.

"I like that, Dad. I've had too many dinners where murder and cartels were the topic of conversation," Erica says.

"Great. So, I'm wondering—since you now know Rafa sent someone to go after Erica, can you safely say he was the one who had Aguilar killed?" Brian asks.

"I'm not ready to make the logical leap just yet," James replies.

"Okay. Why not?" Brian asks.

"I'm just not sure how Rafa could have been in a position to know or do anything about Aguilar. Aguilar was only in Yuma for a couple of days. And I'm still struck by exactly what Aguilar said to me. He said 'it' was bigger than we knew, but he didn't mention Rafa. Maybe Rafa wasn't involved in anything relating to Aguilar," James says.

"Or," Erica inserts, "it's more complex than we know."

"Like what?" Brian quizzes.

"I have no idea," Erica replies.

"Well, who had a reason to want to silence Aguilar?" Brian asks.

"The traffickers?" Erica suggests.

"Maybe, but as your DEA friend said, wouldn't that be aggressive and dangerous for some local traffickers? Wouldn't it put them squarely in front of the local police?" Brian wonders.

"You're suggesting it was someone bigger who wanted Aguilar silenced?" James asks.

"Maybe. Or maybe someone smaller. Maybe it was just a robbery?" Brian suggests.

"Not a robbery, but maybe something less, I don't know, complicated," Erica adds.

"Makes sense," James says.

Brian pauses and reflects. "Before we stop talking about Rafa, I have a few questions that don't pertain to Aguilar but have been bothering me."

"Let's hear 'em," James says.

"Isn't the role of Félix Gallardo in the kidnapping of Agent Camarena key?" Brian asks.

"How so?" Erica inquires.

"Well, it's assumed he had some connection with the CIA, even if attenuated, but at least some connection through—at a minimum—his relationship with Matta Ballesteros, right?" Brian asks.

"Someone has been studying," Erica notes.

"Just some light reading," Brain admits.

"The answer to your question is yes," Erica confirms, "though there can be some legitimate questions as to the depth of his connections to the CIA."

"Fair enough. Are there any such connections to the CIA with Rafa?" Brian asks.

"James?" Erica defers.

"I don't think there is anything specific tying Rafa to the CIA, other than the alleged Rancho Veracruz."

"For which there is precious little, if any, direct evidence," Erica interjects.

"Okay, if we put the purported ranch to the side, is there anything *else*?" Brian re-characterizes.

James ponders for a moment before responding. "Not much material I can think of. Some have alleged they flew marijuana from ranches in Mexico into the US for the CIA, and some of those ranches likely belonged to Rafa. Then there is the assertion that Rafa wanted to move into the cocaine business at or near the time of the kidnapping."

"Which dovetails to my second question. Thank you, James," Brian says.

"Happy to help."

"And the second question is what, Dad?" Erica asks.

"When Rafa fled Mexico after the Camarena murder, why did he go to Costa Rica?" Brian asks.

"It was a foreign country, similar culture and language, and far enough away from Mexico for him to feel safe?" Erica answers.

"But," Brian retorts, "literally a dozen countries fit that description. So, again, why Costa Rica?"

"Let's think about this," James says, taking a long, slow sip from his Old Fashioned. "What do we know happened when he was in Costa Rica? Several of his men bought properties around San Jose, with US dollars."

"And," Erica interjects, "when he was captured at his mansion, there was little security. I recall testimony of five other men in the house and Sara Cosio."

"Maybe he felt safe?" James notes.

"Or protected?" Erica replies.

"Exactly!" says Brian.

"Protected by whom?" Erica asks.

"The Costa Rican government?" Brian suggests.

"Maybe," James answers, "but what would the Costa Rican government have to gain by protecting him?"

"Then who?" Erica asks.

"Wait a second." James takes another drink, pondering. "The Costa Rican government didn't arrest him, right? So, if they had little to gain by harboring him, why didn't they arrest him?

"Maybe they just didn't care?" Erica replies.

"Maybe. Or there was another motivation," James adds.

"And again, I ask, why did Rafa go to Costa Rica?" Brian questions.

"I may see where this is headed. We know, I think, he was flown to Costa Rica by Werner Lotz, and Lotz's alleged connection to the CIA has been discussed for years," James notes.

"There's no way that's just a coincidence," Erica says.

"And there is ample evidence of the CIA being active in its support for the Contras from Costa Rica," James adds.

"Can we say it is at least *possible* that Rafa went to Costa Rica at the direction or suggestion of the CIA?" Brian asks.

"Is it possible? Of course, it's possible," James answers. "But, following your thought, wouldn't that mean there were more connections between the CIA and Rafa than we are aware of?"

"But if so, why was he arrested?" Erica inquires.

"Left hand and right hand," Brian responds.

"After Camarena, the DEA and others were bound and determined to nail Rafa. The CIA would have been powerless to stop them without exposing more issues," Erica states.

"Exactly," Brian concurs.

"Wait, wait, wait," James interjects. "You think the CIA was involved with Rafa in the kidnapping and murder of Agent Camarena?"

"What do you think?" Brian asks.

"Erica can disagree if she wants, but to me the answer is no. A hard no. There still is nothing to link the CIA to Camarena and it defies common sense," James says.

"I agree with that," Erica says. "We've looked, looked hard, at evidence, and there is almost nothing, and if you dare utter the words 'Héctor Berrellez' I'm leaving."

"No, don't do that," Brian laughs. "You've long since convinced me there."

"But is there more to this idea that the CIA was involved with Rafa?" James starts.

"I don't mean to interrupt, baby," Erica interjects, "but do we need to go so far?"

"What do you mean?" Brian asks.

"To follow this chain of thought, can we say Rafa was involved with the CIA? Maybe. But also remember he wasn't the brightest bulb in the box. He could have been manipulated pretty easily. And, as James said, there is Lotz. Either Rafa knew of the connection between Lotz and the CIA or he didn't. Either way, one can envision a scenario where the CIA was pulling the strings," Erica states.

"I'm tracking," James says with a smile.

"And if they were," Erica continues, "then the relationship, whatever it was, could have continued after Rafa's arrest and after his release from prison."

"Yes! I knew that's where you were heading!" James announces.

"If so, what would the relationship have involved?" asks Brian.

"Listen to this," James pronounces. "When I was in Phoenix talking to that reporter who had been friends with Gary Webb, he was focused on the money the CIA made as a result of the drug operations Webb reported on and went so far as to suggest the CIA would have wanted the flow of money to continue over the years."

"Rafa could have been a conduit to do that since everyone is convinced he got back into the business after his release from prison," Erica adds. "And Belmonte did mention that both CDS and the Caborca Cartel have some trafficking routes running through Arizona."

"Let me add one more piece onto this Jenga tower," James offers. "I think the evidence makes it quite likely the CIA worked with or had some kind of an understanding with El Chapo for a significant portion of the time El Chapo was atop the Sinaloa Cartel."

"Though I'm not certain of the timeline," Erica muses, "a direct CIA link from Rafa to El Chapo, which is a link to the CDS, could make a lot of sense."

"Which," Brian states, "leaves me with two questions—who was your attacker working for, and who was running the drugs in Yuma?"

"Aguilar could have walked into the middle of a CIA trafficking operation operating for decades," Erica says.

"Is it possible?" James says quietly. "Could the CIA have killed Aguilar?"

NINETEEN

The following morning, Billy struts into James's office.

"There's the look of a man with some answers," James notes.

"Indeed, I have some," Billy says.

"Great. To which question?" James inquires.

"You said you wanted something out of the ordinary with respect to the CIA and Mexico, and I have some things to share."

"Then, by all means Billy boy, share away," James says.

"To start with, there are some declassified documents some believe indicate former Mexican President Jose Lopez Portillo, who was in office from 1976 to 1982, was a CIA asset. The documents were part of a CIA probe into the assassination of President Kennedy and include a memo from a meeting of CIA agents on November 29, 1976.

"According to the documents, a US intelligence official by the name of Bill Sturbitts reportedly informed his colleagues during a meeting that Mexico was getting a new president, someone who had control of Liaison for many years. Some have asserted there must be a connection since the meeting was just a few days before Lopez Portillo assumed the presidency. And Lopez Portillo was elected when he was the sole PRI candidate. At a minimum, the documents raise questions about whether there was a relationship between the US intelligence community and Lopez Portillo's rise to power," Billy says.

"Okay, and tell me again where this memo came from?" James asks.

"According to the National Archives, the memo in question pertained to a meeting focused on the anticipated release of papers from the CIA's investigation into Lee Harvey Oswald. Oswald, as you know, visited Mexico before the assassination, and as a result, US intelligence conducted extensive surveillance and phone-tapping operations in the country," Billy says.

"Why does absolutely everything having to do with the CIA somehow trace back to the Kennedy assassination?" James asks.

"It all looks like one woven tapestry most people don't see at all, starting someplace before Kennedy and going through Iran-Contra, the Clinton and Bush years, to . . . I don't know where." Billy shrugs.

"You're not turning into a conspiracy theorist, are you?" James asks.

"No, but—"

"But," James interrupts, "the same names keep appearing in different places and different times. But there is a thread."

"Exactly. Take Barry Seal for example."

"I know more about him now than the last time you brought him up. I got crazy and watched the movie," James notes.

Barry Seal is an infamous pilot who flew reconnaissance missions of Sandinista bases for the CIA and went on to run drugs for Panamanian dictator Manuel Noriega and the Medellin Cartel. His notoriety escalated when he was played by Tom Cruise in the 2017 motion picture *American Made*, notwithstanding the real Barry Seal bearing no resemblance to Tom Cruise.

The movie's narrative that Seal was a happy-go-lucky TWA pilot who was recruited by the CIA was more a creature of Hollywood than a factual representation. As a review of the movie from *the Times-Picayune* notes:

[Director Doug] Liman himself has called the film "a fun lie based on a true story," so at least he's honest about his fast-and-looseness—although Seal had such a larger-than-life personality and his exploits were so over-the-top that they probably didn't need embellishment.[1]

Perhaps the most intriguing revelation about the real-life Barry Seal involves his likely connection to something called Operation 40. Operation 40 was a CIA-backed, deep black ops group formed in 1960 after the Cuban Revolution. Ostensibly, it was comprised of Cuban exiles with the intent of fomenting a regime change in Cuba. But evidence suggests the group was involved in much more, functioned for a number of years, and among those alleged to have been members are Félix Rodríguez, Frank Sturgis (one of the Watergate burglars), and Porter Goss—later head of the CIA under President George W. Bush. Naturally, some alleged members have denied the existence of the organization, let alone their involvement.

Notwithstanding such denials, a photograph purported to be of an Operation 40 training site in Florida includes some of the alleged members, as well as one Lee Harvey Oswald. In addition, a woman by the name of Marita Lorenz has claimed she worked with members of Operation 40 and drove in a caravan of two cars to Dallas in November 1963. She also maintained Frank Sturgis was in her car and an occupant in the other car was Oswald himself. Further, once in Dallas, she says her group met with Jack Ruby, the soon-to-be assassin of Oswald.

Suffice it to say, any investigation into Operation 40 leads down a long and windy set of interconnected rabbit holes. So too do the efforts to link Barry Seal to then Arkansas governor Bill Clinton.

A CIA memo from July 1995 summarizes an article from the

1. Mike Scott, "'American Made' Movie Review: Fact, Fiction Collide in Movie Based on the Barry Seal Story," *Times-Picayune*, updated July 7, 2021.

American Spectator, which followed up on prior allegations in the *Wall Street Journal*, this way:

It alleges, explicitly and implicitly, that an aircraft operated by a CIA front company in 1984 used the airfield at Mena, Arkansas, as a starting point for weapons supply flights to the Contras in Nicaragua; on the return flights from Honduras, the aircraft allegedly carried illegal narcotics to Mena. The narcotics runner, Barry Seal, allegedly paid off then-Governor Clinton's protégé, L.D. Brown, and one Dan Lasater, a Clinton contributor.[2]

Whether true or not, the allegations have been made, and several sources have claimed to have connected the dots.

"Then I won't go through all of the claims and allegations surrounding him, but I will note that, by tracking just a few people, one can draw a line from the Cuban Revolution to the Mexican cartels without much trouble," Billy states.

"And with a heavy dose of CIA involvement, I presume?" James asks.

"Definitely. Do you know of El Güero?" Billy asks.

"Héctor Luis Palma Salazar. Sure. I've heard of him. El Chapo's friend," James says.

"More importantly, El Chapo's *former* friend," Billy notes.

Jesús Héctor Luis Palma Salazar was born in Sinaloa probably on April 29. The year was somewhere between 1950 and 1962. He began his life of crime as a car thief and later came to work as a

2. Office of the Central Intelligence Agency, "Briefing for Representative James Leach (R-IA) Regarding [Redacted] in Arkansas in the Late 1980s with NSA," July 21, 1995, https://www.cia.gov/readingroom/docs/DOC_0001289684.pdf.

hitman for Miguel Ángel Félix Gallardo. Later, it is said, he became something of a "logistics manager" in charge of Sonora.

While working for Félix Gallardo, legend says Palma began to work and associate with Joaquin "El Chapo" Guzman.

The Palma myth continues to maintain that a cargo belonging to Félix Gallardo was kept and not delivered as instructed. Some say El Chapo was involved, as was El Lobito Retamoza. In any event, only El Lobito was killed in an apparent act of retribution.

Palma then associated with a Venezuelan named Rafael Clavel Moreno who later became Palma's wife's lover. Clavel is alleged to have convinced the wife to take two million pesos from her accounts and to escape with him to San Francisco, California. But, once they got to a hotel, Clavel cut her throat and sent Palma her preserved head in a cooler.

Fifteen days later, Clavel took Palma's sons, Héctor Jesús and Nataly, to San Cristóbal, Venezuela, and threw them from the bridge of La Concordia, taking a video of the terrifying event to send to Palma.

Clavel was arrested and soon killed. It is believed Clavel had been working for, or at the direction of, Félix Gallardo.

These events precipitated a wild sequence of paybacks and murders. El Güero was said to have been responsible for the murders of Clavel's lawyer, Jesús Güemes, who also may have been an in-law of Félix Gallardo, as well as the murders of nine Arellano family members, a human rights activist, and three Venezuelan students studying at the Autonomous University of Sinaloa.

Palma was also linked to a shooting in a nightclub in Puerto Vallarta, where ten people were killed in an attack aimed at Ramon and Benjamin Arellano Félix.

After this, the Arellano Félix brothers further solidified the organization which came to be known as the Tijuana Cartel, while the Sinaloa Cartel continued to be run by Palma, El Chapo, and El Mayo.

Palma was arrested on June 23, 1995, after a Lear jet he was flying on to attend a wedding party crash-landed. Palma survived the crash-landing and was later arrested by Mexican military officers. El Güero was sentenced to seven years for possession of cocaine and was assigned to Puente Grande, Jalisco, from where El Chapo escaped in 2001.

In 2002, when he was about to leave prison for having completed his sentence, an arrest warrant for extradition by the United States was issued and he was extradited in 2007.

After serving nine years of a seventeen-year sentence in the Atwater Federal Prison, Palma was extradited back to Mexico in June 2016, where he faced new charges relating to the 1995 double murder of police officers in Nayarit.

"Former friend?" James asks. "There must be a story there."

"There is. An old *Rolling Stone* article lays out an interesting series of events, starting with a DEA meeting at Puente Grande prison in Guadalajara which, at the time, housed both El Güero and El Chapo. And, at the time of the meeting, the DEA assumed they were still friends. But, as the story goes, El Chapo told the DEA he and El Güero had not spoken in nearly four years. He said they had stopped being friends after El Güero ordered the killing of El Chapo's brother-in-law without sanction and without El Chapo's blessing. The DEA reported El Chapo said he was forced to break ties with his longtime friend and partner, despite their years of working with one another and their shared hatred of the Arellano-Félix brothers.

"Now here is the interesting part. The report says El Chapo told the agents he was willing to provide information on El Güero if it would help his case, going so far as to pledge that in twenty-four hours he could give the DEA information on the whereabouts of drug storages and weapons caches, and, with a week's notice, he could provide information on the group's entire infrastructure, including the officials protecting them. The DEA agents say they were never able to follow up on his offer because they were called off by one or more US attorneys," Billy says.

"Interesting, but I'm not sure I'm following the connection to the CIA," James says.

"I'm getting there," Billy replies.

"Then by all means, carry on," James encourages Billy.

"El Güero got wind that his old friend had offered to betray him and was less than pleased. No shock there. In response, he seems to have leaked stories to a few Mexican papers maintaining El Chapo had long been cooperating with the DEA and the CIA."

"El Chapo was a CIA asset? I'd heard that allegation before but have never been convinced," James says.

"I'm not prepared to claim he was a CIA asset, but Palma claims there was an arrangement between the two to act in ways benefitting them both," Billy states.

"Including things harmful to El Chapo's enemies, I assume," James adds.

"The DEA alerts the Mexicans of information about other cartels, and the CIA gets inside information," Billy says.

"The policy of divide and conquer, all while El Chapo sits on his perch," James says.

"For as long as he is useful," Billy notes.

"Okay, but wait," James says. "Just to play devil's advocate for a moment, are you sure this isn't just CIA conspiracy paranoia run rampant? I mean, there are people on Facebook, Reddit, and even LinkedIn blaming the CIA for every assassination or mass shooting in the last one hundred years."

"I thought about that too, and I took a deep dive into it. As noted, you can find someone to say almost anything on the internet, but one thing you have impressed upon me from the beginning is that correlation does not equal causation. Many of the claims against the CIA and others are based on coincidences and have little evidence, in any form, to support them. And with so much information out there, one has to be disciplined to separate the wheat from the chaff," Billy says.

"Meaning?" James asks.

"Meaning there are some academics and journalists who have drawn some of these connections, but, if you ask me—"

"I did ask you," James interrupts.

"In my opinion, they draw dubious conclusions and mold their research and the 'facts' they find to the conclusion they want to reach. I tried to do better. Everything I'm telling you is supported by actual evidence or at least semi-credible witnesses. Doesn't mean anyone has to agree with it, but it is not created from air, and it's not just CIA paranoia," Billy says.

"In case there is any doubt, I trust you and your evaluations more than any academic or journalist I don't know, so proceed freely," James says.

"I appreciate that. I also think it goes beyond just El Chapo and the Sinaloa Cartel," Billy says.

"How so?" James asks.

"Let me ask you this, in 1980 what percent of the world's opium supply do you suppose came from Afghanistan?" Billy asks.

"I'd be totally guessing . . . 25 percent?" James says.

"For all intents and purposes, none. Zero," Billy states.

"Seriously?"

"It's true."

"That surprises—no, shocks me," James admits.

"Now," Billy continues, "the CIA started working with the Mujahidin rebels in their anti-Soviet efforts in 1985, more or less. And then the US engaged in various nation building efforts after the war."

"Okay . . ."

"By 1987 or so—it varies by source—but around then, guess the percentage of the world opium market supplied by Afghanistan," Billy says.

"So, going from zero, I'd go to my original answer of 25 percent?" James guesses.

"Sixty percent," Billy states.

"How is that even possible?" James asks.

"I have no idea."

"And the CIA was responsible for it?" James inquires.

"I'm not prepared to go quite that far, but the connection is pretty clear. It's not the only example, and others have made similar claims. I looked at a book called *Politics of Heroin*, and the author maintains the CIA fostered heroin production in Afghanistan for decades to finance operations aimed at containing the spread of communism, and later to finance operations aimed at containing the spread of the Islamic state. He also says that the CIA's role in drug production and trafficking was not limited to Afghanistan, but that the agency followed similar operational processes in Southeast Asia, Central America, and Colombia. And, going back to Afghanistan, several observers have noted that in their efforts to help the Afghans fight off the Russians, the US supported and protected Afghan warlords who became major drug lords," Billy says.

"*Charlie Wilson's War*," James says.

"I think you are dating me a little there. But I have heard of the movie," Billy says.

"That can't date you. It came out in 2007," James says incredulously.

"Yes, but twelve-year-old me was not watching R-rated movies about Afghanistan," Billy says.

"Fair enough."

"One last thing on Afghanistan. In October 2009, several reporters from the *New York Times* reported that unnamed former and current American officials said Ahmed Wali Karzai had received regular payments from the CIA for eight years—starting after his paternal half-brother was elected president—and was involved in the trafficking of opium in Afghanistan. Ahmed Wali Karzai denied the allegations, stating that he had provided intelligence to the United States but was not compensated, and others have questioned the merits of the allegations, but it shows the potential breadth and scope of the CIA's involvement," Billy says.

"Okay, then, just to play this out, the CIA has its tentacles in lots of bad places. To what end?" James asks.

"Money, James. As is so often the case, no matter what angle you look at this, the view always takes you back to money. Drug proceeds can be spent without any congressional appropriations or oversight," Billy explains.

"Dark money," James states.

"Dark money," Billy summarizes, "funds black ops, which promote policies decided upon by people in the shadows, far from the spotlights of political oversight."

TWENTY

DURING VARIOUS PARTS of the year, the Southern California coastal areas are often victim to the weather phenomena colloquially referred to as "June gloom" when overcast skies betray the stereotypical California sunshine.

This June morning is no exception, and Erica wears a powder blue cashmere sweater over her tennis outfit as she sits on the country club patio waiting for Rebecca Talbott to arrive for brunch. Erica and Rebecca were roommates at Stanford and remain close friends.

"Erica!"

"Becca!" The two ladies embrace. "You look amazing."

"Not too bad for a mom of two toddlers," Rebecca asserts.

"Not too bad for anyone," Erica replies as they sit down at the table. "Did you have any trouble getting in?"

"None. You have some clout. I used your name and glided right in."

"Correction. My dad has clout. I just take advantage of the connection."

"Right," Rebecca says dubiously. "So how are you?"

"I'm good," Erica says, smiling.

"Marriage agrees with you."

"I wasn't sure I'd ever want to be married, but now I can't imagine not being together with James."

"I love seeing your smile," Becca says.

"Who'd have every guessed this when we were in college?" Erica asks.

"I know. We were athletes, liberals, feminists. In front of us were the Olympics, fame, politics, making changes to the world," Becca says.

The waitress, Kelli, approaches. "Good morning Ms. Walsh. Would you like some mimosas?"

"Just orange juice for me. I may play some tennis with my dad later this afternoon, and I don't play better when I'm tipsy," Erica says.

"And you, ma'am?" Kelli asks Rebecca.

"I have no excuse, but I too will go with just orange juice."

Kelli pours two glasses. "Just give me a nod when you are ready to order."

"We sure will. Thanks, Kelli," says Erica.

"I do note the use of Ms. Walsh, not Mrs. Butler," Rebecca says.

"One last nod to my feminist roots, I suppose. The same reason I don't use my dad's name either."

"Being your own person," Becca says. "I'll drink to that." Becca holds her glass up, Erica taps it with hers, and the two women drink the juice from their champagne flutes.

"How's Benjamin and the girls?" Erica asks.

"Everyone is good. The girls are growing up too fast, but they are wonderful." Rebecca's eyes twinkle thinking about them.

"I miss them. Is being a mother what you thought it would be?" Erica asks, taking another sip of OJ.

"Are you and James—"

"Just exploring the possibilities," Erica interrupts to answer. "But I am curious. Sometimes even the thought of it is overwhelming."

"You know the saying 'Being a parent is the hardest and most rewarding thing you can do'? For me, some days are hard—times when you just have to walk away. Or times when your heart aches because you can't make all the pain go away, and I'm sure that never changes. But most of the time, I mean the vast majority of the time, I absolutely love being a mom. Being their mom."

"That does make sense, and I'm so happy for you," Erica says.

"They are in daycare now, so I have a bit more free time. I'm still trying to decide exactly what to do with it, but I'm in no rush. Want to know my little secret?" Becca asks, grinning.

"Of course," Erica says.

"Some days," Becca says in a mock whisper, "the best spa and massage in the world can't compare to turning up the AC and the ceiling fan, crawling under the down comforter, and taking an afternoon nap in my own bed, all by myself. No husband. No kids. No pets. Just me."

"Do you miss your job? The office?" Erica asks.

"No. I don't. Some people land in a job that turns into a profession, a career. I did the opposite. By the time we had Semira, the career that I thought would fulfill me for life had become a job I absolutely hated."

"Wow," Erica says. "I knew you weren't satisfied, but I thought it was some of the college idealism wearing off."

"Partially, I think. A lot of people go through it. The world is *not* as we expected it to be," Rebecca states.

"That might be even more true for those privileged few fortunate enough to go to places like Stanford."

"And to be athletes too," Becca adds.

"And *good* athletes too," Erica agrees.

"I thought the PR work I was doing would help people make the world a better place. Wow, if that isn't a naïve statement, I don't know what is." Becca rolls her eyes in self-deprecation.

"Maybe, but it's honest," Erica replies.

"It didn't take long before I figured out that policy takes a backseat to elections, campaigns, fundraising, focus groups, staged media events, and image rehabilitation. For a while it was enough, but, at some point, I stopped caring. More significantly, I found I didn't respect or even like most of the people I was helping. And some I downright hated. Once I realized we helped put a complete imbecile in Congress, I knew I had to leave."

"But *you* didn't vote for the imbecile. The people did," Erica says.

"Now who's being naïve?" Becca teases.

"Okay, but at least the imbecile would have company. I mean, it's not like they were the first one elected."

"Maybe," Becca replies contritely, "but he was the first one I helped put there."

"Fair enough," Erica concedes.

"Getting pregnant with Semira saved my sanity. I intended to go back, but then Benjamin and I decided to have Eva pretty soon after, and I just never did. Now I'm starting to think about how to rekindle the passion I once had, but it'll come in time. I'm in no hurry."

"Sounds great to me," Erica replies.

"Don't think it's totally idyllic. There are days when the noise and the mess is overwhelming."

"OMG. Life isn't perfect. News flash!" Erica mocks.

"Shut up!"

Erica and Becca share a hearty laugh.

"Enough about me. How are you? As busy as ever?" Becca asks.

"Yeah, pretty much," Erica replies. "Work is always busy, and the firm is growing."

"How is it working with your dad *and* your husband?"

"It's good. We all work well together," Erica answers.

"Come on. How is it really?" Becca's eyes narrow, but she's grinning.

"No kidding. I love it. I can see where it wouldn't be for everyone, but at the office, we each have our own lanes, and we stay in them. And, as I said, we work well together. I know what James or my dad needs before they do much of the time. There are other partners I work with too, so it's not just those two all day, every day."

"I remember when you were going to be the star lawyer. Do you ever regret not going that route?" Becca asks.

"Not at all. Never," Erica asserts.

"You don't wish you were the one in court, making the arguments, grilling the witnesses?"

"Someone has been watching too much television," Erica says.

"Maybe but—"

"You know what, Becca, I don't. If you saw the pressure on James's shoulders during a trial or before a big argument—no thanks. At this point, I'll be the supporting wife and damn good paralegal."

"And your dad? How is he?" Becca asks.

"He's great. He says hi in case he doesn't arrive in time to see you."

"Aww, sweet. Is he well?"

"He's great. He never ages, damn him. I have a suspicion he might be dating someone," Erica says.

"Get out!" Becca's eyes widen.

"I know. I don't know for sure, but the signs are there." Erica shrugs.

"Any idea who?" Becca asks.

"None whatsoever."

"Would it bother you?"

"God no. I'd be thrilled for him," Erica says truthfully.

"Do you still have those projects you hint about but never talk about?" Becca inquires.

"They just find us, or I should say James. And it's not so much that I don't want to talk about them, as it is I never want anyone to think anyone else knows anything," Erica admits.

"Sounds dangerous," Becca says.

"Maybe somewhat, but I can tell you James is the most principled person I know, and we try to do the right thing and make a difference," Erica says.

"Batman and Batgirl?"

"Hah. No. I can't convince James to wear the spandex—at least not outside the house. But it has made life more *interesting*, shall we say, and hectic. So, James and I made a deal with each other to totally relax this weekend. James should be on his way to San Diego to meet a friend and head to a wine festival in Temecula, and I'm here with you."

James had left the condo destined for Javi Mirada's house in Solano Beach. With minimal traffic today, James pulls into the driveway, finding him placing a small bag in the trunk of his new, metallic jet-black Porsche 911 Carrera GTS.

"I'm amazed every time I'm here," James comments as he slides out of his car.

"Amazed?" Javi questions.

"This is a big place for one person, and more to the point, apparently public college professors get paid too much?"

"You're funny. Truth is professors aren't paid enough, but consultants and authors can do pretty well," Javi boasts.

"Good to know," James says.

"Besides," Javi adds, "I've seen your place, so shut the hell up."

"Point taken, my friend. Point taken. Are you ready to go?"

"I am," Javi responds, taking James's bag and shutting the trunk. "I'm happy to drive. It will be fun to take the new Porsche out for a good drive."

"If you want to be my chauffeur, who am I to object? Plus, it looks like a sweet ride!"

Erica and Becca are finishing their very leisurely lunch.

"What else is on the agenda for you today?" Erica asks as they stand to walk through the clubhouse.

"Boring mother/wife things. Grocery shopping and trying to get the girls down for naps this afternoon. Benjamin never finds a way to fit their naps in, and then they are terrors in the evening."

"I could use a nap myself," Erica confesses.

"Take advantage of the alone time," Becca says encouragingly

"Oh, I plan to. A sappy rom-com tonight. Sleeping in tomorrow."

"I thought you were going to play tennis with your dad?" Becca asks.

"I'll call him from the car and reschedule. I feel like being lazy."

"All right, what did you do with Erica?"

Upon returning home, Erica is surprised to find a small, padded manila envelope leaning against the condo door, marked only with the words "THE BUTLERS" written in all capital letters.

Calling down to the security desk, Erica asks if anyone had been let up to the floor while she was gone. "No one at all," the guard replies. "It's been a pretty quiet day."

"Huh," Erica replies. "Must be from someone on the floor. No worries."

"No worries. Probably just more advertising," the guard says.

Once inside, Erica opens the package to reveal a plain thumb drive, unlabeled. She sets her purse on the dining room table before taking the drive to the office upstairs. Plugging the drive into the USB extension port on her laptop, she tries to open the drive.

Password protected?! What the hell? There is nothing in the envelope. Think, Erica. Except . . .

Erica types "The Butlers" and presses Enter. Access denied. *What else could it be?* Erica re-types the words using all capital letters and waits as access to the drive is granted.

What in the world? Folders. Lots and lots of folders.

Opening one folder reveals several word documents and a plethora of Excel spreadsheets.

Oh my god. This is . . . amazing.

Pulling her cell phone from her purse, Erica places a call.

"How do you like the car?" Javi asks.

"What's not to like? I love the interior," James says, running his hand gently along the dark red trim of the passenger door.

"It's called Bordeaux Red—appropriate for a wine festival, eh?"

"Appropriate for damn near anything," James replies.

"How is Erica after her attack?"

"You know, she is doing well. I'm surprised how well actually," James answers.

"She is a tough woman, sometimes people don't see it behind the feminine exterior," Javi says admiringly.

"Don't I know it. But by all appearances, she's been able to put her focus on other things and attributes it to a one-time incident."

"Do you think it is?"

"I don't know, to tell you the truth. After Javier was interviewed, it seems like more of a random opportunity for Rafa to exact revenge than a long-term plot for retribution."

"Anything new on the Aguilar front?" Javi inquires.

"No. We know the fentanyl trade was his focus and what got him killed, but not how the pieces fit together. Not yet, at least," James says.

As they drive in the middle lane, a speeding car passes them in the fast lane. "You know my recent pet peeve?" Javi asks.

"Well-to-do college professors in fancy sports cars?" James suggests.

"The complete and total absence of any responsibility to follow the speed limit, or at least be within a reasonable distance of the speed limit," Javi says.

"Because?" James asks.

"Because it's a concrete demonstration of the abdication of the social contract. We could all speed, and very few would be stopped or fined, and the punishment would be relatively minimal. We could, en masse, do lots of things with little fear of punishment. But we don't, or we haven't, because, as a society, we collectively agreed there are certain rules and norms that should be followed for the benefit of all. Does that mean, in an absolute sense, that some freedoms are surrendered? Sure. The freedom to drive as fast as we want, the freedom to drive while intoxicated, the freedom to gather a group of people, transform into a mob, and rob downtown department stores.

"But it's deeper than that. The idea of a social contract is almost as old as human civilizations. Epicurus wrote about natural justice in the fourth century BCE. The concept is explored in the Indian Buddhist text Mahāvastu which dates back to the second century BCE.

"John Locke discussed the state of natural law and believed that individuals in a state of nature would be bound morally, by the Law of Nature, in which man has the inherent power to preserve his property; that is, his life, liberty, and estate against the injuries and attempts of other men. Rousseau, of course, expanded the idea of individuality to include the foundations of society supported by the sovereignty of what he called the general will.

"But the one I like most is Pierre-Joseph Proudhon who saw the social contract not as a foundation for a society or government but as an inherently individualistic concept. People agree to hold up the social contract because it's good for society, yes, but it's just as good for each person as well," Javi concludes.

"You got all of that from one of several thousand people speeding on the freeway every day?" James asks.

"Sorry. Welcome to my inner dialogue. I think about things like this all the time but don't often have the opportunity to expound upon them. Of course, it's not so simple, and some anarchists and extreme libertarians have seized on these ideas in a way I think bastardizes the original concepts, but I knew you would understand," Javi notes.

"One of the many reasons why we are friends," James says.

A few minutes later, the cell phone sitting on James's lap vibrates. "Hey, babe. What's up? I thought you'd be hanging out with Becca most of the day."

"She had some things to do this afternoon, but you are never, ever going to believe what I am looking at!" Erica can hardly contain her excitement.

"I guess you better tell me then."

"A database with what looks to be hundreds, maybe thousands of documents. On first glance, they seem to be evidence of the CIA's role in drug trafficking for the past, I don't know, fifteen, twenty years?"

"Where did this come from? And wait, can I put you on speaker so Javi can hear?"

"Of course. Hi, Javi!"

"Hello, Erica, mi amor." Javi grins.

"Tell us again what you said you are looking at," James requests.

"Let me back up. So I came home from brunch with Becca, and when I got home, there was a small manila envelope leaning on the door. I called security, but they said they had no idea how it got there. Inside the envelope was a flash drive. Nothing else. No instructions or comments whatsoever. I opened it and just started to glance at some of the documents. There are lots of files and folders and documents. Hundreds, maybe thousands of documents. You are going to lose your mind. It's crazy how much stuff is here," Erica says.

"Any idea where it came from?" James asks.

"None whatsoever, but it looks official. I mean it's put together well. Professional," Erica replies.

"And what about the CIA?" James asks.

"I've barely scratched the surface, but every document I've looked at thus far appears to have two things in common: some reference to the CIA, in one form or another, and drugs trafficking from Mexico to the US," Erica explains.

"Wow," Javi chimes in.

"I'm stunned," Erica says.

"What's your plan with them?" James asks.

"I'm not sure. I've left a message for Julia to see if she has any thoughts on how to process this, and I've exited out of the files so she can give me any advice on security issues. Just to be safe, I opened it on my laptop without connecting to the WiFi but using the VPN Julia installed for us. I don't think I want to do more until Julia gives me the okay," Erica says.

"Smart. Being cautious makes sense," Javi offers.

"Okay, well let me know what Julia says please," James requests.

"I will. Drive safe, Javi," Erica replies.

"Always, bella dama. Always."

After James ends the call with Erica, Javi accelerates, and with Andretti-like precision weaves through cars to exit at the next off-ramp.

"Whatcha doin'?" James asks.

"I'm turning back," Javi answers.

"Turning back? But we have plans. Wine and music," James protests.

"Do you think you'll be able to enjoy the festival or anything else while Erica is at home looking through the documents?" Javi asks.

"Probably not," James replies.

"Definitely not, my friend. Which is why I will happily return you to your car, and you can go home and be with your wife."

"But we have rooms paid for in Temecula," James notes.

"You can deal with yours, but I think I can come up with a way to still use mine this weekend," Javi says.

"What's her name?" James asks.

"I haven't decided yet."

Erica hangs up with James, staring at the now blank screen on her laptop.

I didn't count, but it looked like a hundred different folders or more. The number of documents could be in the thousands, and I don't want to try to guess at the number of pages. Slow down, Erica. Before you cause bigger problems, you should wait for Julia. Sounds like a good reason to listen to Becca and take a nap.

Erica removes the thumb drive from the laptop, places it on the desk, and walks across the hall to the bedroom, shedding clothes as she walks.

Erica shuts the door and cocoons herself under her down comforter. She uses her phone to follow Becca's directions, turning up the air conditioning and setting the ceiling fans on medium.

"Alexa, play brown noise."

Becca's right. This is nice. But who the hell sent the drive? And why?

TWENTY-ONE

ERICA SLOWLY WAKES from her nap, rolling over to see that it is only three in the afternoon. *Damn, I wanted to sleep a lot longer.*

After a few minutes of tossing and turning, Erica rises, slips on sweatpants and one of James's IU T-shirts, and then checks her phone. Finding a reply text from Julia, Erica takes her phone and returns to the office, texting Julia back as she sits at the desk.

ERICA

Ok, I'm at the computer but haven't done anything.

JULIA

Perfect. Do you have a USB hub? An external hard drive?

I have both.

What about an extra flash drive?

Yep.

Ok. Plug the drive you received into the hub and run your anti-virus.

Erica follows Julia's simple directions.

ERICA

Done. No risks detected.

JULIA

Great. Now do the same with the new drive.

Done. Same.

Ok, now copy everything from their drive to your drive. This might take a few minutes.

Copying now.

Ok. Text when it's done.

As the timer for the copying slowly winds down, Erica gets antsy. "Alexa, play songs by PJ Harvey." Soon the room is filled with the contralto voice of the English singer-songwriter.

"Alexa, volume up." *Might as well enjoy the ambiance while I wait.*

ERICA

Copied. What now?

JULIA

Take out their drive and hide it somewhere. Then run another anti-virus on both the copied drive and on your external hard drive.

Lucky for me, we just bought a new larger hard drive, so it has little on it. And done. No risks.

Ok. Copy from the USB to the hard drive, and then run your anti-virus again, and then also the one in this link.

Erica waits as the files are copied as Alexa plays "Rid of Me," followed by "Down By the Water," "This is Love," and "On Battleship Hill." *Nice song selections, Alexa!*

ERICA

Done. Still nothing detected.

JULIA

Ok, I think you are probably good to go.
Something would have shown up by now.

Probably?

Ha. You know.

I do, and I owe you!

Text, if you need anything else.

I will. Thanks again.

Content with Julia's pronouncement of relative safety, Erica starts to open folders, sub-folders, and files without any significant plan or methodology. Soon, though, she opens a folder titled "CDS 2008/2009," clicks on one of many files within the folder to find a list of documents, each titled with specific dates. She flips through a document or two before stopping cold.

What the hell? Tim Speer? This can't be what it appears to be. Or . . . maybe it is.

Erica opens a few more folders and more documents. *This is so not good. I'm going to need a cola.*

Erica leaves the office and walks to the landing overlooking the living and dining rooms until a movement below freezes her. Downstairs, a person—probably a man based on size alone—dressed in all black with a black ski mask is looking through the bookshelf and credenza.

Without thinking, Erica instinctively cries out, "Who the hell are you, and what are you doing in my house?"

The masked man turns around and points a gun at Erica. "Damn it." The man pauses before commanding her. "Please put down your phone and come down here." Erica hesitates until the man yells, "Now!"

Erica does as directed, descends the stairs, and follows the point of the gun to the sofa. "How did you get in here?" Erica asks as she sits down.

"That's not important. What is important is the flash drive you received today," the man says.

"Flash drive? I have no idea what you are talking about," Erica says calmly.

"Ms. Walsh, let me be clear. There are no options here. No discussions. I know the flash drive was delivered here earlier today, and I must have it."

"I swear. I don't have any such thing. Nothing was delivered. You are mistaken," Erica states.

The man raises the gun from his side. "You can tell me where the drive is, or I can shoot you and find it myself. Either way, I'm not walking out of here without it."

"You can cut the act now. You won't shoot me," Erica says impatiently.

"Why would you think that?" he asks.

"Because I'm pregnant. I'm having a baby girl, Tim," Erica states.

"What?"

"Take off the goddamn mask, Tim. I know it's you," Erica says.

Tim Speer takes off his mask, stuffing it into his pants pocket. "How'd you know it was me?"

"Of course I knew it was you, and how the hell does it matter one bit? What the hell is this? What is going on? I'm your friend," Erica scolds.

"You weren't supposed to be home. You were supposed to be at your club all afternoon!" Tim says.

"How did you know?" Erica asks.

"Really? *That's* your question?"

"You're right. Don't answer that."

"Look, Erica, I'm sorry but I need the flash drive. It's important," Tim pleads.

"It goddamn better be important for you to break into my house and point a gun at me," she says.

"I'm sorry. I didn't have a choice. I'm in trouble," Tim says.

"You better be in a world of trouble."

"I am," Tim assures her. "It's bad."

"Then you'd better trust me and start talking," Erica demands.

"You can't help. No one can help." Tim looks utterly distraught.

"Well, I guarantee you're not getting the flash drive without telling me what's going on," Erica says.

"So, you do have it?"

"Yes, I have it. But I've just started looking at it."

"Have you seen enough to know why I'm in trouble?" he asks.

Erica sits on the sofa, looking up intently at her friend. "Sit down, Tim, and tell me who put the drive together and why?"

Tim sits in the chair to the right of the sofa, in silence; an aura of doom takes hold as the wispy afternoon clouds serenely float past. His eyes slowly wander around the living room until focusing on a framed concert poster of The Pixies at the Whisky a Go Go in Hollywood.

"I remember that concert. Such an amazing show. I still can't believe James didn't go," Tim says.

"I'll give him credit. He has terrible taste in music, but at least he knows what he likes," Erica says fondly.

"Yeah, and I have a hard time picturing him in the pit at the front of the stage," Tim says shakily.

"Was that almost a smile, Mr. Speer?" Erica asks gently.

"Almost. We've had some good times. Some scary ones too," he says.

"And we will have more of both," Erica says.

"I'm not sure, Erica. I may not have a way out of this."

"I'll say one thing with absolute certainty. You don't know me half as well as I thought you did if you think for one single second we aren't going to try," Erica lectures.

"Okay, you win," Tim announces.

"Then shut up, and start talking."

Tim puffs out his cheeks and blows out hard. "Okay, so, the agency has had a—I don't know—call him a 'consultant,' who has been involved in matters in Mexico and Latin America for years. Apparently, he was also saving lots of information about our activities, and the information would be problematic if made public."

"You broke into my house because the information given to me might be problematic if released? Released by whom? And why was it given to us?" Erica asks.

"It had to have come from the same guy. My only guess is he thinks you and James will do something with it," he admits.

"No offense, but you're being pretty damn nebulous."

"I know but—"

"But you are implicated," Erica finishes.

"Right. And, well, there's more. A lot more . . ." Tim says.

"I'm listening," Erica says.

"This will be a bit of a ramble—maybe more than a bit—but the idea will be obvious. I'll skip the Iran-Contra stuff since it's been discussed at length. But the point is, those actions are only the tip of the iceberg.

"Before I was ever involved, the CIA had established relationships with the cocaine distributors moving coke from South America into the US, with Miguel Angel Félix Gallardo and Matta Ballesteros. After they were taken out of play following the Camarena murder, many others filled the void, including, but not limited to, El Chapo.

"In essence, the agency and those working for it were facilitators. If a product needed to go from point A to point B, they could make it happen, for a fee. Lots of product equals lots of fees. Let me ask you, what operations of the CIA in the last ten years or so are you aware of?" Tim asks.

"Truthfully, probably none," Erica answers.

"Exactly," Tim says. "The agency works in the shadows, and some shadows are darker than others. Congressional budgeting entails reports and oversight and media. I promise you, there are CIA assets and activities in every part of the world—things happening that only a handful of people know about.

"Supplies of cocaine led to supplies of heroin, meth, and then fentanyl. Tomorrow it will be whatever the next new thing is. The point is, once dependent on money, it's impossible to move away from it. As more operations were funded by this money, they wanted more money, and more operations were created.

"I know this because it's been my job for the better part of the last twenty-five years. Identify the sources, secure the routes, receive payment, process retention of said payments.

"Despite being a gringo, I was damn effective at working with on the ground operatives to keep the whole process flowing. For over a decade, I worked with the Rafa Quintero group, both within CDS and in Caborca. We also played both sides of the CDS fence and worked with Los Chapitos when fentanyl was just becoming a thing. I had no idea it would be what it's become.

"A couple of months ago, we got word someone was asking around in a variety of places about fentanyl distribution, including in Yuma. I had a guy in Rafa's organization I trusted who knew the area, so I asked him to go check things out and report back to me," Tim says.

"Oh my God, Tim. Did you kill Aguilar?"

"No! Not intentionally. My guy has family in Yuma, so he went there to see who was asking so many questions," Tim says.

"To get rid of him?" Erica asks.

"No, Erica, no. For information only . . ." Tim shifts in his seat.

"But . . . ?"

"He identified Aguilar as the investigator and then, somehow, connected Aguilar to the imprisonment of his cousin," Tim admits.

"Rafael Caro Quintero?" Erica asks.

"Rafael Caro Quintero. And then he saw a way to exact revenge," Tim says.

"Are you telling me—"

"Revenge against Aguilar, and then, you and James," Tim explains.

"Your guy is Javier de la Cruz?" Erica asks.

"He is . . . and I heard you played wiffle ball with his skull," Tim says.

"Okay," Erica asserts, ignoring his comment, "I want to be sure I have this all straight. A rogue, long-time CIA consultant has proof the agency has been making money off the drug trade for years and has continued to profit from the fentanyl trade."

"Evidence connecting me personally to all of it and—"

"And to Aguilar's death," Erica confirms.

"Making me, a CIA officer, an accessory to the murder of a decorated, retired DEA agent," Tim states.

"Okay, but wait. If Javier was working with you, why did you help us take Rafa?" Erica asks.

"Rafa had long since ceased giving us any information we needed and was turning into a liability. You and James allowed us to get rid of him without the government or the agency appearing to be involved. Javier knew nothing. Suspected nothing," Tim explains.

"And you knew when and where to get us with Rafa because of Javier," Erica says.

"That's right," Tim confirms.

"Son of a bitch," Erica exclaims. "Now that I think about it, I never did see what happened to Javier after you and Aguilar busted into the house."

"Javier slipped to the side so he could provide a story to his comrades we'd tied up," Tim responds.

"I'm still confused. How did he know about Aguilar's connection to Rafa?" Erica asks.

"I'm not sure. He didn't communicate with me after he called to tell me what he'd done to Aguilar. I wasn't sure of anything until he attacked you and then it all added up," Tim says.

"Well, Tim. You were right about one thing. You have one huge problem on your hands," Erica states.

"I know. But I appreciate the corroboration," Tim replies.

"The important question now is how do James and I help you out of it?"

TWENTY-TWO

THE FRONT DOOR to the condo suddenly opens and James walks in, his bag in tow. "Hey, babe! Guess who?"

"Please, no more guessing games," Erica says, rising to greet him, "and why aren't you in Temecula with Javi?"

"Javi thought my mind would be here with you anyway," James says while placing his bag along the wall inside the door. "Oh, hey Tim. What's up?"

"Hi, James. I was just bending Erica's ear on a personal problem. She's a good listener."

"Sorry about the problem, but good to see you." James walks to the kitchen. "I need a Diet Coke. Need anything, hon?"

"No, I'm good. Thanks," Erica says.

"Did Erica offer you anything, Tim?"

"We hadn't quite gotten there, but a Diet Coke sounds good," Tim says.

James retrieves the sodas and returns to the living room, handing one to Tim.

"I need to go upstairs and change out of these travel clothes," James says.

"I'll come with you," Erica says, standing.

"Maybe I should go then," Tim says, also standing.

"Nonsense. Take a load off, relax, and Erica and I will be back down in five minutes. It's been too long, and I'd love to catch up," James says.

"Okay, sounds good." Tim sits back down in his chair and opens his soda as James and Erica ascend the staircase.

Once upstairs, Erica shuts the bedroom door. "We need to talk."

"Sure, what's up?" James asks.

"You might want to sit down," Erica says.

James does as suggested and sits on the end of the bed.

"I haven't looked at many of the documents, but I did find one thing that stands out," Erica says.

"What did you find?" James asks.

"A name," Erica says.

"Whose?" James asks.

"Tim's," Erica answers.

"I don't understand."

"The documents indicate that he was a direct participant in the CIA's interactions with the Mexican cartels and Tim confirmed as much to me," Erica explains.

"Okay, I guess that's not a huge surprise," James reasons.

"But there's more. Javier was working with Tim," Erica says.

"What do you mean by 'working with'?" James asks.

"Javier was Tim's principal contact within Rafa's organization. And …"

"There's *more*?" James exclaims.

"Javier was working with Tim when he went to Yuma to find out who was asking questions," Erica says.

"Does that mean?" James starts.

"Tim sent Javier to Yuma, and that's when Javier killed Aguilar," Erica says.

"We need to call the police, or Belmonte, or—"

"Calm down, James," Erica says.

"Don't tell me to calm down. He killed Aguilar," James says angrily.

Erica places her hands on James's shoulders and pushes him to sit on the end of the bed.

"No, James, he didn't." Erica kneels in front of James.

"Then he got him killed," James says.

"Tim did not kill Aguilar. Javier killed him. And Javier has a permanent concussion and will be enjoying penitentiary food for a very long time. The others responsible for Aguilar are the bastards who sold Robbie the drugs. Those are the ones you should be angry at, not Tim. Let's send them to jail. Whether at this moment you like it or not, Tim is our friend, and we should help him.

"James, I love you more than anything, and you are the most principled person I know. But sometimes, those principles get in your way. Not everything is black or white, right or wrong. This, my love, is when you need to look deep inside yourself and find what is the right thing for you to do. For *us* to do," Erica states.

James reflects for a moment. His mind plays a quick highlight reel of their time with Aguilar and Tim in Mexico, most notably in the hangar when the security guard came to check on things and sent James to hide. Now, in this moment, James understands, in a way he never had before, the way Tim must have felt when he was determined to protect James, all of them, no matter who or what had been at the hangar door.

"Let me ask you this. Since Aguilar's passing, if you were in real trouble, is there anyone anywhere you'd want to have your back more than Tim and Bobby?" Erica asks. "And when we were in Mexico, Aguilar trusted Tim completely, trusted him with his life."

James remains quiet, in thought.

"Damn it. You're right. Tim has a problem. We have a problem. But I still have questions," he says.

"As well you should, but then ask Tim directly, as we help him."

Tim is still in his chair, looking blankly over the Pacific Ocean when Erica and James return.

"Tim, I gave James the highlights of our discussion and—"

"And," James interrupts as he and Erica sit on the sofa, "you lied to us. You've been lying to me since the first moment I emailed you at your 'office.'"

"I know, James, and I understand. All I can say is that I *had* to lie. I had to lie to both of you. To a lot of people," Tim admits.

"I know, Tim, I do, but I can't pretend it doesn't bother me or that there isn't a part of me that is furious," James says.

"James—" Tim utters before being stopped.

"Let me finish. I grew up in an orphanage and then was placed in a lot of foster homes in Indiana. When I was in sixth or maybe seventh grade, I was sent to a foster house that had another boy staying there. Grant was his name. Grant and I got pretty close, but then, after about six months, as often happened, I was moved to a different home.

"Grant and I didn't see each other much after that. One day I was riding my bike near a park, and I saw Grant squaring off against two older boys. I raced to where he was, threw down my bike, and stood next to Grant. Let's say we threw the first and last punches. I never asked Grant what the issue was with the other boys or how it started. It didn't matter. He was my friend. I stood by his side.

"I also know, as Erica so convincingly explained to me, that you've been a good friend. More importantly, I know, and I mean *I know*, you would never have done anything to hurt Aguilar. So, let's find those responsible," James says.

"I don't know what to say. Thank you. Both of you," Tim says.

The two men shake hands and then embrace, patting each other on the back.

"I hate to interrupt this Hallmark moment," Erica interjects, "but, unless I'm mistaken, we still have files with your name all over them, and we still have no way to identify the people who killed Aguilar."

"And I hate to make this worse but—"

"Seriously, Tim? It gets worse?" Erica interrupts with guttural exasperation.

"How so?" James asks.

"If one connects the dots in these documents, a widespread pattern of CIA involvement in drug proliferation since the 70s emerges. It goes way beyond me and way beyond Mexico," Tim says.

"I think you'd better explain," James says.

"Okay, but get comfortable," Tim warns. "I'm sure you already know Jesus Vicente Zambada-Niebla, also known as 'El Vicentillo.' In addition to being the son of Ismael 'El Mayo' Zambada-Garcia, he was alleged to be the logistics coordinator in charge of the drug shipments from Latin America to the United States. He also was said to have been close to El Chapo, and in his guilty plea, spoke about working with El Chapo."

"Most of that is public information and pretty established, right?" Erica asks.

"It is," Tim agrees. "But here is something the public doesn't know. Some would contend El Vicentillo provided credible, detailed information to support his allegation that Operation Fast and Furious was part of an agreement between American agencies and the Sinaloa cartel to finance and arm the cartel in exchange for information used to take down rival cartels, as part of a divide-and-conquer strategy."

Operation Fast and Furious was conducted as part of Project Gunrunner, a program of the United States Bureau of Alcohol, Tobacco, and Firearms (ATF), as part of the Department of Justice's broader Southwest border counternarcotics strategy. Project Gunrunner begun in 2005 and was designed to allow traceable firearms to go to Mexican low-ranking drug cartel members—straw buyers—with the intent that doing so would help lead law enforcement to higher-ranking cartel-related criminals.

The Fast and Furious operation started around 2009 and came to light in 2010 when two of the weapons linked to Fast and Furious were found near the scene of the murder of Border Patrol Agent Brian Terry in Arizona. Terry's killing resulted in an ATF whistleblower claiming the agency had lost track of many of the guns it had allowed criminals to obtain. A congressional investigation through the House Oversight Committee commenced after those allegations came to light.

Investigations, including one conducted by the Department of Justice, revealed the Fast and Furious program facilitated the sale of nearly two thousand guns for more than $1.5 million. Hundreds of these guns later were recovered in the United States and Mexico.

The report issued by the inspector general focused blame on ATF headquarters, the agency's Phoenix, Arizona, field office, and the US Attorney's office in Arizona. Following the report, as well as a subsequent three-part congressional report, there remains disagreement on several key allegations. For example, some have maintained that ATF officials intentionally did not intercept guns bought by straw buyers before they got into the hands of drug cartels. ATF agents, on the other hand, claim they seized weapons at every available opportunity but prosecutors and lax gun laws hindered their ability to perform their duties at every stage of the operation.

In the end, more than a dozen DOJ and ATF officials were punished for their roles in Operation Fast and Furious. Within minutes of the release of the IG's report, it was announced that acting ATF chief Kenneth Melson was retiring and another official, Deputy Assistant Attorney General Jason Weinstein, had resigned.

The report claimed Weinstein and Melson were among fourteen people responsible for the ATF allowing illegal firearms to enter Mexico and for their reckless disregard for public safety in doing so. The report also contended that Weinstein failed to pass along key information about the flawed tactics being used in Fast and

Furious, while Melson and other ATF officials failed to properly supervise the probe.

More significantly, the report's executive summary asserted that this was not a one-off operation executed by a single ATF office in Phoenix; it was a coordinated strategy created and implemented by those at the top of the DOJ in order to identify leaders of a major gun trafficking ring. Th decision to shift the focus from arresting straw buyers to identifying leaders of illegal trafficking networks was deliberate and tactical.

The joint House and Senate's final report on the congressional investigation of conduct in Operation Fast and Furious—encompassing 2,359 pages, including 211 pages of text with 692 footnotes, 266 exhibits, and three appendices—alleges numerous errors and decisions by ATF officials and the Arizona US Attorney's Office led to serious problems—including inter-agency communication failures between ATF, DEA, and FBI.

Darrell Issa, then the House Oversight Committee chairman, had this to say:

ATF and the Arizona US Attorney's Office failed to consider and protect the safety of Americans, Mexicans, and fellow law enforcement personnel throughout Operation Fast and Furious. Testimony and a persistent reluctance to fully cooperate make clear that many officials at ATF and the Department of Justice would have preferred to quietly sweep this matter under the rug. Though they are among the most vocal objectors to oversight by Congress, this investigation has also shown that both agencies are among those most in need of additional scrutiny and attention from Congress.[1]

The Fast and Furious operation resurfaced in connection with court filings for and testimony by El Vicentillo. According to El Vicentillo, for more than a decade, a deal was in place for the

1. House Committee on Oversight and Accountability, "Congressional Investigators Release First Part of Final Joint Report on Operation Fast and Furious," Press Release: July 31, 2012, https://oversight.house.gov/release/congressional-investigators-release-first-part-of-final-joint-report-on-operation-fast-and-furious/.

Sinaloa cartel to provide information about rival Mexican cartels to the DEA in exchange for the US government agreeing not to interfere with Sinaloa shipments into the United States and the dismissal of criminal charges against certain cartel participants.

In a series of court filings in a criminal case against El Vicentillo filed in the federal court in Chicago, he went further and asserted the US efforts were part of a strategy previously employed by the US government in combatting Colombian drug cartels whereby the government would divide and conquer by making sweetheart deals with one cartel in order to gain information to be used in destroying the cooperating cartel's rivals.

The Mexican newspaper *El Universal* conducted an extensive investigation and concluded that the DEA, in fact, had entered into agreements with the CDS dating back to 2000 and continuing at least through 2012. The *El Universal* investigative reports included certain statements from an alleged CDS lawyer, Humberto Loya-Castro, who was ultimately indicted in the Chicago case. Loya-Castro claimed that DEA agents made a deal with Sinaloa Cartel and himself that they would not interfere with CDS drug trafficking, not pursue prosecution or detainment of him, El Chapo, El Mayo, and other Sinaloa leaders in exchange for information about rival cartels drug-trafficking activities. Loya-Castro also claimed that the agents told him that this arrangement had been approved by high-ranking officials and federal prosecutors.

"We're aware of the rumors that El Chapo was protected by one or more American agencies for providing information, at least for a while," Erica notes.

"I can assure you there are more than just rumors and innuendo. There has long been credible evidence that various agencies of the United States entered into agreements with cartel leaders to act as informants against rival cartels who received benefits in return, including access to thousands of weapons. El Vicentillo went so far as to say he and other CDS leaders were immune from arrest as long as they provided information to US agents. This went on from 2004 to around 2009, more or less, and though the dividing lines are a bit fuzzy, it dovetailed with Operation Fast and Furious, which covered the period from, I don't know, 2006 to 2011, or thereabout," Tim states.

"And you know all of this because you were one of the liaisons between the US agencies and the cartels," James half proclaims, half questions.

"Right. Initially, I liaised with El Chapo himself, and those close to him, very close to him, and then it evolved. It was more involved than that, but you get the gist. And for the record, it makes some degree of sense. Pick the least offensive, most cooperative group, allow them to operate, and take down others. I mean, come on, we got the Zetas, the BLO, and others because of this."

"While El Chapo got rich and smuggled tons of drugs into the US," Erica inserts.

"Yes," Tim concedes, "but those drugs were coming anyway. Someone was going to supply the demand. Someone was going to make money meeting the demand. And look where it got Chapo. I've been to Super Max. It's not pretty."

"The war on drugs is far more complicated than America good, Mexican cartels bad. I do understand," Erica says.

"Look, Erica, I'm not trying to say I am proud with all that was done . . ." Tim rubs his palm across his forehead and through his hair.

"But it will be your fingerprints on a lot of this if these documents are released," James says.

"That's right, James. I'll be the Ollie North of this generation," Tim says.

TWENTY-THREE

"LET ME RECAP, just to be clear," Erica says with an ironic twinkle in her eye. "We need to come up with a plan to nail those responsible for running the fentanyl that killed Robbie, and those who murdered Aguilar, expose CIA corruption, prevent Javier from talking, and keep Tim's mug from being the lead on every news program in America."

"That's about right, and it would be good if we could do it in the next hour or so," James adds.

"Piece of cake, right?" Tim says.

"I think I have an idea on how to expose the CIA, but not with Tim's name all over the documents," James asserts. "Is there a way to excise his name from the files?"

"I have no idea," Erica replies, "but we know someone who probably does."

"Julia?" James responds.

"Yep. I'm texting her right now."

"Julia?" Tim asks.

"Julia is Bobby's friend who happens to be a computer genius. She has helped us out on some sensitive matters, including connecting with Rafa. She is very good and very discreet," James explains.

"Works for me," Tim replies.

"Julia helped me when I first started looking at the documents. She says she can be here in about an hour," Erica says, looking up from her phone.

"Perfect," James says. "I think I might have an idea on how to expose the CIA but it might be better for Tim—plausible deniability and all—if I handle that upstairs and leave you two to Javier."

"Okay, but what about Yuma?" Erica asks.

"I happen to have the new US Attorney for the Southern District of California on speed dial. I bet we can come up with a plan," James says.

"Okay, babe. We'll leave those to you," Erica says.

James kisses Erica and ascends the stairs. "Don't leave without saying goodbye, Tim."

"Not a chance."

"This is Brian Wilson."

"Brian, it's James Butler."

"Hi, James. How are you?"

"I'm good, and I have a proposition for you," James says.

"I'm listening," Brian says.

"I have come into the possession of a collection of documents—internal CIA files that reveal the depth and breadth of the agency's involvement in drug trafficking," James says.

"Do they support Gary's assertions?" Brian asks.

"I'm not sure. I only just got them and have only scratched the surface of looking at them," James says.

"Okay. So why call me?" Brian asks.

"I am going to want these documents to come out, but I need them to be presented by someone credible and at the right time," James explains.

"I'm not sure I'm either credible or well-known enough," Brian says.

"But if they support Webb's reporting, you'd be the perfect one to present them," James says.

"Why don't you do it yourself?" Brian asks.

"Let's just say I'd prefer to remain in the background on this one. But I can help you analyze the documents and facilitate the reveal."

"I don't know, James. I'm retired. I live a quiet life. I'm not sure I'm prepared for something like this—for the scrutiny or the pressure."

"I understand, Brian. I really do, and I won't pressure you to do anything you don't want to do. But I think back to our conversation on your patio, where you enlightened me on many things the CIA and other agencies have done that have not been widely exposed and are just wrong. Not kinda wrong but a complete betrayal of purpose. The opportunities to expose this malfeasance don't appear often," James says.

"You're right, they don't, but look what happens when they do, and someone tries. Gary's career was ruined, Brian says. "Iran Contra led to congressional grandstanding and reports and a few fall guys, but nothing really changed—obviously. I could go down the list and cite example after example. I have to ask myself, is it really worth it?"

"I'm not going to argue with you, and if you don't want to do it, I'll accept that. But let me ask you this, even at the end, after all that had happened to him, did Gary regret writing his articles?" James asks.

"I think he regretted the way many things were handled, and maybe even some of the choices he made, but I don't think he ever regretted the work itself," Brian says.

"As I see it," James says, "he wasn't perfect, but he did the right things for the right reasons and got persecuted for it. This is a chance to right that wrong and do something positive for his legacy."

"You make a good point. Okay, James. I'm sold. Nervous but sold," Brian says.

"Great. You are going to be dumbfounded when you see these," James says.

"I hope so. When would you expect this to go down?" Brian asks.

"We are going to need a couple of weeks to get the documents to you in a way that gives you cover and to arrange the release. But I have people working on that as we speak," James says.

"I trust you've done your best, but, if this doesn't go as planned, it could take a bad turn for both of us," Brian says.

"I know, Brian. I know. I'll touch base early next week on how to facilitate all of this."

"You know Javier," Erica says to Tim. "Any thoughts on how we handle this?"

"These people react to two things—money and fear," Tim states.

"I'm not paying him anything, so we are going to have to scare him. But how do we do that while he is in custody? Jailhouse thugs to intimidate him would be a bit cliché," Erica muses.

"And it wouldn't help. You don't threaten him. You threaten his family."

"Tim! I'd never, ever, under any circumstances be involved in something where his family was harmed."

"I'm not saying that, Erica. I wouldn't allow that to happen either."

"Okay, good. But maybe you should explain," Erica says.

"We would never hurt his family, but we need to make him think we would. He has a wife and twin girls. I've met them all. Javier is a thug, but he's a good family man, and his girls, Elena and Amelia, are as cute and sweet as imaginable," Tim says.

"Then you can't be involved directly," Erica states.

"Why not?" Tim inquires.

"Tim, if you've met the girls, Javier will know you couldn't harm them. He's a gutless thug, but he's not stupid," Erica says.

"Then how?" Tim asks.

"Me," Erica says.

"You? I don't see you as the threatening type," Tim says.

"Pssh. I already played fungo with his head. He threatened my life. He threatened James. I think I can pull it off," Erica says.

"Then I know how to help and make it real," Tim claims.

"Perfect," Erica says.

"But," Tim adds, "he's still in custody."

"I wonder if Agent Belmonte could facilitate something?" Erica asks.

"I don't know. Do you think he'd be receptive?" Tim wonders.

"Let's find out," Erica asserts.

"Steve Williams's office."

"Hi Stacy, it's James Butler. Any chance Steve is available?"

"It's your lucky day, James. You caught him in the middle of a very short window between meetings."

"I'll keep it short," James promises.

"No worries. I'll put you through," Stacy says before transferring the call.

"James, good to hear from you," Steve's booming voice comes over the phone.

"Thank you. It's a thrill to be speaking to the United States Attorney Stephen Paul Williams."

"Is it absolutely necessary to say that every time we talk?" Steve asks.

"I'm sure it will get old. Eventually." James grins.

"In all seriousness, James, my schedule is pretty tight. What's up?"

"What if I told you I think I could set up a major bust of a fentanyl ring in Yuma, Arizona?" James asks.

"I'd say you should be talking to the US Attorney in Phoenix, Gary Restaino, or to the Yuma Police or County Sheriff," Steve says.

"And if I thought the bust would involve elements from Mexico, including figures that are under indictment in the Southern and Central Districts of California?" James asks.

"Then I'd be interested in hearing more," Steve says.

"There are nuances to this that make it . . . unique," James says.

"Why would I have thought anything else? James, my responsibilities are different now," Steve states.

"We'd also be arresting those responsible for Aguilar's murder," James says.

"Okay, James. I'm listening."

Walking down the stairs to find Erica, Tim, and Julia at the table, James proclaims, "I'm batting two for two. How'd you do?"

"Good job," Erica replies. "We have a plan to deal with Javier and Julia just got here."

"Nice to see you, Julia."

"You too, James."

"Tim and I were just explaining the desire to scrub some names from the documents," Erica says.

"Without making it *look* like the intent was to omit a specific name or names," Tim adds.

"So, what do you think?" James asks Julia.

"This is a lot of data. But I think I could use a tool to look for proper names. We could start with names we know and train it to look for others," Julia explains.

"Train it?" James asks.

"It's called AI, dear," Erica answers. "You're behind the technology curve."

"So far behind," James agrees. "Do you think that would work, Julia?"

"Absolutely," Julia says.

"Then the next question is how long? And what do you do with the names?" James asks.

"James, why don't you let me and Julia work on this, and you can work on your batting average upstairs?" Erica suggests.

"It does make sense, James," Tim agrees with a laugh.

James puts up his hands in surrender. "Okay, you win. I am out of the computer information process. But I think I have a good plan for what to do next, when you are done."

"Just as I expected," Tim interjects. "But I need to get going and keep up appearances."

"Okay. Take care, Tim," Erica says looking at the computer monitor with Julia.

James and Tim walk to the door. "I don't want to say anything to Erica, but I might be hard to reach for a while, depending on how things go down."

"I'll talk to her about it later. Be careful," James says.

"I will. And thank you. In my business, you're expected to use and be used by people. You have to be guarded and careful. You don't have friends," Tim states.

"I'm your friend Tim, and I'm going to do everything I can to see to it that you get through this as unscathed as possible," James says.

"I love you, man," Tim says, walking out the door.

James watches Tim disappear into the elevator. "Be safe, my friend. Be safe."

James returns to his office upstairs while Julia and Erica continue to work with the data on the drive.

"I wish there was a way to know where this material came

from. Or better yet, how to identify the source," Erica muses more to herself than to Julia.

"That might not be as hard as you think," Julia replies.

"I like the sound of that," Erica says.

"You know about metadata, right?" Julia asks.

"Sure—data about other data imbedded in programs and documents," Erica answers.

"Correct. In addition to and somewhat similar to metadata, which is more program-based information, computers also create identifying information. That information can sometimes be used to 'back door' into the original source," Julia says.

"Do I want to know how that is done?" Erica asks.

"Doubtful," Julia says. "But here's where it gets cool. If—and right now, it is only an if—we can access the system and do so without being detected, then it's possible to leave some presents."

"Such as?" Erica asks.

"Well, for example, would you ever want it to be altered when someone looks at or edits the information?" Julia inquires.

"Maybe."

"Or how would you like to freeze a user out if they tried to access certain information or whatever?" Julia asks.

"Now that I like. A lot." Erica pauses for a moment. "You do know that this information probably came from a government agency somewhere, right?"

"I assumed so," Julia states.

"Does that make it harder?" Erica asks.

"It makes it less legal, but not more difficult. Surprisingly, government agencies are not very good at protecting their own systems or information," Julia says.

"I would never ask you to do something you're uncomfortable with," Erica says.

"I know. But I heard just enough earlier to know I can help, and I can make someone miserable for messing with your friend. So, tell me Erica, do you want semi-legal and slightly problematic for the person or not legal but unpleasant?" Julia asks.

"Extremely unpleasant. The more unpleasant the better," Erica responds.

TWENTY-FOUR

The Santa Ana City Jail, located on Civic Center Drive and two blocks from Santa Ana Stadium, is operated under the jurisdiction of the Santa Ana Police Department. Though individuals detained for California misdemeanor and felony offenses sometimes are booked into this correctional facility, the jail houses detainees accused of or sentenced for federal crimes. Those held at the jail may be brought in by the US Marshals Service, the FBI, or even the DEA.

Erica and Tim wait on the south side of the facility, facing West Sixth Street, expecting to meet Belmonte.

"Thanks for setting this up, Agent Belmonte," Erica says as he approaches.

"It's far from standard protocol, but this is an appropriate exception," Belmonte states.

"No cameras or recordings, right?" Erica asks.

"That's correct, Ms. Walsh. Just you and Mr. de la Cruz," Belmonte says.

"Do we want to know how you pulled this off?" Erica asks.

"Don't ask; don't tell," Belmonte says.

Looking to Tim, Erica asks, "Do you have the photos?"

"Right here," Tim replies, handing a manila folder to Erica.

"All right, I guess now is the time," Erica says.

"I do have to come in with you, but I'll stand in a corner. He's cuffed, but I still can't let a civilian in the room alone," Belmonte says.

"It's okay. Just don't stop me. Please," Erica asks.

Belmonte starts to open the door. "The floor is yours."

Erica and Belmonte enter the small interrogation room with a small table in the middle. Javier is cuffed to the table. Belmonte shuts the door, taking his place against the wall just inside the door.

"Hola, Javier," Belmonte says.

"You know him?" Erica asks.

"I busted him in Phoenix about seven or eight years ago," Belmonte says.

"You might have said something," Erica says.

"I didn't realize anything until you called with your request, and then it all came together," Belmonte states.

"A few other things are making sense now too. But that's for later," Erica turns from Belmonte to face Javier.

"Chica," Javier says with a slight smirk.

Sitting down in the chair across from Javier, while maintaining firm eye contact, Erica replies in near perfect Spanish. "Hi, Javier. How's your head? Still have a headache?"

"*Puta*," Javier spits out the word.

"Big talk for a man handcuffed to a table," Erica says.

"Let me go and see what happens," Javier says.

"We did that dance once," Erica states. "And you lost. Badly and painfully."

"What do you want?" Javier asks.

"To start with, I want to know how you knew about Aguilar?" Erica asks.

"Who?" Javier scoffs.

"The man you killed in Yuma. My friend." Erica stares into him.

"Oh, the dumb son of a bitch who was asking too many questions," Javier replies.

"How did you know who he was?" Erica asks.

"I didn't. But Señor Quintero did," Javier says.

"How?" Erica presses.

"I sent a picture of the man asking questions. He said, 'that's the guy who kidnapped me.' He told me all about the people that did that to him," Javier explains.

"How does that make sense? Rafa's in jail," Erica says.

"Stupid chica. He's still Rafa. He still knows." Javier smiles at Erica as he talks.

"Except I think you're lying. You didn't send a thing to Rafa. Oh, Javier, you're so stupid it's beyond predictable. Remember Carl, the security guard at my office building you paid off? He told the police you said you hadn't talked to Rafa in months, that Rafa had disavowed you. So, I know someone else told you. Who gave you instructions? Who were you working for?" Erica asks.

"I work for Rafa and only Rafa," Javier states.

"Wrong. I know for a fact that for years you've been working with and providing information to the CIA," Erica says. "I wonder if you told Rafa about that work. Do you think he'd be happy if he found out?"

"Only information that impacted other cartels. Never anything to hurt Rafa."

"How did you pass him information?" Erica asks.

"Which one?" Javier asks.

"What do you mean 'which one?'" Erica asks.

"There were two," Javier explains.

"Two men from the CIA?" Erica asks.

"Sí," Javier says.

"Okay, how did you pass information on to *them*?" Erica asks.

"Chica, you aren't answering my question—which one?" Javier gives her a look, imploring her to take his meaning.

"Did you pass different information to each one?" Erica asks.

"Sí. Only what they asked for at the time."

"Did you pass information to the two of them at the same time?"

"No, never," Javier replies.

"Did you meet with them together?" Erica asks.

"No."

"Okay. What did the men look like?"

"The first one is a very tall gringo," Javier answers.

"Tim?"

"Sí."

"And the other?" Erica asks

"Shorter, younger. Not as friendly," Javier says.

"You said Tim was the first one. Was he your first connection with the CIA?" Erica asks.

"Yes, then Art came later," Javier explains.

"And you never met with Tim and Art together?" Erica asks.

"No, Art said they were in separate investigations, and I shouldn't say anything to Tim because it would harm both investigations," Javier explains.

"You believed that?" Erica asks.

"I didn't care. Two people were paying me," Javier says.

"Who told you to go to Yuma in the first place?" Erica asks.

"Tim."

"Did you tell him when you'd found the man or send him a picture?" Erica asks.

"No, once I was there, Art said I was to talk to only him and that it was an order from high up. I sent a picture to Art, and later he said I needed to kill the man," Javier says.

"Did he say why?" Erica asks.

"No. I don't ask such questions."

"Who else did you tell about him?"

"No one, chica. I just did what I was told and shot him. I didn't need to tell anyone else," Javier explains.

"Tell you what, Javier, if you call me chica one more time, I'm going to go get my bat and take a few more swings at that thick skull of yours," Erica offers.

Javier looks to Belmonte. "Are you going to let her threaten me?"

"I don't know what you're talking about," Belmonte replies, continuing to lean against the wall. "You and this nice lady are having a perfectly pleasant conversation."

"Worthless cop," Javier says.

"I'd be careful there, Javier. I'm the only thing standing between you and a severe beating," Belmonte warns.

"Fine." Javier turns back to Erica. "I've told you what I know. What else do you want?"

"I want you to call all of your people and tell them to leave me, my family, and my friends alone," Erica explains.

"Never!" Javier says with venom.

"Oh, you stupid little man." Erica opens the file.

"What is that?" he asks.

"Just some pictures. Let's see, this one is your wife, right? And this one is your twin girls. Elena and Amelia, right? I'll admit, I can't remember which is which. But I do know this is their school." Erica lays the pictures one by one in front of Javier.

"How do you have those?" Javier asks.

"Did you really think I don't have connections? Ways of finding your family? Ways to make your pathetic life even more miserable? What's wrong? You're not smiling any more, are you?" Erica asks.

"What do you want?" Javier snarls.

"I already told you. I want to be left alone. *Completely* alone," Erica says.

"Or what?" Javier asks.

"If anything happens to anyone close to me, I mean anything at all, and I don't care who does it—if anything happens, I'm coming after you. After your family," Erica explains.

"You would never," Javier says.

"You killed my friend. You came after me, in my office. You threatened my husband!" Erica leans forward. "Look at me. Do not make the mistake of doubting me for a single second. I'll have your family hurt, and I'll bring the pictures to you myself. I'll show them to you right here."

"You can't threaten me. There are laws. People will know," Javier says.

"You are so naïve. It's just you and me. No one's listening," Erica says with a sneer.

Javier looks to Belmonte, who responds, "I'm sorry, I wasn't paying attention. Did you say something?"

"No one will know," Erica continues. "No one will believe you. But, if you don't believe me, I'll leave and come back tomorrow with proof that I'm serious. Dead serious. I think Amelia is the blonde. She's such a pretty girl. School starts at 8:30 a.m.?"

"Okay. Okay! I'll tell my people to back off," Javier says.

"Not good enough, Javier. You're going to tell them to make sure nothing untoward happens to me or my family. Nothing. Anything happens, I blame you. Not your fault? I still blame you. Do you understand?" Erica asks.

"Sí," Javier says.

"No. Say it. Say it!" Erica smacks her palm on the table.

"Nothing happens to you or your family. Nothing," Javier promises.

"That's right, Javier. And one more thing."

"What?"

"I'm going to follow you. Whatever prison you go to, I'll know, and I'll know the warden, the cell block commander—I'll know every person that you come into contact with. You will never be alone. If you do anything, I'll know. Step out of line, I'll know, and I will make you pay. Understand?" Erica asks.

Javier looks down at the table.

"Do you understand?!" Erica shouts, pounding the table.

"I understand."

Erica collects the photographs and returns them to the folder before standing and walking to the door. "Sleep well, Javier," she says.

Belmonte opens the door, allowing Erica to exit in front of him, the door shutting behind him.

"Holy cow, Tim," Belmonte asserts. "Your friend here was a complete and total badass."

"I've seen her in that mode before. Not a lady to be taken lightly," Tim replies.

Belmonte concurs. "Quite impressive, Erica. I almost believed you really would go after his family."

Erica begins the walk down the hall to the exit. "Who says I wouldn't?"

Back in her office, the adrenaline from Erica's confrontation with Javier is slowly dissipating from her veins. Her futile efforts to get some productive work done are mercifully interrupted by a call on her cell phone.

Fresno? I don't know anyone from Fresno who'd be calling my cell.

The call rings until it disconnects, followed immediately by another call from the same number.

Persistent.

"Erica Walsh."

"Erica, hi. It's Bill Belmonte."

"Agent Belmonte. I didn't recognize this number," Erica says.

"It's a very old but very safe number, if you get my drift," Belmonte says.

"Understood," Erica says. "What's up?"

"Who else besides you and me knew about our meeting with Javier today?"

"Other than Tim, only James."

"No one else?" Belmonte asks.

"No one." Erica affirms. "I told my dad Javier was the one who attacked me here in the office, but I didn't tell him about the meeting. I wasn't sure he would approve of the methods. Why? What's going on?"

"You remember after Javier was arrested, I worked with the local AUSA to indict him on federal charges to keep him under our control?" Belmonte asks.

"Yes, I do recall you mentioning it," Erica says.

"Well, I just had a telephone call with the agent in charge of the Los Angeles Division. He called me because the deputy administrator in DC called him because the head administrator called *him* after she received a call from the director of national intelligence," Belmonte says.

"I think I'm following."

"The point of that daisy chain of communication is that the DEA has been aske—in a very persuasive way—to back off any investigation into or prosecution of our friend Mr. de la Cruz and, at the request of the DNI, Javier will soon be transferred to a different but unknown facility," Belmonte states.

"What the literal hell?" Erica exclaims.

"I'm not sure, I'm really not. But it seems someone with some power wants Javier protected."

"Any idea who?"

"At the moment, regrettably, none. But at this point, I think it best to keep the distribution of information to a need-to-know basis," Belmonte advises.

"Understood. I'll convey the message to James. Thanks for the head's up," Erica says.

"Of course. Be careful, Erica, and I'll be in touch soon."

As soon as the call with Belmonte ends, Erica calls James on the office phone.

"Hey, what's up?" James asks.

"Belmonte just called. We need to talk. I'm heading to your office. Can you call Tim?" Erica asks.

"On it," James replies.

Erica nearly jogs down the hall, past the lunchroom and into James's office, shutting the door behind her.

"What did Belmonte say?" James asks.

"Tim on?" Erica asks.

"He said he'd call back in two minutes or less. I think the exact phrase was one minute forty-three seconds, but you get the idea."

"Let's wait for him so I don't have to try to explain twice. If that's okay with you?" Erica asks.

"Sure," James says.

"Is that music playing in your office? You never listen to music at work?"

"I do on rare occasions."

"That's Alice Merton. How are you even aware of her music?" Erica asks, gobsmacked.

"I'm not, but I met Detective Torres at a Starbucks this morning and it was playing, and I liked it. I asked a Gen Z barista who the artist was and played it when I got in," James says.

"I'm in shock."

"I'm evolving," James says, his words interrupted by the playing of the Johnny Rivers hit "Secret Agent Man" from his cell phone. "Alexa, off. Tim, hi, thanks for calling back. Erica is here with some information to share."

"Hi, Erica. What's going on?" Tim says.

"After we left the jail today, I went back to the office to work, and a few minutes ago, Belmonte called me to tell me that the DEA had been quote, 'Requested,' end quote to refrain from investigating or prosecuting Javier and that Javier was being moved to a different facility. Belmonte said the directive apparently came from the DNI. He called me from a burner phone and suggested we keep the circle of information as small as possible," Erica explains.

"Holy crap," Tim says.

"Any idea who could have that kind of juice?" James asks.

"None in particular," Tim says.

"You didn't tell anyone about meeting Javier?" Erica asks.

"Of course not," Tim replies.

"Then how did anyone—" Erica begins.

"I have no idea," Tim interrupts.

"One thing seems certain," James says. "Aguilar was spot on. It is bigger than we knew."

TWENTY-FIVE

A CLOSURE on I-8 outside El Cajon convinced James and Bobby to leave earlier than planned and on a different route. Rather than heading south to San Diego, James takes the Riverside Freeway to I-215 until it merges into I-10. From there it is a drive through the California desert past Palm Springs, Palm Desert, Indio, and Blythe. At a tiny Arizona town named Quartzsite, I-10 intersects with Highway 95, which James will take south to Yuma. The Tesla's air conditioning is on high, beating back the 100-degree weather outside.

"I'm not saying I've been counting," James says, "but in the last few minutes, you've checked your phone four times, adjusted the AC a couple of times, and changed your seat position at least twice. You are unusually not calm."

"In the NFL I watched film relentlessly—day and night. It was my mission to understand everything I could so I could anticipate and account for every variable. I knew where to look, what to read, what to expect. With my business, I look for certainty and try to take away all of the variables so that everything is as ordered and stable as it can be. That's what my clients demand and deserve.

"But here, there are about three dozen variables I can picture off the top of my head. Add in a fluid situation with people we don't know or understand, and, yeah, you could say I'm not calm." Bobby pauses for a moment. "Do you think the information from Guillermo is good?"

"It better be. I'll be out of favors for years if it doesn't happen as planned," James states.

"You trust him?" Bobby asks.

"I do. He helped with Erica, and he knows I'll repay it, so I think our interests are aligned. Besides, at this point, I don't see how we have a choice," James admits.

"If you're confident, I'm all in, but I'd be less twitchy if we were going to be wired, with the police right outside monitoring everything," Bobby suggests.

"I know that makes more sense, and to tell the truth, it's mostly how I sold it to Erica. But Guillermo was worried about any of his people getting pinched, so it had to be done this way," James explains.

The men are a couple hours outside Yuma when James receives a text. "Okay, Guillermo says the meeting is at 8 p.m. and has an address. We are meeting a Tony Treyes. Guillermo says he is right the connection to the traffickers."

"Eight o'clock. Right after sunset. Great," Bobby says.

"I'm texting Steve now," James says.

At 7:15 p.m., as they approach the outskirts of Yuma, James gets another text from Guillermo. "Oh, hell."

"What's up?" Bobby asks.

"Guillermo says the meet has been moved to 7:30," James says.

"Tell him we can't get there?" Bobby suggests.

"Already on it." A few moments pass before James has a return text. "He says it's 7:30 or never. I'm texting Steve now."

"Good idea."

"Steve says they are all set for eight. He'll try to move it up, but we might have to stall for a few minutes."

"Stall? Stall?" Bobby proclaims. "Let's just stall drug dealers making a transaction, like that's an easy thing to do."

"What do I tell Guillermo?" James asks.

"I say we tell him we will hustle and be there at 7:30, unless you disagree," Bobby says.

"Hell no." James texts for a moment. "Done."

A few minutes before 7:30 p.m., James and Bobby are near the address. James stops a block short of the destination: a metallic barn on the edge of town. "Are you ready?" he asks.

"We're only going to have one chance. Let's do this," Bobby responds.

"Let's do this," James agrees, applying pressure to the gas pedal.

A block down the road is a long driveway leading toward the barn sitting in the dusky light. James parks, and the two men walk toward the front of the barn, where they find two men, obviously armed, standing post.

"We are here to meet Tony Treyes. Guillermo sent us," James says.

"We need to pat you down," one of the men says.

"No problem," James replies. "We aren't armed."

The men do the pat down, and then one opens the barn door. "In the back."

James and Bobby walk slowly to the back of the mostly dark barn, where they find a man sitting under a long fluorescent light at a folding table with another man standing guard over his left shoulder.

"James and Bobby?" asks the seated man.

"I'm James, he's Bobby, which would make you Tony," James answers.

"Have a seat," Tony says. "Guillermo says I should trust you."

"I'm happy to hear that," James says as he and Bobby sit in the two folding chairs across from Tony.

"So, tell me what you are looking for," Tony requests.

"We are looking to acquire some fentanyl that our connections in Los Angeles will re-sell," James says.

"Straight or with cocaine?" asks Tony.

"Both. But neither deadly," James says.

"That's not an issue, but why not go through Guillermo?" Tony asks.

"There are a couple of reasons," James explains matter-of-factly. "No offense to Guillermo, but he doesn't really fit in with the people we want to sell to. Plus, if Guillermo gets the product from you and then sells it to me, I'm paying a mark-up I would rather pass on to the end user and not pay upfront," James explains.

Before Tony responds, James and Bobby are startled by a disturbance from the back.

"Is that Tony T. back there? It's been a long time," calls a voice.

Bobby looks behind him, then immediately turns around. "Oh, hell," he whispers to James.

"What?" James whispers back.

"The jackasses from the convenience store," Bobby says.

James looks behind him, watching as Ricky and Leo approach.

"Sorry to interrupt, Tony, but when we heard you were in town, we had to say hi," Leo exclaims.

Ricky is a step ahead and immediately recognizes James and Bobby. "You?!"

"You know them?" Tony asks.

"These too assholes were asking questions about that dead guy. They came into the store a couple weeks ago," Ricky says.

"Asking questions about a murder and now trying to buy product? I smell a cop," Tony says while getting to his feet.

"We aren't cops. I swear," James says, standing as well.

"Sit your ass down. You don't move until I tell you." Tony reaches behind him and pulls a gun from his waistband. "Are you wired? Are there cops outside?"

"We are not wired, and we're not here with cops," Bobby says.

"That's because they *are* cops," Leo says.

"No," James repeats.

"Let's kill them right here," Leo says. "Stand up," he orders James and Bobby, who comply.

"I don't want to kill no cops, especially not here," Tony says.

"Fine then, I'll shoot them," Leo says.

"Stop right there!" a voice from the dark yells. Slowly, a figure emerges from the darkness. "Put your guns down, and back away from these men."

"Who the hell are you to tell me what to do?" Tony protests.

"The name is Cedric."

"So?" Tony scoffs.

"Cedric Carter. People around here used to call me C-3."

"Oh, shit. I'm sorry, Mr. Carter," Tony says.

"What do you mean, 'Sorry, Mr. Carter'? We the only ones with guns," Leo says impatiently.

"You better shut up before your punk ass gets killed," Cedric warns.

"I don't know who you think you are," Leo says.

"When I was young, C-3 wasn't *just* my name. It was what I did to people who challenged me—crush, cripple, and cancel.

Leo raises the gun to eye level. "Well, you ain't young no more."

"You're pointing a gun at me? You must be even dumber than you look. Just because I don't have a gun doesn't mean I don't have guns," Cedric says.

With those words, two very large men, dressed in all black, carrying AK-47s emerge from the darkness behind Cedric. "Are we going to have a problem here?" Cedric asks Tony.

"No, Mr. Carter," Tony says solemnly.

"Then you two put your guns away and step away from these morons," Cedric says.

Tony and his guard follow Cedric's directions while Ricky and Leo hold onto their guns but lower them to their sides.

"What about my men outside?" Tony asks.

"They're fine. Just a bit tied up at the moment," Cedric replies. "Are you okay, Bobby?"

"We're good now, Cedric. Thanks," Bobby says.

Cedric looks at Tony. "Are you going to take their guns, or am I?"

"I will." Tony approaches Ricky and Leo. "Hand them over."

Ricky hands his gun to Tony, while Leo hesitates.

"Leo," Ricky says imploringly.

"No, damn it. I don't want to let these losers walk away," Leo says.

"Leo, if you don't want to die where you stand, hand it over now," Tony states. Leo hands over his gun with the grimace of a disappointed toddler. Tony hands the guns to Cedric, who hands them to James.

"Cedric," James says, "in about five minutes, this place is going to be crawling with DEA agents. Our objective here was to get the men that had Aguilar killed. These two boneheads showed up at just the right time," James says, pointing toward Ricky and Leo. "I bet they can lead us to the suppliers in the area, and I've already told Williams about them."

"If so," Bobby notes, "we can keep your promise to Guillermo and let Tony fade away into the night."

"Agreed," James says.

"What do you say, Tony. Do you want to leave with your men?" Cedric asks.

"Yes, we do," Tony says.

"Then leave these two with us, and get out now," Cedric instructs.

James has an epiphany. *I'm so stupid. I never put it together until now. Cedric was Bobby's friend who saved us after we crossed the border with Rafa.*

"Of course, man," Tony agrees.

"And you mention this to no one, and if you ever see either of these men again, you walk the other way. Understood?" Cedric asks.

"Got it," Tony answers.

"No, no, no. Not 'got it.' I asked if you understand," Cedric says calmly.

"I understand," Tony confirms.

"Then get out of here. Now," Cedric states.

Tony and his bodyguard run toward the barn door and soon are out of sight.

"What do you want with these two?" Cedric asks James.

"The DEA has questions for them, as does the local sheriff. We plan to turn them over," James says.

"You suck, man. Especially you," Leo barks to Bobby.

"Are you talking to me?" Bobby asks incredulously.

"Yeah, you. You're big, but that doesn't mean you're tough. Tough comes from the streets," Leo says.

"Tough comes from your mother's cooking. And you wouldn't survive thirty seconds on the real streets. You think Yuma is tough?" Bobby asks.

"Talk is cheap, old man," Leo says.

"Cedric. Do you mind if I take a moment here?" Bobby asks.

"Have at it, hoss," Cedric says.

With those words, Leo tries to sucker punch Bobby, who moves almost imperceptibly as Leo's punch glances innocently off Bobby's chin.

"Just as I thought." Bobby throws a quick one-two combination to Leo's ribs and chin, sending him to the ground, writhing in pain. Bobby looks toward James. "I think we are done here."

"You been training with Mike Tyson?" Cedric asks. "That was pretty."

"Thanks, but you should go too. I don't know when the cops will be here, but I suspect you and your friends don't want to be here when they do," Bobby says.

"Agreed," Cedric says nodding to his men. "I'll be in touch."

"Sound good, and thank you," Bobby says.

"Yes, thank you," James agrees.

"I do what I can to make things better, and I move in mysterious ways." With those words, Cedric and his men stride to the door and slip out into the darkness.

Bobby sits down next to James who is holding a gun on Ricky and Leo. "How long do you expect?"

"I'd think not long," James replies.

No more than a minute passes when the men are startled by a noise from outside.

"This is the DEA. We have the barn surrounded. Put down any weapons and stand with your hands in the air," calls a voice over a megaphone.

"I think you'd be right," Bobby replies. "I don't know about you, but I'm standing with my hands in the air."

James sets the two guns on the table and moves away to a point where he can see the door, watch Leo and Ricky, and be visible to anyone entering.

Soon two men in SWAT gear, shining flashlights, enter the barn, followed by Steve Williams flanked by two men wearing DEA jackets, and a woman wearing an FBI jacket.

"James?" Williams calls out.

"Back here," James replies. "No one is armed."

James and Bobby drop their arms once Williams approaches. Williams surveys the area. "Are those the two?"

"That's them," James answers.

"Charming, I'm sure. James this is Heather Rice, she's an AUSA in this region and an ally. Technically this is her operation. The sheriff's office has men following right behind."

"I was expecting more men," Rice says.

"Five minutes earlier and you would have found them," James replies. "But we did the best we could."

"Let's have a chat with these two," Williams says.

Rice looks to the DEA agents, as the SWAT members finish a search of the barn. "Let's cuff those two and bring them over here," she instructs. Leo and Ricky are set against a wall in front of Williams and Rice, with Leo grimacing.

"What's wrong with him?" Williams asks.

"Let's say he took a swing at the wrong person at the wrong time," James replies.

"Who the hell are you?" Leo asks.

"Me?" Rice replies. "I'm the one who decides if you spent the rest of your life in a federal penitentiary or not."

In the background, James whispers to Bobby. "Should we start counting the cliches?"

"Life?" Ricky whines.

"Life. You see, I have enough to charge you with felony murder, conspiracy to import cocaine, drug trafficking, and anything else I can think of."

"Murder? We didn't murder anyone," Ricky protests.

"Maybe not, but your dumb ass business partners did, and that makes you as guilty as if you pulled the trigger yourself. Unless I decide otherwise. But, hey, that's up to you two geniuses."

"Us? How?" Ricky asks.

"Shut up, Ricky. He's playing you," Leo admonishes. "You've got nothing on us."

"He's probably right, Ricky. I mean look how far you've gotten following his lead thus far?" Rice turns to look back at James and Bobby. "Too stupid to help themselves. Oh well."

"I bet Ricky would love a prison cell somewhere cold. Do you think you could find him a cell in Montana?" James asks.

"That's a great idea. I'm sure that could be arranged," Rice says.

"Come on, man," Ricky whines, looking to Williams.

"Don't talk to me," Williams says. "She's the one who decides your fate, not me."

"I can be your worst enemy, Ricky. Or you can help me. The choice is yours," Rice offers.

"That's at least three," Bobby whispers.

"What help?" Ricky asks.

"Damn it, Ricky. Shut your mouth!" Leo yells.

"That's it," Rice shouts to Leo. "I'm sick to death of you." Looking at the two agents standing next to Leo, she barks, "Take him out of here!"

One of the agents stands Leo up and starts walking toward the barn entrance. "If Ricky here is going to Montana, let's send this dumbass to North Dakota. I'm sure he'll love how the inmates stay warm up there."

"Wait, wait, wait. What can you do to help?" Leo asks.

"That's the wrong question. It's not what I can do for you because I promise I'm not doing a damn thing for you until you cooperate, and I mean *really* cooperate," Rice explains.

Leo hesitates for a moment.

"Too late," Rice snaps her fingers as the agent tugs on Leo.

"Okay, you win. Please. I'll help. What do you need?" Leo asks.

Rice stays silent as the agent leads Leo almost to the barn door.

"Please," Leo begs. "Anything. I'll cooperate."

The agent looks back to Rice who smiles before the agent guides Leo back and shoves him to the ground next to Ricky.

"You, my new friend, are going to make a phone call to your associates across the border. The ones that supply you. And you are going to tell them you are being raided and need their help," Rice says.

"You're crazy. They'll kill me if I lie to them."

"If you think things will be better in the pen for the next forty or fifty years …"

"*Puta*!" Leo shakes his head. "Prison is better than dead."

Rice bends to face Leo. "Listen, you stupid son of a bitch. You are in a lot of trouble, and I'm more than willing to dedicate my time to making sure it never, ever gets better. Do you understand me?"

"I can't. You don't understand!"

"Wrong numb nuts. I understand too well," Rice looks to the cell phones sitting on the ledge. "Which phone is yours? Oh wait. Let me guess. This one must be yours." Rice holds up a black iPhone adorned with a swastika emblem on the back. "You have one chance and one chance only. Make the call now, right now, or these men are going to take you, and you will never see the outside of a prison again. Ever!"

"Fine. I'll call," Leo says.

The DEA agent stands Leo up and unlocks his cuffs.

"Call the main man," Rice instructs. "Not a lieutenant. Not a sicario. Your main contact. Tell him your stash is being stolen and you need help. Men. Lots of men and you need right now."

Leo starts to scroll on his phone looking for the number. As he hits dial, Williams issues a warning. "One false word, and you are done. Look at me. You will be *done*. Understand? And we know Spanish."

Leo nods and then turns his attention to his phone. "*Compañero. Necesito ayuda. Rápido. Una banda del norte intentó asaltar nuestro alijo. Debe haber diez de ellos. Solo podemos mantenerlos a raya por tanto tiempo. ¡Por favor!*"

"What did he say?" James whispers to the nearest DEA agent.

"Send help," the agent replies.

Leo listens for a moment. "*Sí. Gracias. Sí. El granero rojo.*"

Leo hangs up the phone and hands it to the agent. "They are coming."

"Very good, Leo. You sounded properly scared. Take them away," Rice says.

Leo is re-cuffed.

"Wait, we helped you," Ricky pleads.

"And I'll uphold my end of the bargain, later, if they come," Rice explains.

The agents lead the two men out of the barn with Rice, Williams, Bobby, and James following.

"Things may get a bit crazy here soon," Williams tells James. "You and Bobby should leave now. Can you find someplace to hang out in town until this wraps up? In case we need you for anything."

"Our plan was to get out of Dodge soon," James replies.

"But," Bobby interjects, "I could use a drink and some food before we hit the road."

"Tell you what, why don't you go find something to eat. Text me where you are, and I'll meet up with you in an hour or so?" Williams suggests.

"Works for us," James says.

Williams starts shouting directions and runs off toward the field.

"So, Bobby, where in Yuma says, 'Congratulations you busted a drug ring and didn't die'?"

The Wednesday evening crowd at Hooter's has since left as James and Bobby sit quietly, watching a random baseball game on the television on the wall in front of their high-top table.

"Hooters? Really?" Williams smirks, walking to the table.

"Who knew how long you'd be, and this is as good a place to wait as any," James says.

"Fair enough," Williams agrees, sitting on a stool.

"And?" Bobby asks.

"We nabbed four guys in addition to your two friends and confiscated distributable quantities of cocaine and meth," Williams states.

"No fentanyl?" James wonders.

"Not that was apparent. It's possible there is some in the drugs we found, but we won't know that until we can run lab tests. But —and I want you to know this, James—there is no doubt that this group was moving a lot of drugs, including fentanyl," Williams says.

"Probably never will be a direct link to Aguilar's grandnephew though," James says remorsefully.

"Maybe not, but we just took a lot of drugs off the streets," reassures Williams.

"What about the Mexico crew?" Bobby asks.

"I'm glad you asked. Two cars stopped in the US and three more in Mexico. In total, fifteen in custody, all with cartel ties," Williams says.

"That's great news," Bobby responds.

"Why some in Mexico?" James asks.

"It's part of the process, James. We had to alert border patrol on both sides and give the south side something," Williams explains.

"Makes sense," James takes a drink of beer. "By the way, nice watch."

"Hah, I was wondering if you'd notice. I didn't wear it for the raid, but it felt like a good occasion to take it out." Williams holds up his wrist so they can properly admire it.

"It's insured, right?" James asks.

"Indeed. And I haven't thanked you for that nice added expense," Williams says.

"I know this whole event was unusual . . ." James starts to explain.

"Unusual? Not a single part of this was standard or regulation at all. We were fortunate that the Yuma Police and the Yuma County Sheriff's Department could not have been more helpful and understanding, not to mention my compatriot, Gary Restaino, and especially Heather," Williams says.

"She was impressive. I'd hate to see her and Erica working together," Bobby says.

"If either ever runs for office, I'll send a good donation," James says.

"Thank goodness the results make everything look good. The prize was worth the price," Williams says.

"I supposed it was," James remarks.

"I need to head back. Are you guys good to drive home?" Williams asks, eyeing James's beer.

James shows Williams his bottle. "Non-alcoholic. All good."

"Good. I'll touch base in a day or two, but this was great. Thanks for all the help," Williams says.

"Yep. Say hi to Carol and the kids for me. You won't forget about the other thing, right?" James inquires.

"Will do, and no I won't," Williams promises.

Williams shakes hands with James and Bobby and walks to the door. Turning back, he looks to James who is looking dejectedly at the television screen above him. Williams pauses and walks back to the table.

"James?" Williams asks.

"Yeah?" James says, turning to Williams.

"Are you good?" William eyes him closely.

"Yeah, I'm fine," James says.

"Then what?" Williams asks.

"I wanted to tie it all together," James admits.

"And what, you only jailed Aguilar's killer and disrupted the drug ring that killed his relative," Williams says.

"I know. I understand," James says.

"No, James, I don't think you do. In my world, victories come in increments. It's not like your trials where you win or lose, and, in your case, usually win. When it comes to fighting drugs and the traffickers, the wins are smaller, at the margins, and we all pray, each day, that they amount to something that makes a difference. And we live for those occasions when the win is bigger, more clear cut. James, in our world, this was a win. A big win. You did good."

TWENTY-SIX

"You have done nothing with the information I gave you." James's mystery contact is concerned.

"You sent the thumb drive?" James asks.

"I thought you'd assume that."

"Well, thank you for the confidence but we weren't at all sure. Since we weren't sure where it came from, we hadn't yet decided how best to use it," James explains.

"I am hoping you release it to the press so the world can see the symbiotic and problematic relationship the CIA has maintained with the Mexican cartels for decades."

"How do you have these materials?" James asks.

"It's probably best for everyone concerned if I don't share too much, but I will say you can rely on their authenticity and accuracy."

"You want this exposed why exactly?" James asks.

"Americans are dying and have been dying for years from the drugs flowing, virtually unabated, from Mexico to the US. Years ago, it was heroin and marijuana, then cocaine, then meth and fentanyl, and no one knows what it'll be tomorrow.

"Drug trafficking is probably never going to stop, but we can ebb the tide if there is a concerted effort on both sides of the border. But the documents you now have in your possession show, conclusively and in detail, that every effort of law enforcement was resisted and countered by an immoral alliance between the cartels and the CIA.

"That alliance allowed traffickers to move more drugs into the US than they ever could have alone, profiting millions upon millions of dollars, while killing American men, women, and children.

"The CIA took its cut, netting untraceable funds to funnel to unsupervised and unauthorized activities around the globe. It simply must stop. If it doesn't, I fear for the future of this country, if not this hemisphere."

"That is powerful and hard to argue with," James admits.

"Look, I'm no saint nor an innocent. All of our intelligence agencies are in difficult times, facing perilous decisions. Some require, shall we say, harsher actions than others. It is easy to second guess on a case-by-case basis, but this is a long-standing operational directive that benefits the cartels and the CIA and no one else."

"Until recently, I had only a vague idea of the quantities of drugs being trafficked into the US and the resulting deaths. It is staggering—and sobering," James says.

"It's not just drugs flowing from Mexico, you know. Guns are trafficked in staggering quantities as well, just in the other direction."

It is estimated that as many as one million guns cross from the US into Mexico every year. Most of those guns come from and enter Mexico through Texas, which has a strong gun culture.

Unknown to many Americans, the Mexican constitution allows for legal possession of one small-caliber firearm with several important caveats: the owner must be a Mexican citizen or a foreigner with legal residency status, the firearm must be of small caliber as cited by the regulations, it must be registered with the army, and critically, the firearm is not to be carried in the street. The purpose of the law is to provide for self-defense within the confines of one's own home.

Most interestingly, though, Mexico, a nation of one hundred thirty million people, has a single store permitted to sell guns. The store sits on a military base in Mexico City, was selling fewer than forty guns a day in recent years, and is prohibited from advertising.

It is no surprise then that about 70 percent of guns seized in Mexico from 2014 to 2018 and submitted for tracing had originally come from the US, according to ATF officials.

Easy access to a legal inventory in Texas and lucrative prices on the secondary market has resulted in many Mexican border towns being flooded with guns.

Carlos Peña Ortiz was once mayor of Reynosa, a Mexican town along the US border eleven miles away from a Texas gun store where residents and visitors can buy guns. Peña Ortiz once described the problem: "The financial incentive to smuggle weapons into Mexico is high and purchasing them in Texas and driving a few miles is too easy."[1] Peña Ortiz saw many rifles styled after AK-47s purchased in the US then taken to Mexico and resold at three or four times the sales price.

In July 2022, federal agents discovered a massive gun smuggling operation with ties to the Mexican cartel inside a home in southwest Arlington. According to media reports, at the home, inside a closet, ATF agents found one hundred fifty empty gun boxes. Jose Carlos Rivas-Chairez, a Mexican citizen who lived at the home, paid more than a half-dozen US residents to buy guns for him and admitted he disabled the guns, wrapped them in plastic, hid them in car tires, and smuggled them to Mexico. The ATF special agent in charge said when federal law enforcement ramped

1. Sam Garcia, "How Texas's Gun Laws Allow Mexican Cartels to Arm Themselves to the Teeth," *The Guardian*, October 17, 2022.

up gun trafficking efforts in border cities, the cartels started looking north into the Dallas / Fort Worth area for straw buyers.

Operation Southbound is a federal operation implemented with the goal of disrupting gun trafficking to Mexico. The operation resulted in the seizure of some two thousand firearms from October 2022 to March 2023—a 65 percent increase compared to the same period the year prior.

Operation Without a Trace, an operation by Homeland Security Investigations and US Customs and Border Protection to intercept illegal guns, is said to have resulted in 534 investigations and the seizure of $29 million. Further, more than twelve hundred guns, forty-seven hundred magazines for semi-automatic and automatic weapons, and seven hundred thousand rounds of ammunition were seized, all of which were believed to have been headed to Mexico.

Following a CBS investigation exposing Americans helping Mexican drug cartels smuggle weapons across the southern border, Senator Chuck Grassley, a Republican from Iowa, sent a letter to the head of the ATF expressing concern over reports that the ATF had defunded and shut down an interagency effort, Project Thor, an interagency initiative launched in 2018 aimed at identifying and dismantling the supply chains across the US that provided weapons to Mexican drug cartels. The effort was denied funding for fiscal year 2022 by ATF.

In his letter to ATF director Steven Dettelbach, Senator Grassley accused the bureau of directing resources away from targeting criminal actors to focus on law-abiding gun owners and sellers instead, citing its revocation of federal firearms licenses and a proposed rule that broadens the definition of who is required to become a federal firearms licensee.

During a trip to Mexico with other US officials, Attorney General Merrick Garland said that the trafficking of military-grade weapons into Mexica was a serious danger to both the United States and Mexico. "So, we will do everything in our power to stop the unlawful trafficking of weapons to the drug traffickers as part of our fight to break up every link of the chain of the drug traffickers."[2]

One commonly ignored issue is the role of corruption in the smuggling of guns into Mexico. As is the case with illegal drugs, most guns move into Mexico by land through ports of entry. All of the same issues that exist for the interdiction of drugs at busy ports of entry, many with high volumes of commercial traffic, apply to guns.

Anecdotal evidence indicates the vast majority of gun seizures occur on the US side of the border. Many of the cartels have a long-recognized history of corrupting police and government officials. There is no reason to believe the flow of guns into Mexico is not enhanced by cartel financed corruption of customs and border officials in Mexico.

"But why expose the operations this way? Why don't you make it public or be a whistleblower?" James asks.

"I like my career. Almost all of what I've worked on was for a good purpose. We've made the world better and America safer. Every organization goes askew at times. But that doesn't make it all bad, and it doesn't lead me to want to cast aside all the work I've done."

"Okay, that does make sense. Let me think on the best way to do this, but we will handle it," James says.

"That's all I ask, James. Just do what you think is right, and we will be good."

After the call ends, James leans back in his oversized office chair, letting out a deep guttural yawn. Closing his eyes for a

2. Melissa Quinn and E.D. Cauchi, "Grassley Pushes Biden Administration for Information on Gun Trafficking into Mexico after CBS Reports Investigation," *CBS News*, October 10, 2023, https://www.cbsnews.com/news/gun-trafficking-mexico-atf-chuck-grassley-cbs-reports/.

moment, James shakes his body back to life, sits up, and dials a number on his office phone.

"Hola."

"Rosalia, it's James."

"James, how are you?"

"I'm good. I have some news for you," James says.

"Okay," Rosalia replies with obvious hesitancy.

"The first thing to know is that the person who killed Joe is in custody and likely will be spending the rest of his life in prison. I can give you a lot more details if you want me to," James says.

"No, James, I don't. Joe's gone. All I care about now is that there is some justice," Rosalia says.

"You also should know that many of the traffickers who moved the drugs that could well have been the ones that killed Robby are also in custody, both in the US and in Mexico."

"How did you know about Robby?" Rosalia asks.

"It took a while to unravel, but that's why Joe was in Yuma. He was trying to track down the source of the drugs that killed Robby," James explains.

"I had no idea," Rosalia says, her voice quivering.

"As I said, it took Erica and me a while to get to the bottom of it, and then we were fortunate to finish what he started, with the help of some very kind and talented friends," James says.

"Thank you, James," Rosalia says.

"We all wanted to do right by him. The last thing for you to know is that in the next day or two, there is going to be a press conference where a reporter is going to present to the world evidence that the CIA was involved with Mexican drug traffickers for many years," James says.

"What does that have to do with Joe?" Rosalia asks.

"Without going into detail, none of those revelations would have come to light if Joe hadn't started investigating in Yuma. Joe was a hero in life and in death," James says.

"That means so much to me, James," Rosalia says, weeping.

"For obvious reasons, most of this really should stay between us. We don't want anyone else getting caught up in this mess," James says.

"I understand, James. Joe was proud of you and would be proud of how you furthered his memory in my heart," Rosalia says.

"Joe meant a lot to me, and you do too," James says.

"Promise me you and Erica will visit soon," Rosalia requests.

"We will, and Erica wanted me to tell you she will call you tomorrow," James says.

"Be well, James."

"You too, Rosalia."

"Oh, hell. He's the CIA contractor or consultant; I can't remember which," Erica proclaims.

"The what?" James asks.

"Sorry. When Tim and I were talking, he said the drive was sent by a contractor or consultant who worked with the CIA. I got the sense that person had a lot of power and access," Erica says.

James holds a finger to his lips and points to the patio. Erica follows him outside, and James slides the door shut behind them.

"It makes sense," James says in a whisper. "Tim and Aguilar knew where we were because the CIA started tracking us sometime after I first met Tim in his office. This mystery man could find us then because he had access to that same monitoring. That's how he knew how to lead us and how Tim and Aguilar knew about our plans for Mazatlán."

"They probably have us bugged. What do we do now?" Erica asks.

"I sure as hell am not going to be led around like some show dog. First, let's get Bobby over here to sweep for bugs. And the office too. After we are cleared, let's call Brian Wilson and arrange his press conference so he can tell the world his friend Gary Webb was closer to the truth than anyone knew," James says.

"Without exposing Tim," Erica clarifies.

"Right. If Julia is as good as I think she is, we might just pull it off," James states.

"What about Tim?" Erica asks.

"I'm going to go for a walk and call him now. Let him know the plan," James says.

"It's going to be tricky for him no matter what we do," Erica says.

"I know, and I'm sure he understands that," James says. "Can you handle things with Bobby?"

"I can, and I will. You talk to Tim and make sure he knows we have his back. I'm going to call Belmonte and fill him in," Erica says.

"Good idea. But isn't it a bit late?"

"Yeah, but Belmonte said he often works late, so I might as well try now."

James rides the elevator down to the lobby, then walks through the clubhouse and out to the pool area. Finding the area abnormally quiet, James takes a chair to the farthest end of the pool and dials Tim.

"James, what's up?" Tim answers.

"We need to talk."

"Sounds ominous."

"Remember how, when we were in Mexico, Erica and I alluded to someone giving us information?" James asks.

"I do remember that," Tim replies. "I also remember dropping the subject when you didn't want to share."

"I know. Well, the person who's been feeding us tips appears to be the same person who sent us the thumb drive," James says.

"Oh, hell! That's not good. Not good at all," Tim says.

"It gets worse," James says.

"Really? How does it get worse?"

"He's getting impatient with the fact that I haven't 'used' the information yet," James says.

"Not a surprise." Tim pauses for a moment. "What are you going to do?"

"We are going to follow the plan. Erica and Julia have removed your name—heck, everyone's names—from the documents. I paid Julia very well, by the way, and you owe me. Then Webb's reporter friend is going to tell the world about the CIA's bad acts without ever having seen or heard your name," James says.

"Okay. That all sounds good," Tim says.

"But . . .?" James asks.

"But Arthur—that's his name, by the way. Arthur Collins," Tim says.

"Sounds British and made up," James says.

"Probably is," Tim agrees.

"He doesn't sound British," James says.

"In any event, he still has my name and access to all the old records," Tim says.

"Right. We have a little surprise for him that may impact his ability to use those documents going forward. But, and you know this as well as I do, even if we stay in front of this as best we can, we still might not be able to prevent you from being exposed." James takes a deep breath. "You're my friend. You're Erica's friend. You were Aguilar's friend. If there is a better path, we will find it."

"James, relax. I'm a spy. It goes with the territory. I've taken steps. Do what you think is best and let the chips falls where they may," Tim says.

"Are you sure?" James asks.

"I'm sure," Tim confirms.

"What is Arthur's problem with you?" James asks.

"I don't think it is me exactly. At some point, I think, maybe he lost faith in what the agency was doing. The line between the good guys and the bad guys got blurrier, and his faith in the mission waned."

With James gone, Erica calls Belmonte at his office.

"Agent Pfeiffer."

"I'm sorry," Erica says, "Agent Pfeiffer?"

"Yes, ma'am. DEA Agent Scott Pfeiffer."

"I'm terribly sorry. I was trying to reach Agent Belmonte. I thought this was his number," Erica says.

"Let me transfer you to someone who can help."

After a few moments of silence, another voice takes over. "DEA."

"Yes, I am trying to reach Agent Bill Belmonte," Erica says.

"I'm sorry. Agent Belmonte has been transferred."

"Transferred? To where?" Erica asks.

"I'm not at liberty to disclose that information."

"Okay, can you give me his new telephone number?" Erica asks.

"I'm sorry, I'm not at liberty to disclose that information."

"Okay, I get it. Thank you."

Erica hangs up and searches her cell phone for the number Belmonte had used to call her, the one he said was "safe." Finding it, she quickly hits call but hears only a voice mail message.

"This is Bill. Leave me a message, and I'll get back to you soon."

"Bill, it's Erica. I'm worried about you. Please call me back as soon as possible."

TWENTY-SEVEN

"THANK you all for coming today on such short notice. My name is Brian Wilson, and Gary Webb was a friend of mine."

A whisper of the Santa Ana winds turning this June day oppressively hot floats through downtown Los Angels. Wilson stands on the white marble steps of the Downtown Los Angeles Federal Courthouse on Main Street before a small gathering of print and television media.

"Today, I am announcing that at 5 p.m. local time, I will publish on a new website the first installment of a series that, based on a trove of discovered documents, establishes that Gary was correct, and the CIA was responsible for much of the proliferation of crack cocaine in our nation's inner cities and did so in order to surreptitiously fund the Contras in Nicaragua.

"But, Gary, God bless his soul, had seen only the tip of the proverbial iceberg. My reporting will go far beyond America's inner cities and the Nicaraguan Contras and expose the CIA's toxic alliance with drug traffickers around the globe. The CIA, and other intelligence agencies of the United States, have been key actors behind the proliferation of narcotics throughout the world since the end of World War II and have used their control of these trades to fund a wide range of covert black ops in this hemisphere and across the world, including operations against US allies and in contravention to stated foreign policies.

"From Operation Gladio to the onset of opium production in Afghanistan, to Colombian cocaine and Mexican marijuana, to the Fast and Furious Operations and a divide-and-conquer strategy that allowed certain drug dealers to reap the rewards of billions of dollars in profits, the CIA's fingerprints are a defining and consistent feature of the expansion of narcotics trafficking across the globe.

"Closely intertwined with these efforts, the CIA has also engaged in a series of clandestine actions to topple regimes. Some, like the overthrowing of the prime minister of Iran, are well-known. Others, such as the disposition and eventual murder of Congolese prime minister Patrice Lumumba, are less known. But they all are significant and present a clear picture of an intelligence community often operating outside its authorization and contrary to its enacting mission.

"In the articles to come, I will present internal CIA documents to paint a picture of a government agency acting outside its authorized scope, without oversight, and with virtual impunity. Governments, policies, and American ideals became meaningless to a select few, erroneously convinced of the righteousness of their path and the morale deficiencies of those who dared to question their motives or actions. Theirs is a path accelerated by the events of November 1963 and propelled in the decades since by blood money from drug trafficking, while turning a blind eye to the death and destruction left in their wake, both in the United States and across the world," Brian states.

"My friend Gary was able to piece together the damning evidence of the CIA's malfeasance, even if not all of his allegations hit their marks. But Gary was neither the first nor the last. Others have risked their careers and even lives to expose the truth. The reporting to come, by me and the journalists who I have no doubt will pursue the evidence further than have I, is made to honor them: their courage, their dedication, and their unwavering faith that the United States of America stands for liberty, justice, and, yes, even truth, and their dedication to exposing those governmental elements that fall short of that ideal."

"How did you come into possession of the documents to which you refer?" a young woman from NBC asks.

"They were delivered to me anonymously on a computer disc that appears to be untraceable," Brian explains.

"You mentioned operations. What about personnel? Do you know who was in charge of or involved in the operations?" a reporter from the *LA Times* asks.

"Interestingly enough, the documents provide operational names, dates, locations, and details, but, as best I can tell, every name of a living person has been changed to a character from a superhero story," Wilson replies.

"A superhero story?" asks another reporter.

"In most instances where there is or should be the name of a person involved, the names have been replaced by the name of a character from the worlds of DC and Marvel comics. We have Batman, Superman, Wonder Woman, Iron Man, and so on. But, it's critical to state, only the names are affected. It appears clear that everything else needed to identify and trace the operations is present and laid out in great detail," Wilson says.

"From the materials you have reviewed, did the CIA commit any crimes of either US or international law?" asks a man from *Buzzfeed*.

Rebecca Talbot, who has been standing one step up on the stairs and just over Wilson's left shoulder, moves forward to the microphone to speak. "Mr. Wilson is not going to opine on the legality of any of the actions by the CIA revealed by the documents. That's a determination to be made by others at another time. Mr. Wilson's point is that the documents demonstrate elements of the CIA acted contrary to stated national policies and in ways that directly benefitted criminal organizations, most notably Mexican cartels, the same cartels that have flooded American streets with illegal drugs costing Americans hundreds of thousands of lives and millions, if not billions, of dollars."

After listening to the first few press questions from the back, James quietly steps away, turning right to walk down Main Street toward City Hall. Passing a doorway, James stops upon hearing a friendly voice.

"Mr. Wilson was pretty good. When I heard Brian Wilson would be performing today, I was pretty excited, but I thought he would sing Beach Boys songs. I was hoping for 'Good Vibrations.' The courthouse did seem like an odd venue."

"Tim, how are you?" James asks.

"I'm good. Dealing with the fallout. But good. Let's walk," Tim says.

"Should you be seen walking the streets?" James questions semi-humorously.

"Relax, James. It's all good," Tim says.

"We kept your name out of it," James says.

"I heard. Thanks, but comic book characters?" Tim asks.

"Julia and Erica came up with that idea. Julia said AI tools made it pretty easy, but that's way outside my technical knowledge," James says.

"However, it was done, I do appreciate it," Tim says.

"I intentionally did not look at the details until after the names were changed, so I don't know what you did other than what you told Erica and me. And I don't care," James says truthfully.

"I told you most of it, and you know my roles. I'm a facilitator and fixer. I execute plans. I don't define agenda, and I don't set policy on a large or small scale," Tim says.

"Either way, it wouldn't affect our friendship," James says.

"I know. There are things I've been involved in that I'm not proud of. At first, I was just doing what I was told. Now, I'm not

William Calley, and I'm not asserting a Nuremberg Defense, but back then I was young, idealistic, and impressionable."

Superior orders, or more colloquially "just following orders," is a concept of criminal law asserting a person, whether a member of the military, law enforcement, or the civilian population, should not be considered guilty of committing actions that were ordered by a superior officer or official.

One of the most notable uses of this concept was by defendants during the post-World War II Nuremberg trials in 1945 and 1946. These trials generally determined that the defense of superior orders was not sufficient to avoid punishment but could be enough to reduce a punishment or sentence. Nevertheless, the use of the defense was so prominent that the assertion became commonly referred to as the Nuremberg Defense.

The concept of superior orders also was applied to an infamous tragedy from the Vietnam conflict. Following the Mỹ Lai massacre in 1968, the defense in the court-martial of William Calley sought to apply the doctrine as a defense. In some ways, the outcome of the Mỹ Lai trial was contrary to the principals of the laws of war set forth in the Nuremberg tribunal. Secretary of the Army Howard Callaway was quoted in the New York Times as stating that Calley's sentence was reduced because Calley believed that what he did was a part of his orders. Calley was said to have used the exact phrase "just following orders" when confronted by another American soldier about the ongoing massacre.

A number of subsequent decisions have modified these principles to hold that the justification for acts done pursuant to orders does not exist if the order was of such a nature that a man of ordinary sense and understanding would know it to be illegal.

From this perspective, an order from a superior may have a basis in the laws of a nation. But Nuremberg Principle IV acknowledges that, at the same time, such an order may also be unlawful under prevailing international law. These principles thus seem to create an inherent dilemma—to refuse to follow a valid order could subject one to punishment at a national level, but to follow the order risks punishment under international law. Principle IV further states: "The fact that a person acted pursuant to order of his Government or of a superior does not relieve him from responsibility under international law, provided a moral choice was in fact possible to him."[1]

"I thought you were a SEAL before you ever got involved with the CIA?" James asks.

"Well, the truth is a little different. I was recruited to Langley in college and stayed with them while I was in the SEALs and my time in Central America," Tim explains.

"So then when you were 'exiled' to the Balkans, it wasn't so much a punishment as it was a mission?" James asks.

"More or less. I was still working, but by then I'd ruffled a few too many feathers. It was not a desirable location," Tim says.

"Not a hot spot for CIA officers? "James teases.

"Funny, but no. Point is, I'd been with the agency for a long time, and for better or worse, I usually thought I was doing the right thing, at least in the big picture. And, believe it or not, we did quite a bit of good. That doesn't make all of my crooked straight, but it does help me sleep at night," Tim says.

"Understood. I didn't need an explanation, but thanks," James says.

"You know this isn't going to stop him," Tim says.

"Arthur? No, I don't suspect it will," James replies. "Can he cause you much harm?"

"Me?" Tim asks with a laugh. "Not much. Changes will be

1. Wikipedia, s.v. "Nuremberg Principles," last modified April 2, 2024, https://en.wikipedia.org/wiki/Nuremberg_principles.

coming, but I do have a very particular set of skills. Skills I have acquired over a very long career. Skills that make me a nightmare if on the open market. There will be a home for me somewhere."

"Good to know, Liam. Good to know," James says.

"I'm more worried about you and Erica," Tim says.

"We will be fine. It helps to know the players and motivations now. And we might still have a trick or two up our sleeves," James says.

"I wouldn't doubt the two of you for a second," Tim says.

"I do have a few unanswered questions," James says.

"About me?" Tim asks.

"No, in general. About Aguilar," James says.

"Let's hear them," Tim says.

"I think the big one is how did Javier know Aguilar was a part of the group that snagged Rafa? I mean, he never saw Aguilar in Mexico. Erica says he told her he sent a picture of the guy asking questions to Rafa who identified Aguilar, but that doesn't make any sense to me."

"Why would he send a picture of someone asking questions about fentanyl to Rafa in jail?" Tim asks.

"Exactly," James says.

"The answer, I think," Tim states, "is that he wouldn't send a picture to Rafa, but he *would* send one to his CIA handler."

"But you were his handler, and you said he never communicated with you once he was in Yuma," James asks.

"Was I though? Or better said, was I the only one?" wonders Tim.

"Ahhh! That's right, Erica said he alluded to another handler. How did I forget that?" James says, internally scolding himself.

"Don't beat yourself up, there has been *a lot* going on. What if Arthur was monitoring enough of my work that he knew I'd sent Javier to look into the person asking the questions? Maybe he got the picture from Javier and knew it was Aguilar and knew of his role in Rafa's incarceration?" Tim posits.

"But that's a well-kept secret, or so I thought," James says.

"Truth is James, there are few well-kept secrets within the intelligence community or within the CIA more specifically. Not to mention the amount of gossip, innuendo, and plain speculation," Tim states.

"But why kill Aguilar?" James asks.

"I'm afraid I'm stumped there too. Ask Arthur the next time you talk to him," Tim suggests.

"I just may do that," James says.

"I was kidding, but it would be interesting to hear his response. I probably should disappear. I'm not too worried but don't want to be reckless," Tim says.

"One last thing, real fast?" James asks.

"Sure."

"Did you look at the documents on the drive?" James asks.

"No, I was only told what was on it. I saw just a smidgen at your house. Why?" Tim asks.

"Erica has looked more than me, but my perception is that there are a huge number of documents. Could your name really have been on all of them?" James asks.

"Why does that matter?" Tim asks.

"I'm not sure. It's nothing specific," James says, "but something doesn't feel quite right."

I don't know." Tim shrugs. "I'm probably on a lot, and I just assumed what I'd heard was true. What are you thinking?"

"I'm not sure," James says. "Just trying to consider all the angles."

"You do that, but now, I really must be going," Tim says.

"Okay. You take care of yourself. If you don't, Erica will be really pissed off," James warns.

"I would not want that. It's been nice to catch up, James. You know—"

"I know. Now go," James says.

The men turn to walk in opposite directions, until Tim turns around. "And James?"

"Yeah?" James says, turning toward Tim.

"You are going to be a great father."

TWENTY-EIGHT

James's and Erica's heads are buried in their laptops as they sit on the sofa, the screen door to the patio letting in the cool, autumn air, when James receives a text from Tim: *If you are near a TV, turn on Channel 4 news. After the commercial break.*

James shows the text to Erica while retrieving the remote and turning on the big screen.

"We've been following the stunning revelation last week of documents indicating that the CIA has been responsible for the importation of vast quantities of drugs from Mexico for many years and profited from those transactions. Now, in a Channel 4 exclusive, we have learned that a CIA officer responsible for many of these activities, which are alleged to have funded off-the-book operations around the world, has been fronting as a private investigator in Pacific Palisades. We went to the offices of Tim Speer to ask him about these allegations and his role but, when we arrived at his tony office, it was empty and abandoned."

James turns off the television. "Damn it."

"You had to figure it was going to come out," Erica says

"I did, but I was still hopeful," James admits.

James's cell phone rings. "It's Tim," he says to Erica while putting the call on speaker.

"Tim!" James says.

"Did you hear that? I had a 'tony' office. That's good right?" Tim laughs.

"You're conspicuously upbeat, considering," Erica chimes in.

"Ah, don't worry about it. I expected this and am prepared," Tim says.

"How did you know when the piece was going to air?" Erica asks.

"An anonymous tip," Tim answers.

"Right, real anonymous," Erica comments.

"I'm not sure I understand the full objective here," James says.

"I'm not completely certain myself, but Arthur seems to have decided that the CIA was misguided in its efforts in Mexico, notwithstanding his participation over the years," Tim scoffs.

"Arthur?" Erica asks.

"Yes, the consultant. Arthur Collins," Tim answers.

"I don't think I had heard his name before. He was just, well, 'he,'" Erica says.

"Why the change of heart?" James asks.

"No idea. It's all gone down pretty fast, so I haven't been able to connect the dots," Tim says.

"What are you going to do? Where are you going?" Erica asks.

"I can't tell you that," Tim says.

"I understand. But please take care of yourself," Erica says.

"Of course, I will. I've watched every episode of *Burn Notice*," Tim replies.

"We'll meet you in Miami then," James observes.

"Maybe not Miami, but I'll see you soon. When are you due, Erica?" Tim asks.

"November 27."

"Oh, close to Thanksgiving!" Tim says excitedly.

"No, she's due exactly on Thanksgiving," James says.

"That's poetic. I'm happy for both of you. Very happy. Take good care, you two," Tim says.

With those words, the phone goes silent. James plops back down on the sofa.

"He'll be fine," Erica reassures him.

"Tim has nine lives. I just wonder how many he's used up."

Erica and James sit in silence for a minute, ruminating over recent events.

"James, I think I understand a lot now," Erica says.

"Me too, but you go first," James offers.

"After Belmonte and I visited Javier in jail, I told you he said something about another CIA handler or connection, right?" Erica asks.

"Yes, I remember that," James says.

"But I don't think I mentioned his name," Erica says.

"Arthur?" James asks.

"Close. Art," Erica says.

"Wow. So, our friend Arthur, in addition to working with Tim on assignments in Mexico, was working against him or at least separate from him," James says.

"Right, but to what end?" Erica asks.

"I'm not sure I have a good answer prior to Aguilar asking questions, but from then on I have a theory," James says.

"Let's hear it."

"Posit this. CIA has been involved in Mexico and with the traffickers for years, well beyond what Tim knows about or was involved in. Aguilar starts asking questions which could expose some or many of those activities. Arthur identifies Aguilar in some way and becomes so concerned that he might be on to something that he has Javier kill him," James says.

"Then why send us the files?" Erica asks.

"Outside people might start looking into things. He can protect his identity and protect much of the information by presenting Tim to the world with enough documents to make it all look legit," James explains.

"But won't that lead to investigations, congressional, internal, or otherwise?" Erica asks.

"Perhaps, but how many of those investigations are going to even think about looking beyond Tim, who they have been gifted on a silver platter, and that is even more the case if some of those doing the investigations actually approve of or condone the CIA's actions," James states.

"Okay, then why Tim?" Erica asks.

"I think Tim was involved enough that the allegations seem plausible. Heck, even Tim accepts it. But when we talked the other day, I asked him if he looked through the documents on the drive, and he said only a few of them. How hard would it have been to insert Tim's name on more than he was involved in, knowing that he couldn't deny a lot and attempts to disclaim involvement on other aspects would be received skeptically at best?" James says.

"I think I should have asked Javier one other question," Erica says.

"That question would be what?" James asks.

"Who sent him to kill me?" Erica asks.

"If it wasn't Rafa, then it had to have been Arthur," James surmises.

"My thought exactly," Erica agrees.

"Well, then, my dear Sherlock, why did Aguilar tell me it was 'bigger than we knew'?" James asks.

"It's rather quite elementary. Aguilar was a more intuitive investigator than Arthur or anyone else realized. Aguilar became aware that he was being watched and/or followed in Yuma, went back to San Antonio, and used his old connections to dig up information about some of the CIA's involvement in the drug trade, in addition to what is available on the web. He knew he was walking into a dangerous situation in Yuma but went back the last time not to investigate fentanyl but to investigate the CIA's role. When he realized his life was in danger that night, he called you to warn you—to warn us. I think he was likely going to try to leave Yuma immediately after the call. He thought he had time, or had given Javier the slip, but Javier caught up to him," Erica says.

"I like it. Two questions though. First, how did Javier know it was me on the line when Aguilar was shot?" James asks.

"Arthur might have told him to look out for us, under the assumption that Arthur knew some or all about Mexico and Rafa," Erica answers.

"I can work with that. Then how did Javier know to call me when Bobby and I were leaving Yuma?" James asks.

"Same answer. Arthur," Erica says.

"Or, I gave my business card to two people. Larry, the hotel clerk, and the woman at the restaurant," James suggests.

"One of them must have been connected to the guys at the gas station," Erica says.

"Larry. That weaselly SOB." James reflects for a moment before exclaiming, "Oh, of course."

"What?"

"He said he wasn't aware Aguilar had stayed at the hotel before he was murdered, but said he recognized Aguilar's picture from the news. I can't believe Bobby and I didn't press him on the idea that no one else who worked at the hotel mentioned that Aguilar stayed there. It's a small town. Someone who worked there would have said something," James says.

"Unless he already knew or had even interacted with Aguilar at the hotel and lied to you," Erica says.

"In that case, the two thugs in Yuma could well be connected to the traffickers, and totally unaware of any CIA involvement," James says.

"Agreed. So, what do we do now?" Erica asks.

"Well, we messed up part of his plan through the press conference. It's going to be harder to sweep things under the rug now with all the eyes on the materials," James suggests.

"I think it's time to screw with him a bit more," Erica says, picking up her phone. "Julia," she notes.

ERICA

Hi Julia. Do you have the computer virus ready?

JULIA

I do. Ready to go at any time.

And you are sure it won't be traced back to you?

Positive. It's going to bounce off so many cells and through so many VPNs it will be untraceable. You're comfortable with the effect?

Very comfortable with the intended effect. In fact, it's going to make me feel warm and fuzzy inside.

Very well. Just tell me when.

Fire when ready.

Gone!

Thanks Julia. Look for a transfer coming your way tomorrow.

Thank you. I appreciate it.

James and I appreciate you.

"Julia says the virus has been sent. If you listen carefully, you should be hearing screams of horror from Arthur soon," Erica tells James.

"He's not going to be happy," James says.

"No, not happy at all," Erica agrees.

"He may come after us," James states.

"And if he does?" Erica asks.

"We push back even harder."

TWENTY-NINE

"THAT WAS A STUPID STUNT, JAMES," Arthur says.

"Stupid? I thought Brian was very photogenic and articulate," James says.

"I'm not talking about the press conference. I'm talking about my files," Arthur says.

"What about your files?" James asks.

"They're gone. Deleted. Destroyed," Arthur says.

"Really? I hate it when that happens. Did you back them up? Maybe on a cloud site . . . Spooks are Us? I'm sure you'll restore some of them," James says.

"Yes, I'll get them back, but it will take time and resources," Arthur says bitterly.

"That's really too bad," James says.

"I know it was you. Or someone helping you," Arthur says.

"Why would I do that?" James asks.

"I don't know, James. I thought we had a nice discussion the last time we talked," Arthur says.

"It was nice, but then I was thinking about it later and realized something important," James says.

"What was that?" Arthur asks.

"That you were lying to me the entire time," James says.

"I'm offended. I would never," Arthur protests.

"Give it a rest, Arthur," James says coolly.

"What?" Arthur asks. There's a commotion over the phone, like he's dropped something or maybe slammed something down.

"That's right. I know who you are and what your plan was," James says.

"And what do you think that plan was?" Arthur asks.

"Tim Speer might have thought he was running things in Mexico, but he was really being played like a pawn in a chess game," James says.

"By whom?" Arthur asks.

"Well, you, of course. But then Aguilar starts looking at things in Arizona, and you are worried he might find something, so you have him killed. Then, the *coup de gras* was pinning it all on the person you programmed to do your dirty work," James says.

"I may have underestimated you, James. But you are still playing a dangerous game, above your capabilities," Arthur says.

"I doubt that, but, since we now understand each other, I am curious how you were able to manage Aguilar's movements in Yuma, at least on the last trip," James says.

"As so often is the case, it's much simpler than you might think. I just called him and told him I was Bill Belmonte. Belmonte had arrested Javier years earlier, so it would make sense if he asked anyone. And, I'll let you in on a secret. Tell someone you are DEA in person, and they are likely to ask for identification. But no one ever questions it when you call them. It's odd but true," Arthur says.

"But Aguilar had Belmonte's number in his files. Belmonte's correct number," James says.

"Yes, and he had it in his phone too. I used that number to call and talk to him," Arthur explains.

"But, how?" James asks.

"Let's say I have access to sources of information and technologies you cannot imagine. You'd do well to remember that," Arthur warns.

"That's why Javier took his cell phone after he shot him," James says, comprehension washing over him.

"Right, and a notebook you didn't even know about," Arthur says.

"But why kill him? Why not just manipulate him out of the way?" James asks.

"Loose ends, James. I can't afford loose ends," Arthur says.

"You killed a decorated DEA agent. He was a lot more than loose ends," James says.

"That's the difference between you and me," Arthur explains. "You are emotional. In my world, emotions lead to operational failures and can get you killed. I dealt with the situation according to my training and experience."

"But here is where it *is* emotional, Arthur. You sent Javier after my wife, in my offices," James says.

"That was Caro Quintero," Arthur says.

"Nice try, but it was you cloaked in whatever deceptions you like. The moment Javier set a foot in my office, you crossed a line from which you can never walk back," James says.

"That sounds like a threat," Arthur says.

"Good. Then you heard me correctly," James states.

"You are playing on a level you cannot even comprehend. If you threaten me, I threaten back. If you push me, I push back. Harder. I'm reminded of the line often attributed to Machiavelli: 'Power is the pivot on which everything hinges. He who has the power is always right; the weaker is always wrong.'" Arthur says.

"Ignoring that your quote is almost universally misunderstood, including, apparently, by you, I have a quote of my own," James says.

"Oh?"

"There was an old television show I really liked. The story isn't important, but there was one particular line in an episode I really like, and I find it uniquely applicable," James says.

"Oh? What's that?"

"It's from a tough guy character who had just been threatened, and he says something like, 'Any time. Any place. If you're feeling froggish little man, then leap.'"

Erica and Brian's legal assistant, Jessica Sievers, arrive back at the office after a quick lunch at a bistro near South Coast Plaza. After some chit-chat in the lobby, Erica walks back to her office, sits at her desk, and takes her cell phone from her purse, which she places in a desk drawer. Looking at the phone before shutting the drawer, Erica is surprised and relieved to see a voicemail from Belmonte:

"Erica, hi, it's Bill Belmonte. Sorry to have been radio silent for a bit but that's how things work in this business at times. I really didn't mean to worry you. I'm fine, and I will be, but I worry about you and James. There seems to be a lot of activity underneath the surface surrounding the Aguilar case. I'll be back in touch soon and we can talk more then. Take care."

Erica reflects momentarily before returning the call to Belmonte's "safe" phone. Erica is shocked when she gets a recording, not Belmonte:

"We're sorry. The number you have reached has been disconnected or is no longer in service. If you feel you have reached this recording in error, please check the number, and try again."

Erica hangs up and immediately redials, only to reach the same recording.

Erica then sends an email to Belmonte's DEA address. Instantaneously, she receives a reply email: Agent Belmonte can no longer be reached at this email address. For further information, please call 202-555-1111.

Oh Bill, I'm so sorry if we caused you harm.

James has wrapped up a lunch meeting at Great Maple at Fashion Island. On this sunny day, he has eschewed his normal suit for a lavender polo shirt and black slacks. As fortune had it, James was able to find a parking spot in the lot immediately adjacent to the restaurant. Leaving his companion at the door, James strolls toward his car, enjoying the beauty of the day. Reaching his car, James climbs in and presses the start button when the tranquility is pierced by the sirens from two Newport Beach police cars, lights flashing, that stop to pin James into his parking spot. James puts his hands on the steering wheel.

"Get out the car with your hands up," an officer instructs over the car's loudspeaker.

James does as directed and climbs out of the car, hands high above his head, palms clearly visible. "What's going on? What's this about?"

"Shut up, turn around, and hands on the car," says the voice over the loudspeaker.

James complies, leaning against his car. A tall, lanky male officer cuffs James, turns him around, and leads him several feet from the car.

Another officer immediately searches the main compartment of the car. "Nothing here," she shouts.

"Can we search your trunk?" the tall officer asks James.

"Not unless you tell me what you are looking for," James says.

"We had a tip that this car had a kidnapped child in it," the female officer says.

"What do you mean this car?" James asks.

"The tip included the license plate number," the tall officer says.

"That's convenient. Look in the trunk. Look anywhere you want. There's not a child in the car; in fact, there's never been a child in that car," James says.

The female officer pops the trunk and looks inside. "There's no child, but there is something suspicious." She holds up a brick-sized bundle tightly wrapped in plastic wrap. "Could be marijuana."

A third car, unmarked but with police lights flashing, enters the scene, and out exits Detective David Torres. "What do we have here?" he asks approaching the scene.

"Suspect is cooperating. No child found, but a suspicious item found in the trunk," the female officer says.

"Can you say what it is for sure?" Torres asks.

"No, but it could be marijuana," she answers.

"Have you conducted an extensive search of the car?" Torres asks.

"No, not yet," she says.

"You wouldn't mind, would you James?" Torres asks.

"Mind, why would I possibly mind?" James questions.

"Before you do that, uncuff Mr. Butler, and I'll stay with him," Torres says.

The female officer does as she's told, then joins the other officer in the car search.

"What do you make of this, James?" Torres inquires.

"An anonymous tip, with a license plate number, by someone who knew where I was having lunch, and a mystery package left in plain sight. What does that say to you?" James posits.

"Sounds like someone set you up," Torres responds.

"My thought exactly," James says.

"Any ideas?" Torres asks.

"Maybe, but I'd prefer not to guess at this point," James says.

"Fair enough. What if the package contains something illegal?" Torres asks.

"I've got a hunch it won't but, if it does, I'll deal with it," James says.

"*We'll* deal with it. I'm not going to participate in a set up if I can avoid it," Torres says.

"I appreciate that," James says.

"The car is clean. I mean spic and span clean," the tall officer reports back to Torres.

"What can I say? I like a clean car," James says.

"All right. You take the package to the lab and get them to process it immediately and deliver the results to me and only to me. Understood?" Torres orders.

"Yes, sir. Understood," both officers respond in unison.

"I'll take Mr. Butler with me. I'll need his car key and his phone from the car. We can leave his car here for now," Torres says.

"Am I under arrest?" James asks.

"No, you're not, at the moment, but I'm going to need to take you into the station while we run tests to see what's in this package," Torres explains.

"And if I refuse?" James asks.

"You're not going to make things difficult for me, are you?" Torres asks.

"No, I'm not, but I wanted to see you sweat a little," James says. "Can I have my phone to call Brian and have him meet us at the station? Since I'm not under arrest."

"Sure. You can call him from the car. I'll drive you to the station unless you'd prefer a ride in a squad car," Torres says.

"Your car will be just fine," James says.

A few minutes later, Torres's car turns off Jamboree Road onto Santa Barbara Drive in front of the police station.

"I've always thought this was an odd location for a police station," James observes. "Across the street in one direction is a Land Rover dealership and in the other direction is the Newport Beach Country Club golf course. Who said, 'Here is where our police department shall be?'"

Torres ignores James's comment and parks in the side parking lot. Torres opens the back door to let James out, and the two walk into the station.

"I'm glad I got a haircut yesterday," James says. "I'll look good for the mugshot."

"You know the procedure . . . no arrest, no mugshot," Torres explains.

"No exceptions? I was thinking it might make for a nice Christmas card," James says.

"No exceptions. You're taking this pretty well, considering," Torres observes.

"I didn't do anything, and I have a pretty good idea who's behind this, so no need to panic. Yet," James says.

"Follow me. I'm going to put you in an interrogation room until I can get a determination on the contents of that pack," Torres says.

"No problem. Will you let Brian in when he gets here?" James requests.

"Of course," Torres agrees.

After a few restless minutes alone in the interrogation room, James is relieved to hear a knock on the door, followed by Brian Castle entering the room and sitting across from James at the table.

"I always knew you'd end up like this, but I didn't expect it to be so soon," Brian jests.

"Not funny. But thanks for coming," James says.

"Of course. So, what happened?" Brian asks.

"An 'anonymous' tip said there was a kidnapped child in my car. The tip included my license plate number. I was getting ready to drive back to the office after a lunch meeting, but, before I could even get out of the parking spot, I was blocked by two squad cars and officers with drawn guns. They quickly determined there was no child in the car, but while looking they found a bundle of, let's say, plants in the trunk. Fortunately for me, Dave, or I should say, Detective Torres, arrived, and I agreed to come in while they determined the nature of the aforementioned plants," James answers.

"Seems like a classic set up," Brian says.

"It was. Even Torres said so, which probably is the only reason I'm not in cuffs or under arrest," James says.

"Who do you suspect is behind this?" Brian asks.

"I have a pretty good idea, but this might not be the best place to say more. I don't trust that no one is listening," James says.

"Enough said. Did Erica tell you about her call from Agent Belmonte?" Brian asks.

"No, she didn't. I've been running around all day, and we've barely spoken," James says.

"Apparently, Belmonte left her a voicemail saying he was okay but worried about you and Erica. But when Erica tried to call him back just a few minutes later, she got a recording that the number had been disconnected."

"Oh no. That is troubling. Deeply troubling."

"I assume it's all connected—Aguilar, Javier, Speer, this, Belmonte, all of it," Brian says.

"I think so. Intricately connected," James agrees.

With those words, Detective Torres returns to the interrogation room. "You're free to go."

"What about the package from his car?" Brian asks.

"The lab says it was a combination of industrial hemp, a plant called kenaf, and mint. Not marijuana and not illegal. But it did smell nice. Here is the fob to your car," Torres says.

"Good to hear. I'll take up the issue of the detainment later," Brian responds.

"I'm sure you will," Torres says. "I'm sorry, James. My hands were tied."

"Don't worry about it, Dave. You were doing your job. We're good," James says.

James and Brian walk through the station, using the main exit facing south to Santa Barbara Drive.

"Will you take me to my car? It should still be in the parking lot, still in the spot where it was parked," James says.

"Of course. I'm parked on the side, way in the back," Brian says.

Once safely in Brian's car, Brian revisits the conversation from the interrogation room. "You said you have a good idea who is behind this. Who do you think?"

"The CIA consultant, Arthur. Erica and I have consciously not given you too many details, but I think he is the one pulling the strings behind everything."

"Then why set you up with something not illegal?" Brian asks.

"To prove he can. It's a warning of sorts," James says.

"But if you are now mortal enemies, why not get you arrested? Wouldn't that be his best revenge?"

"My best guess, because he thinks I might still be of value to him," James reasons.

"In ways you have no idea of at present?" Brian asks.

"Correct," James confirms.

"Or when he might have a need for that value to him?" Brain asks.

"Also correct."

"You, my friend, are in a very precarious and dangerous position."

THIRTY

THE UNITED STATES District Court for the Central District of California covers a wide swath of Southern California, encompassing the counties of Los Angeles, Orange, Ventura, Santa Barbara, San Louis Obispo, San Bernardino and Riverside Counites. The district's western division has two main locations in Los Angeles. The First Street US Courthouse is in the Civic Center District of downtown Los Angeles and opened in October 2016. The main federal courthouse is the Edward R. Roybal Federal Building and United States Courthouse. Named after a prominent congressman, the Roybal Building is located on Temple Street in downtown Los Angeles and opened in 1992.

Today, James is appearing in front of US Magistrate Judge Shelley Hoffman in Courtroom 790 in the Roybal Building for a late afternoon hearing. He parks in the public lots across Temple and steps across the street, then through security. Taking the elevator to the seventh floor, James steps off to find a quiet and vacant hallway; even this busy courthouse is quiet on this Friday afternoon near Christmas. James proceeds to Courtroom 790, gives the clerk his business card, and requests that his client, who has been a resident of the nearby Metropolitan Detention Center, be brought up from the holding cells in the lower level of the building.

After only a few minutes wait, his client arrives and is seated at the defense table. The assistant United States attorney arrives moments, later followed by the appearance of the magistrate judge.

"All rise. This court is now in session. The Honorable Shelley Hoffman presiding."

"Please be seated. We are here in the case of *US v. Miguel de Leon Herrara,* Case No. 2024CR14332. Can I have appearances of counsel?" the judge requests.

"AUSA Katherine Boyd for the United States, your honor."

"Good afternoon, Judge. James Butler for the defendant who is present and, I should note, does not need an interpreter."

"Thank you both. I understand the parties have reached a plea agreement?" asks the judge.

"Yes, your honor," Ms. Boyd says. "The defendant has agreed to plead guilty to counts one and two, both misdemeanors, with time served for count one and a suspended sentence of three years supervised probation for count two, and count three, which was a felony, will be dismissed."

"Is that your understanding, Mr. Butler?" the judge asks.

"It is with one additional note, your honor. Mr. de Leon is permitted to transfer his probation to a federal court in Mexico, which has already been arranged and approved, and serve the term of his suspended sentence in Mexico. Mr. de Leon has been made very well aware that any criminal infraction of any kind occurring in Mexico, or anywhere else for that matter, will result in the revocation of his sentence and his prompt return to the United States and to this court, pursuant to which he has agreed to a prospective of waiver of any rights he would have to contest extradition," James states.

"I agree with Mr. Butler's comments, your honor," Ms. Boyd confirms.

"Very well. I must say, from my vantage point, this is a

generous deal from the government. I assume this has been appropriately vetted and approved and that you believe this reduced sentence and plea agreement is in the government's best interest?" the judge asks.

"It has been approved at the highest levels. The government recognizes that this is a bit outside the box, but believes it is in the best interests of everyone involved," James says.

"That's good enough for me. It does not strike me as unconscionable. I've read the plea agreement, but would you like to present a factual proffer?"

Ms. Boyd reads the proffer, a statement of the essential facts of the case against the defendant, and James concurs on behalf of his client, at which time the judge asks Miguel to rise. Miguel rises and stands, with James next to him, as the judge advises him of his rights, the rights he is giving up, and the voluntary nature of his plea. At that point, Miguel pleads guilty, and the agreed upon sentence is formally imposed, though a federal judge is not bound by the agreement of the parties on a sentence.

"Is there anything else from the government?" Judge Hoffman asks.

"Nothing further, your honor."

"Mr. Butler, anything from the defense?"

"Nothing additional, your honor, but I thank you for the accommodations in getting this scheduled," James says.

"Happy to help, Counsel. We are adjourned. Good luck, Mr. de Leon," the judge says.

"What happens now?" Miguel asks.

"You'll go back to the MDC but should be released in an hour or so, and I'll be there waiting for you," James explains.

"Great. Thank you," Miguel says.

"Save that for when you are out," James says before turning to Ms. Boyd. "Thanks for the help, Katy."

"Happy to do it, James. Always good to help a fellow Hoosier," Katy replies.

"I think it's a good deal, and I believe in Miguel," James says.

"I think it's a good deal, and I believe in you," Ms. Boyd says. "Not to mention that it's almost never a bad career move to do a favor for a newly appointed US Attorney."

A little more than two hours later, James waits outside the processing unit at the MDC, which sits little more than a block away from the Roybal Courthouse. After a few minutes, the door opens, and Miguel appears, papers and a small bag of possessions in hand.

"Mr. Butler. Thank you," Miguel hugs James.

"It's my pleasure. Someone wants to see you but not here," James says.

"Okay, where?" Miguel asks.

"Follow me," James says.

James leads the way out of the main MDC doors and turns right, heading back toward the courthouse and his car. Once in the car, James exits the parking lot onto East Temple, followed by a quick right onto North Main Street for the two-minute drive to the Casa La Golondrina Mexican Café, a Main Street institution since 1924.

"What are we doing here?" Miguel asks.

"You'll see, but before we go, I want to say something to you," James says.

"Sure, what?" Miguel asks.

"Several people, whom you will never meet or even hear of, did favors for me to help you today. I did all of this in the belief that you are a good man who made a mistake. But I also did it because your brother did a stand-up thing for me. He asked me to look into your case and see if I could help. It would be a terrible thing if his belief in you was not warranted. Don't let him down. Go to Mexico and lead a good life that will make him—and you—proud," James says.

Miguel starts to speak but is stopped.

"You don't need to say a thing. Just do the right thing," James says.

James gets out of the car, followed by Miguel. At the front door, James opens the door for Miguel, who walks inside to cheers from several people inside.

Guillermo approaches and wraps Miguel in a bear hug.

"I am so happy to see you," Guillermo says.

"Me too. I can't tell you how much. I am never going back," Miguel promises.

"Thank you, James. For everything," Guillermo says.

"I'm happy I could help. But now I'm going to leave you two to celebrate. Miguel, please, don't screw up, and don't violate your parole," James says.

"I won't. I promise," Miguel says, shaking James's hand.

"Damn straight he won't," Guillermo reiterates.

As James starts to open the door, Guillermo reaches out to shake hands.

"You did my brother a solid. That means a lot. If you ever need me, I'm there, *mi hermano*," Guillermo says.

"I'm happy I could help," James says.

"You did more than help. You gave my brother a chance, a chance at a new and better life," Guillermo says.

"I never had a brother. It's nice to see the bond you two have," James says.

"You don't understand. In my world, I trust family and few others. Trust can be a dangerous thing. Trust in the wrong person can get you killed," Guillermo explains.

"Miguel deserved a second chance," James says.

"Listen to me, James. Where I'm from, we have two families—the one you are born into and the one that you share your life with, the one you trust with your life. You're not *family*, but you're family. You're my brother."

James leaves the restaurant and walks back across the street to get to his car. In the parking lot, James notices an utterly plain beige Ford Taurus on the other side of the parking lot.

That car looks a lot like the really ugly car I saw parked outside the courthouse.

James walks past his car, then circles around to walk back across the street to the food trucks in the plaza. James buys some street corn and walks back toward his car, this time detouring toward the beige car. Getting closer to try to look into the car through its tinted windows, James casually continues to eat his street corn.

What the? It's almost 90 degrees outside but there are two people sitting in that car with the windows almost all the way rolled up. Something is not right.

James returns to his car, pulls back onto Main Street and drives to the Chevron gas station about a mile up the street. James watches as the beige car passes by the station. James enters the station and buys a bottle of Coke Zero and a prepaid phone. James takes the phone out of the package in the store, disposing of the packaging in the store.

Once back in his car, James looks on his phone for Bobby's number to send a text. *Bobby. It's James. Can you call me at this number in 5 minutes? Very important.*

James starts his car, connects the new phone to the car's Bluetooth and pulls out onto North Main. Driving down the one-way street, James passes the beige car, parked about three quarters of a block up the street. James passes the car, makes a right onto North Alameda to East Commercial Street, until he can merge onto the 101 Freeway and head back toward Orange County. While making the left onto Commercial Street, James is certain he sees the beige car waiting at the Alameda Street turn signal.

Soon James gets the call he was hoping for. "Bobby. Thanks for calling me."

"What's going on? You have me worried, and why this phone number?"

"I'm in LA, and a beige Taurus with two occupants has been following me most of the day. I stopped at a gas station and bought a pre-paid phone in case they are able to monitor calls from my phone," James says.

"You're learning. What do you want to do?" Bobby asks.

"I want to put an end to this crap and find out who these two are working for," James says.

"Okay, do you remember that warehouse I started my business in?" Bobby asks.

"The one off Alisos in Mission Viejo?" James asks.

"That's it. Pull up to the garage door, and I'll handle the rest," Bobby says.

"Do I want to ask?"

"Trust me."

"Completely," James says.

James takes the slow drive down the 5 Freeway into Orange County, exiting at the Alicia Parkway exit. He turns left onto the parkway then left again at Via Fabricante A right shortly before Los Alisos takes James into an industrial park. James drives toward the back where he sees Bobby standing outside an apparently vacant warehouse. James pulls up close to Bobby, lowering his window.

"Pull into the warehouse, drive about mid-way into the warehouse, and stay in your car," Bobby instructs.

"Got it." James drives forward, parking in the warehouse where he can see Bobby, his window still rolled down.

Moments later, James sees Bobby holding out his hand in the universally recognized stop position. The beige car slowly approaches Bobby.

"What's the problem?" The car's driver yells at Bobby. "Let us pass by!"

"I don't think so," Bobby replies. "You need to pull into this garage."

"Not gonna happen," the driver replies.

"It wasn't a request," Bobby barks. With his words, four men in masks carrying pistols surround the car. "I said, pull into the garage. Now!"

"Okay. We don't want any trouble."

"Pull in very slowly, and there won't be trouble," Bobby explains.

The beige car slowly turns toward the garage, following Bobby who walks in front of the car with the four men continuing to cover the car. Once inside, the garage door is closed.

"Get out of the car with your hands in plain sight," Bobby instructs.

The men do as they are told. As each steps out of the car, they are frisked by Bobby's men. James leaves his car to approach the men, now leaning against their car.

"You're making a mistake, Mr. Butler," the driver says.

"Really? You think so?" James asks. "It doesn't seem that way right now."

"Why have you been following James?" Bobby asks.

"What agency do you work for?" James asks.

"We don't work for an agency," the driver says defiantly.

"I don't give a damn who you don't work for, and these games are pissing me off!" Bobby yells. "Who directed you to follow James? Tell me now, or neither of you leave here with all your body parts."

"We were hired by someone we don't know," claims the driver.

"I don't believe for a second that you don't know who you work for. I want a name. I want the name of the person in the CIA that hired you." Bobby's anger is palpable.

"Look," the driver says with a reluctant sigh, "all I can tell you is that we were hired by someone who identified himself as a CIA contractor for what he called a 'side' project. But we never met him in person."

"The CIA cannot legally surveil American citizens," James notes.

"As I said, we don't work for the CIA."

"When did Arthur hire you?" James asks.

"Last week. We only started following you two days ago."

"How do you report back?" James asks.

"We have a phone."

"Let me see it," James says.

"It's in the car."

"Get it," James says.

"Wait," Bobby commands, with a head gesture to one of his men. The masked man goes to the other side of the car, opens the door, and positions himself to aim his gun into the car. "Slowly get the phone and *only* the phone," Bobby instructs.

The man crawls into the car through the passenger door, and reemerges with the phone, showing it to James.

"Unlock it and hand it to me." James inspects the phone after it is handed to him. "How do you communicate with him?"

"We text. There is only one number on the phone: 'The Prince.'"

"Subtle," James notes. "Both of you against the car," James instructs while holding up the phone to take a picture. James snaps a picture, attaches it to a text message to The Prince, and taps a message: *I met your friends today. Back off or I'll expose everything. I'll start by delivering these two to the nearest US Attorneys office. You stop, I'll stop.*

Moments later, there is a simple reply: *Ok.*

James hands the phone to Bobby. "Can we destroy this?"

"We can do that," Bobby replies, taking the phone from James. "What about these two?"

"I think we can let them go if they give assurances they will never come near me or you again," James answers.

"What about it?" Bobby asks the men. "Do you want to leave, or should my men explain to you the ramifications of messing with the wrong people?"

"We are done," the driver says. "We won't bother any of you again. I can promise you that."

"What about you?" Bobby asks the other man, who has remained silent.

"I promise," he says, nodding in fervent agreement.

"And you'll forget everything about James and this meeting?" Bobby reiterates.

"Yes," the men answer in unison.

"Fine, get the hell out of here, and pray neither James nor I ever see you again."

The two men scramble into their car and back out of the now opened garage door.

"Think they stay quiet?" James asks while watching the car exit the garage.

"Yes, I do," Bobby answers. "Guns and force can turn tough men weak. Those weren't tough men."

THIRTY-ONE

A SEASONABLY MILD November day greets Erica and James as they explore downtown San Antonio after spending the night at the Historic Menger Hotel directly adjacent to the Alamo and Alamo Plaza.

Built in 1859, the Menger Hotel is the longest actively running hotel west of the Mississippi. Over its history, it has hosted numerous dignitaries, including Presidents Ulysses Grant, Benjamin Harrison, Theodore Roosevelt, Woodrow Wilson, William H. Taft, William McKinley, Harry Truman, Richard Nixon, Ronald Reagan, Lyndon Johnson, George H. W. Bush, and Bill Clinton; military figures, including Sam Houston, Robert E. Lee, and William Hood Simpson; and other public figures, including Oscar Wilde.

The Menger also has a cherry-wood bar modeled after the House of Lords taproom in London. In 1898, Colonel Leonard Wood and his lieutenant-colonel (and future president of the United States), Theodore Roosevelt, set up an enlistment table at the Menger Bar where they recruited over 1,250 men to form the 1st US Volunteer Cavalry, better known as the Rough Riders, who achieved fame for their contributions at the Battle of San Juan Hill during the Spanish-American War. Two bullet holes in the bar's wall are said to have been from accidental discharges during this recruiting process.

James and Erica spent the prior evening visiting the Alamo and taking in the sights along the San Antonio Riverwalk. Dinner at Biga on the Banks, recommended highly by the Menger's bartender, consisted of habanero jerk scallops for an appetizer, spiced South Texas antelope and Lockhart quail for James, and baked Scottish salmon for Erica. Erica enjoyed a mocktail while James indulged in two well-crafted Old Fashioneds.

Today, sightseeing gives way to a trip to the Fort Sam Houston National Cemetery to pay their respects to Aguilar. James parks the rental car far away from Aguilar's burial site.

"It's a nice day for a walk with my family," James says as he opens the door for Erica.

"Just what an absurdly large pregnant woman wants to hear," she says.

"Do you want me to pull closer?" James offers.

"No," Erica says, "a walk actually would be nice. Much better than sitting in the car."

Hand in hand, James and Erica slowly walk toward the large magnolia adjacent to Aguilar's site.

"We haven't talked about it much, but Arthur has been noticeably and thankfully quiet for a while now. Do you think he's given up?" Erica asks.

"I doubt it. As I told Brian, I think he still believes he can use us to his benefit at some point in the future," James answers.

"So, we wait until he appears again?" Erica asks.

"Afraid so. But I think he is done testing us," James says.

"Well," Erica reflects, "at least that's good."

"I'm also feeling better with all of the security measures at the office and those Bobby has implemented at home," James says.

"I sleep better with them too," Erica agrees.

"It is a little odd."

"What's that?"

"It's been a couple of months now, and we've gotten back to

some semblance of normal. Sometimes I wake in the middle of the night, worried about what might happen next," James admits.

"I do too, some days, but then I think about all the great things in our lives, the things we've accomplished, and this wonderful baby girl coming to share this with us, and I think normal is wonderful," Erica says.

"Well said. I think I can get used to it."

James and Erica reach Aguilar's site. A modestly sized but ornate headstone is now in place. Interestingly, the headstones at this cemetery are federal property, and any marking of or damage to a headstone is a violation of federal law.

"The headstone is beautiful," Erica says.

"It's interesting that we only knew Aguilar for a couple of years, but I feel like he was with us for much longer," James says.

"He was with us for so many important things. Mexico, Rafa, our wedding. Big events," Erica reasons.

"Combined with his big personality."

"Very true." Erica pauses. "He would have appreciated all you did for him in his death."

"All *we* did. We did this together, and I'm proud of what we accomplished," James says.

"That's progress, my love."

"Progress?"

"For a while it bothered me that you so clearly wanted to have done more," Erica says.

"I still wish we had been able to do more, but we did everything we could. I dare say more than anyone else could," James says.

"I agree." Erica gives James a hug that becomes a long embrace.

James briefly opens his eyes and sees movement several yards away near another large magnolia.

"Without making it obvious, please turn around and look behind you," James whispers. "Look at the man by the tree."

Erica looks, but tells James, "I don't see anyone."

James looks back toward the tree in astonishment, but he too sees nothing.

"Who was it?" Erica asks.

"I must be losing my mind, but I would have sworn Tim was standing right over there," James says.

"Are you sure?" Erica asks.

"Obviously not. But I really thought so."

"That's weird, but, if he was here, he's gone now."

THIRTY-TWO

JAMES SHUTS the rear passenger door on the Tesla and trots to the driver's side. Starting the car, James guides the car out of the circle driveway, down a narrow connecting road to the main street.

"I know they say the baby seat is supposed to face back," James states, "but it just seems so strange to not be able to look back and check on her. Besides, I love looking at her chubby face, even in the rear-view mirror."

"I agree. Maybe I should have ridden in the back seat with her? Should we stop?" Erica asks.

"Nah, it's a short drive. I'm sure it's fine," James says.

"Are all new parents this jittery?" Erica wonders.

"I think the good ones are. Besides, the car seat has a safety rating that would let us put her in a NASCAR race."

"Okay." Erica sighs. "I'll try to relax."

James drives down Cul de Sac Oceancrest to Pelican Hill Road North to Newport Coast Drive downhill to Pacific Coast Highway.

"It was nice to see your dad with Susan at the Christmas dinner. She seemed very at home," James says.

"Dad seemed very happy, and that's what matters," Erica replies.

"Of course, it is. I like her. She's not super chatty, but she's nice. They make a good couple," James offers.

"Dad waited so long to introduce us that I almost started to worry," Erica says.

"What . . . he'd saved some DNA from your mom and cloned her?" James jests.

"No, goofball. But maybe there was some reason he was concerned we wouldn't hit it off. But then when we met, we hit it off, and I realized he just wanted to be sure it was a real thing before imposing it on me," Erica says.

"It will be nice to spend some more time with her in a quieter environment," James observes.

"Yes, Dad's 'quiet and intimate' Christmas dinner was anything but," Erica says.

At PCH, James turns right and stops at the light to turn onto MacArthur Boulevard. After a green turn light, MacArthur leads to the Farmhouse at Roger's Gardens, a farm-to-table restaurant in Corona del Mar helmed by Chef Rich Mead. Since their move from the condo, the restaurant has become one of James and Erica's favorites.

The restaurant has a post-Christmas glow and a bustling Sunday brunch crowd.

"Mr. and Mrs. Butler. What a delight to see you," Alexandra, the restaurant's front-end manager approaches to greet them. "How's the baby?"

"Sleeping peacefully, thank goodness," Erica replies.

"Then I shall not disturb her, but maybe I'll be able to see her later," Alexandra says.

"Of course," Erica says.

"Diedre? Will you take the Butlers to number three on the patio?"

"Of course." Diedre turns to James and Erica. "Right this way, and congratulations."

"Thank you," James replies.

The restaurant retains the Christmas decorations, but the weather bears no hint of winter. As such, Erica had reserved a table on the back patio where there would be more room. Diedre guides them through the main dining room maze of tables, trees, plants, and flowers.

"Here you are," Diedre says as they reach the patio. "Will the baby be warm enough?"

"She is well bundled under there, so I think we will be okay. My dad and his date will be joining us soon," Erica says.

"I'll show them back as soon as they arrive," Diedre says.

"Thank you, Diedre," James says.

Diedre leaves and is soon replaced by their waiter.

"Michael, good to see you," Erica says.

"Thanks for requesting me, Mr. and Mrs. Butler. How are we all today?"

"Couldn't be better," James says.

"Unless we had mimosas," Erica says.

"Coming right up. And you are expecting two more?" Michael asks.

"Yes, we are, and you might as well bring some for them," Erica says.

"Just hook us up, Mike," James says.

"On it," Michael replies before moving inside.

Erica adjusts the baby seat on the chair next to her. "Do you ever look at this tiny person and think 'this is ours'?"

"All the time, my love." James reaches for Erica's hand, caressing her fingers with his thumb.

Erica looks up to find Brian and Susan Newell approaching.

The four enjoy appetizers, mimosas, and a free-flowing conversation until Michael arrives with a bottle of champagne.

"More champagne for the mimosas?" James asks.

"No, James," Brian replies, "this is very good champagne, and it's not for the mimosas but for a celebratory toast."

As Brian talks, Michael retrieves four new champagne flutes, pops the cork, and pours glasses of champagne for everyone.

"A toast? To what?" James asks.

"Not until we all have our glasses," Brian replies.

Michael distributes the glasses and slips away.

"Okay, now?" James asks.

"Erica, do you want to tell him?" Brian asks.

I thought Brian and Susan were engaged, but I guess not, James thinks.

"I'd love to," Erica says conspiratorially. "Dad called me last night and said the partners had an informal meeting last night—some would call it a party, but he said it was a meeting—and at the meeting, he stepped down as managing partner, and the partners decided to take a vote, and they elected a new managing partner."

"Who?" James asks.

"You!" Erica exclaims.

"Congratulations, James," Brian says. "A new father, and the new managing partner. I couldn't be prouder or happier for you."

"I'm stunned, and I don't know what to say," James says.

"Then drink up instead!" Brian raises his glass.

"To James!" The four toast in unison before sipping their drinks.

"Managing partner?" James says. "Heck, I haven't even been in the office much recently."

"That's the best kind of manager," Brian jokes. "The vote was unanimous."

"Really? Even Ben? He doesn't like me much," James says.

"It's not that he doesn't like you. Different practice areas. Different eras. Different personalities. Okay, he doesn't like you much." James and Brian laugh in unison. "Seriously though, the partners all said they wanted someone who has a profound respect for the firm and its long-term future and would put his or her soul into it. That, my friend, is you. Even Ben said so."

"I'm touched, and more than a bit floored," James admits.

"Not to change the subject, but how's the new house, Erica?" Susan asks.

"It's great. We love it, except that it's a lot more work than the condo. Once we finish decorating, we will have a nice dinner, and I'll give you a personal tour," Erica says.

"I'd like that. Thank you," Susan says.

Alexandra approaches the table. "I'm very sorry to interrupt, Mr. Butler, but someone dropped this off and asked me to deliver it to you personally," she says, handing James a gift-wrapped box. "He was very insistent that I deliver it and that I do so straight away. And, Mrs. Butler, he said to tell you congratulations."

"Did he give a name or say who he was?" James asks.

"No. He just handed me the box, and said he was in a hurry, but you'd understand," Alexandra explains.

"What did he look like?" Erica asks.

"Tall, athletic. A bit older, and maybe I shouldn't say this, but really good looking," Alexandra says.

"Tim!" James and Erica blurt out together.

James bolts up and races to the front of the restaurant, only to see a car driving away. It passes out of sight as James looks on before he walks back to the table.

"You couldn't catch him?" Erica asks.

"No, but I might have seen him driving away," James says.

"We might as well open the gift," Erica says.

"Are you sure it's safe?" Susan asks.

"Yes, we are," James says.

Erica slowly and carefully unwraps the box. Inside is a smaller box, taped shut, with a tag on it.

"The tag says it's for you, James," she says handing the box to him, before returning her attention to the larger box. "Oh, my goodness. Look, James." Erica holds up a light sage green blanket with the words *Margaret Faith* in pink cursive letters. "It's absolutely beautiful."

James struggles to open the small box while watching Erica. "It is a very pretty blanket."

"Look, Dad, Susan."

"Margaret Faith," Brian comments. "I just love that name. Your mom would too."

"It was James's idea. He gets all of the credit," Erica replies.

Turning back to James, Erica reflects, "I wish we could thank Tim."

James pries open his box exposing a generic-looking cell phone.

"Not to worry. I'm pretty sure we will be hearing from Tim again."

EPILOGUE

Relaxing at home with Margaret playing in her crib next to him, James is startled by the ringing of the phone—not his phone but *that* phone.

"Hey, man, how the heck are you?" James says.

"Umm, I'm good. Is this James Butler?"

"Yes, this is James. I'm sorry, I was expecting someone else."

"I know this is out of the blue, but my name is Jeffrey Goldman. I'm an attorney in New York City, and I have been appointed as defense counsel in an interesting case here in New York."

"No offense, Mr. Goldman, but 'appointed counsel' sounds like a defendant that doesn't pay, and that's not my normal client. Plus, I never take cases on the East Coast," James says.

"I understand, Mr. Butler. I looked at your credentials, and I'm impressed, and I wouldn't have called you except for something odd that happened yesterday," Mr. Goldman says.

"Something odd? What was that?" James asks.

"I visited my client, and he handed me a cryptic note. Someone he didn't know gave it to him and said it would be important to his case," Mr. Goldman explains.

"What did the note say?" James asks.

"Well, it has your name and this number and . . ."

"And what?" James asks.

"Two more names. The first is 'Tim Speer.' I've never heard of him, and I didn't do a search for him before calling you," Mr. Goldman says.

"That's okay. I know Tim. What about the other name?" James asks.

"It's not a full name. Now that I look at it, it might not even be a name. It just says 'Kiki.'"

"I'll be there on Monday."

THANK YOU!

Thank you for reading! If you enjoyed this book, please leave a review on Amazon, Goodreads, BookBub, The Story Graph, or anywhere else you like to track your recent reads. Alternatively, you could post online or tell a friend about it. This helps our authors more than you may know.

- *The Team at Torchflame Books*

BIBLIOGRAPHY

Attwood, Shaun. Clinton Bush and CIA Conspiracies: From the Boys on the Tracks to Jeffrey Epstein. Gadfly Press, 2019.

Attwood, Shaun. American Made: Who Killed Barry Seal? Pablo Escobar or George H. W. Bush. CreateSpace Publishing, 2016.

Beith, Malcolm. The Last Narc: Inside the Hunt for El Chapo, the World's Most Wanted Drug Lord. New York: Grove Press, 2010.

Bernstein, Carl. "The CIA and the Media." Rolling Stone. June 27, 2007.

Ganser, Daniele. NATO's Secret Armies: Operation GLADIO and Terrorism in Western Europe. Boca Raton: Routledge 2005.

Grillo, Ioan. El Narco: Inside Mexico's Criminal Insurgency. New York: Bloomsbury Publishing, 2011.

Hernandez, Anabel. Narcoland: The Mexican Drug Lords and Their Godfathers. London: Verso, 2013.

Hurowitz, Noah. "Inside Drug Kingpin El Chapo's Secret 1998 Meeting With the DEA." Rolling Stone. July 8, 2021.

Kuykendall, James. ¿O Plata o Plomo?. Xlibris Corporation, 2005.

Langton, Jerry. Gangland: The Rise of the Mexican Drug Cartels from El Paso to Vancouver. Toronto: HarperCollins Canada, 2013.

Marshall, Jonathan. Dark Quadrant: Organized Crime, Big Business, and the Corruption of American Democracy. Lanham, MD: Rowman and Littlefield, 2021.

Reed, Terry, and John Cummings. Compromised: Clinton, Bush and the CIA. New York: S.P.I. Books, 1994.

Shannon, Elaine. Desperados. New York: Penguin Book USA Inc. 1988.

Smith, Benjamin T. The Dope: The Real History of the Mexican Drug Trade. Norton, W.W. & Company, Inc., 2022.

Walsh, Lawrence E. Firewall: The Iran-Contra Conspiracy and Cover-Up. Norton, W.W. & Company, Inc.,1998.

Webb, Gary. Dark Alliance: The CIA, the Contras, and the Crack Cocaine Explosion. New York: Seven Stories Press, 1998.

Wilford, Hugh. The Mighty Wurlitzer: How the CIA Played America. Cambridge: Harvard University Press, 2008.

H. Select Comm. to Investigate Covert Arms Transactions with Iran and S. Select Comm. on Secret Military Assistance to Iran and the Nicaraguan Opposition. H.R. Rep. No. 100-433. S. Rep. No. 100-216. (1987).

Subcommittee on Terrorism, Narcotics and International Operations of the Committee on Foreign Relations, United States Senate. S. Rep. No. 100-165. (1989).

House Permanent Select Comm. on Intelligence. Prepared statement of Frederick P. Hitz, Inspector General Central Intelligence Agency. (1998).

ACKNOWLEDGMENTS

This book, like its predecessor, would not have been possible without the support and encouragement of many people, far too many to name here, but each and every one is appreciated.

Mark Ulmer has listened to a great number of my theories and thoughts on the subjects discussed in this book and has offered valuable insights and critiques. The support and assistance of Jesus Martinez has been invaluable. Thank you to Jim Lacy for keeping me somewhat grounded by running me ragged on the tennis court. My deep appreciation goes to Vikki Hofer for her encouragement, support, and generosity of spirit, and shout out to all of the good people at "The Mutt".

I have been extremely fortunate to have shared thoughts, ideas, and information with a number of professionals and have learned from and been enriched by each encounter. Those who deserve recognition include Ioan Gillo and Professor Benjamin Smith, as well as many to whom I am extremely grateful but will not name here for reasons I am confident they understand.

I am indebted to everyone at Torchflame Books, and especially to Chelsea Robinson for her invaluable and incredibly thoughtful editing. Teri Rider and Jori Hanna have done so much to help see this book come to life.

My family has been incredibly supportive, and their encouragement has been a continuing source of inspiration.

Finally, to Nathen Baalman, whose research and support from before *Someone Had to Die* was finalized through the drafting of this book and means more to me than I ever could put into words. Rest in peace.

ABOUT THE AUTHOR

Jack Luellen is a Denver, Colorado, attorney with more than 30 years of experience. In practice, Jack has tried cases to courts and juries, and has written hundreds of briefs, motions, and memoranda, to state and federal courts, including federal courts of appeal and the United States Supreme Court.

In 1990, Jack first started working on cases related to the 1985 kidnapping and murder of DEA Agent Enrique Camarena and has investigated the case in the years since that time. Jack's investigations have taken him to foreign countries and included interviews with witnesses both notorious and infamous. This work was the background for his first James Butler mystery *Someone Had to Die.*

Jack's investigations into the world of Mexican cartels, and continuing research into the Camarena murder form the foundation for his sequel novel, *Someone Had to Lie.*

Jack is the proud father of an amazing daughter.

Connect with him online at www.jackluellen.com.

ALSO BY JACK LUELLEN

Though the murder of DEA Special Agent Enrique Camarena occurred more than 35 years ago, James Butler can't shake the nagging feeling that maybe the investigators missed something. The more James digs into this cold case, the more unwanted attention he gathers from powerful forces on both sides of the border who would prefer to keep the case closed.

Someone Had to Die follows a fictional lawyer as he digs into the true story of Special Agent Enrique "Kiki" Camarena's abduction and murder in 1985, drawing from and exposing interviews and facts never before published.

www.ingramcontent.com/pod-product-compliance
Lightning Source LLC
LaVergne TN
LVHW050753260125
802031LV00004B/14

9781611533705